Nancy Atherton is the much-loved author of twenty Aunt Dimity mysteries. The first book in the series, *Aunt Dimity's Death*, was voted one of the century's 100 Favourite Mysteries by the Independent Mystery Booksellers Association. She lives in Colorado, USA.

Discover more about Aunt Dimity and Nancy Atherton online at www.aunt-dimity.com.

Praise for Nancy Atherton's Aunt Dimity series:

'Atherton's a spellbinding storyteller, and *Aunt Dimity and the Summer King* is a thoroughly enchanting read' *Crimespree Magazine*

'A complete and utter gem' *Suspense Magazine*

'Perfect for those who prefer charmingly low-key puzzles to blood-soaked chills and thrills' *Kirkus Reviews*

'An antidote to cynicism and divisiveness' *Cozy Library*

'Honestly, reading just doesn't get any sweeter than this. Take a break from the serial killers . . . and let Nancy Atherton and Aunt Dimity remind you of the reason you got hooked on books in the first place' *CrimeCritics.com*

'We all wish we had an Aunt Dimity' *escapewithdollycas.com*

*By Nancy Atherton and featuring Aunt Dimity*

# NANCY ATHERTON

## Aunt Dimity & the Summer King

**headline**

First published in Great Britain in 2015 by
HEADLINE PUBLISHING GROUP

First published in paperback in 2016 by
HEADLINE PUBLISHING GROUP

2

Cataloguing in Publication Data is available from the British Library

ISBN 978 1 4722 1633 5

Printed in Great Britain by Clays Ltd, St Ives plc

HEADLINE PUBLISHING GROUP
An Hachette UK Company
Carmelite House
50 Victoria Embankment
London EC4Y 0DZ

www.headline.co.uk
www.hachette.co.uk

For Chloë and Emma,
who will always be my kittens

# One

Every back road is somebody's main road. No matter how rough or remote it might be, a road always leads somewhere, and for someone, that somewhere is home.

I lived on a back road, a narrow, twisting lane bordered by hedgerows, lush pastures, and shadowy woodlands. My home was a honey-colored cottage in the Cotswolds, a region of rolling hills and patchwork fields in England's West Midlands, and my little lane was used chiefly by my family, my friends, and my neighbors.

Bewildered strangers occasionally knocked on my door to ask for directions, but they left as quickly as they came. They had no reason to linger—no castle, no cathedral, no Bronze Age barrow or seaside promenade to pique their interest. There was nothing special about my corner of the Cotswolds, apart from its tranquil beauty and the unchanging, ever-changing cycle of country life.

My husband, Bill, and I were Americans, as were our nine-year-old twins, Will and Rob, but we'd lived in England long enough to be accepted as honorary natives by our neighbors. Our cottage was situated near the small village of Finch, a place so tiny and of so little consequence to the world at large that most mapmakers forgot to include it on their maps.

Finch was, of course, of tremendous consequence to those of us who lived there. It was the center of our universe, the hub around which we revolved. We might not be able to name the newest celebrity, but we knew everything worth knowing about one another.

We knew whose dog had acquired fleas, whose roof had sprung a leak, and whose chrysanthemums had been fatally stricken with root rot mere moments after such catastrophes took place. We knew who could be relied upon to make six dozen flawless strawberry tarts for the flower show's bake sale and who couldn't be trusted to bake a single macaroon without setting the oven ablaze. We knew whose children and grandchildren were delightful and whose were to be avoided like the plague, and we shared our knowledge with a diligence that put the Internet to shame.

Local gossip was the stuff of life in Finch, a sport, an art form, a currency that never lost its value. We didn't need celebrities to entertain us. We found ourselves endlessly fascinating.

Finch wouldn't suit everyone—those desiring privacy, for example, would find the lack of it hard to bear—but it suited Bill and me down to the ground. Bill ran the European branch of his family's venerable Boston law firm from an office overlooking the village green; Will and Rob attended Morningside School in the nearby market town of Upper Deeping; and I juggled a multitude of roles—wife, mother, friend, neighbor, community volunteer, gossip gatherer, and devoted daughter-in-law.

Bill's father, William Willis, Sr., lived up the lane from us, in Fairworth House, a splendidly restored Georgian mansion surrounded by an impeccably maintained estate. Willis, Sr., had spent most of his adult life in Boston as the head of the family firm, but he'd moved to England upon his retirement in order to be near his grandchildren.

My father-in-law was an old-fashioned, courtly gentleman, a handsome widower, and a doting grandfather. I adored him, as did nearly every widow and spinster in Finch. Many a heart had been broken when Willis, Sr., had bestowed his upon the celebrated watercolorist Amelia Thistle. Amelia had taken nearly two years to return the favor, but Willis, Sr.'s patient pursuit of her had eventually paid off. He had proposed, she had accepted, and the date of the wedding had been set.

Bill was delighted by the match. He looked forward to being his father's best man as eagerly as I looked forward to being Amelia's matron of honor. Will and Rob were somewhat less enthusiastic about fulfilling their forthcoming roles as Grandpa's ring-bearers, but Amelia had bought their cooperation by promising to hide a handful of their favorite cookies in her bouquet. For a woman who'd never had children of her own, Amelia possessed a rare gift for dealing with nine-year-olds.

Although Willis, Sr., was no longer the head of the family firm, he was still regarded as the head of the family and attendance at his nuptials was considered compulsory. Flocks of aunts, uncles, and cousins would soon be descending on Finch to pay homage to the paterfamilias, an event that did not fill Bill with unalloyed joy. While he got along well with most of his relatives, he actively disliked two of his aunts. He referred to them as the Harpies, but only when Will, Rob, and his father were out of earshot.

Though Aunt Honoria and Aunt Charlotte had been widowed for many years, they had, in their youth, married men from their own social milieu. They believed that Bill had let his old-money Boston Brahmin family down when he'd married a middle-class girl from Chicago. Had they been openly hostile to me, Willis, Sr., would have come down on them like a ton of bricks, so they disguised their disdain with artful expressions of "concern" for me, the unfortunate outsider.

They criticized my posture, my table manners, my dress sense, and my speech, but they did so solicitously, as if they were bringing enlightenment to a savage who'd been raised on a desert island by a troop of baboons. Willis, Sr., who could usually spot a hidden agenda from a mile off, was blind to his sisters' shenanigans. He saw Charlotte and Honoria through rose-colored glasses, but they made my easygoing husband see red.

Bill's aunts had never darkened our doorway in England—they rarely left Boston—and he was not looking forward to their first visit. He made his misgivings known to me as we strolled along our little lane one day, three weeks before the wedding.

It was a glorious Saturday morning in early June. After dropping the boys off at the local stables for their weekly riding lessons, Bill had decided to clear up some neglected paperwork that awaited him at his office in Finch. He didn't usually walk to the village and I didn't usually accompany him, but the weather was superb and we'd both felt like stretching our legs.

My mind was on other things when Bill spoke, so his words seemed to come out of nowhere, like a bolt from the blue.

"If the Harpies are rude to you," he declared, "I'll strangle them."

"I should hope so," I said lightly, but one glance at my husband's thunderous expression told me that he was not in the mood for levity. "What brought your aunts to mind?"

"A phone call from Father," he replied. "Honoria and Charlotte will be arriving at Fairworth House on Monday."

"Monday?" I said, my heart sinking. "Why so soon?"

"They *say* they're coming early to help Amelia with the wedding, but you and I know they'll do nothing but nitpick and nag." Bill laughed bitterly. "I wouldn't put it past them to spend the next three weeks trying to talk Father out of marrying Amelia."

"Fat chance," I said scornfully.

" 'An *artist* in the family,' " said Bill, mimicking Honoria's pene-
trating nasal drawl. " 'What on earth were you *thinking*, William?
We could understand it if she *dabbled*. Everyone *dabbles*. But she *sells*
her paintings. For *money*. My dear, it simply isn't *done!* ' "

"They wouldn't be stupid enough to talk like that in front of your
father, would they?" I asked incredulously.

"I almost wish they would," said Bill. "It'd be a treat to watch
Father kick them out of Fairworth."

"If they spout off about Amelia, he will," I said. "And they won't
be able to stay with us because we don't have a guest room anymore."

"Yet another reason to be thankful for my beautiful wife," Bill
acknowledged, "and my beautiful, beautiful daughter."

My husband's entire aspect changed as he gazed down at the precious passenger I was pushing along in the pram. His shoulders relaxed, his fists unclenched, and his thunderous expression gave way
to one of pure adoration. Bill was in love as he had never been in love
before and I felt not the slightest twinge of jealousy because I, too,
was besotted.

Don't get me wrong. We loved our sons ferociously, but our baby
girl had come to us long after we'd abandoned hope of having another child. Her late arrival had secured a special place in our hearts
for her. Because of her, Bill had done the unthinkable: He'd cut back
on his workload in order to spend less time at the beck and call of his
demanding clients and more time at home with his family. It was a
choice the Harpies would never understand, but I did, and I approved
of it with all my heart.

Our daughter had been christened Elizabeth Dimity, after my
late mother and a dear friend, but Will and Rob had dubbed her Bess.
I suspected they'd done so for the pleasure of calling her Bessy Boots,

Messy Bessy, and a host of other big-brotherly nicknames, but Bess she had been from that day forward.

Bess had entered the world on a stormy, snowy night in late February—a scant fifteen weeks ago—but we felt as if we'd known her forever. She had her father's velvety brown eyes, my rosy complexion, and a wispy crop of silky, softly curling dark-brown hair.

"She *is* beautiful, isn't she?" I crooned.

"She's incomparably beautiful," Bill agreed, "and highly intelligent."

"And even-tempered," I added.

"And healthy and strong and good-humored," Bill continued.

"And kind and patient and wise," I went on.

"Our Bess," Bill concluded, "is as perfectly perfect as perfect can be."

We looked at each other and laughed. We wouldn't allow ourselves to become baby-bores in public, but we were free to sing Bess's praises in private, secure in the knowledge that every word we said was true.

"She's also considerate," I pointed out. "If we hadn't turned our guest room into her nursery, we would have had to offer it to one of your cousins."

"Thank God for small blessings," Bill murmured, beaming at Bess. "I don't know where Father will put everyone," he added, shaking his head. "Fairworth House is big, but it isn't big enough to accomodate his out-of-town guests as well as Amelia's."

"He could put someone in the old nursery," I suggested facetiously. Willis, Sr., had refurbished the nursery in Fairworth House with his granddaughter's comfort in mind. It came in handy when our visits coincided with Bess's nap times, but it wasn't a bedroom for grown-ups.

"Are you serious?" Bill asked, eyeing me doubtfully.

"I was attempting to be humorous," I said, sighing. "An attempt which has clearly failed. The serious answer is: Amelia has booked hotel rooms in Oxford and Upper Deeping for those who accepted their invitations promptly. Late responders will have to fend for themselves."

"I suppose they could rent the empty cottages," said Bill.

A sense of unease rippled through me. The empty cottages worried me far more than Bill's aunts. Honoria and Charlotte would be gone shortly after the wedding, but the cottages were part of a troubling trend.

Two cottages stood empty in Finch and they had done so for five months. Their former owners had either passed away or moved away, and though the little dwellings were attractive and in good repair, no new owners had come to claim them.

I couldn't understand it. Finch might be small, but it was not without resources. Taxman's Emporium stocked everything from baked beans to freckle cream, Peacock's pub was renowned for its pub grub and ales, and Sally Cook's tearoom was a pastry lover's delight. Finch had its own church, post office, and greengrocer's shop and it boasted the finest handyman in the county. Mr. Barlow, the retired mechanic who served as our church sexton, could turn his hand to just about any job.

Finch even had an international contingent. Bree Pym was from New Zealand, Jack MacBride was from Australia, and my family represented the United States, as did my best friend, Emma Harris, who lived up the lane from us in Anscombe Manor, where she'd established the riding academy Will and Rob attended. Our village was, in its own way, quite cosmopolitan.

Granted, there was no school, but the old schoolhouse was still very much in use as our village hall. The flower show, the Nativity play, and numerous bake sales were held there, and committees met beneath its roof to plan the year's village activities.

Finch was surrounded by farmland, but Oxford wasn't far away and Upper Deeping was even closer. It seemed to me that a relatively short drive to work was a small price to pay for a home in such a beautiful setting.

Fishermen could cast their lures into the Little Deeping River, cyclists could pedal in peace along uncrowded lanes, hikers could ramble to their hearts' content on a network of lovely trails, and children could play in safety on the village green while the elderly swapped stories on the bench near the war memorial. All in all, Finch had a lot to offer.

Yet the two cottages remained empty.

"There shouldn't be *any* empty cottages in Finch," I said. "They should've been snapped up ages ago. What's wrong with people, Bill? Why doesn't anyone want to live here?"

"No idea," said Bill. "And it's too nice a day to waste fretting over a problem we can't solve."

I fell silent, but I didn't stop fretting. It distressed me to see Ivy Cottage and Rose Cottage uninhabited. Their blank windows seemed to peer reproachfully at passersby, as if the village had somehow let them down. Amelia's home, Pussywillows, would soon be on the market as well and I couldn't help wondering if it would find a buyer. The thought of *three* perfectly good cottages standing vacant for months on end was as depressing as it was perplexing.

Bill spoke of everything but the empty cottages as we strolled past Emma Harris's long, curving drive, Bree Pym's redbrick house, and the wrought-iron gates guarding the entrance to Willis, Sr.'s estate. We were within a few yards of the humpbacked bridge that crossed the Little Deeping when I came to a halt.

"Here's where we part ways," I said to Bill, nodding toward the trees on our right. "If you squint, you'll see an old cart track hidden away in there. Bess and I are heading for parts unknown."

Bill pushed aside the branches of the bushy bay tree that concealed the track's narrow entrance.

"I'm glad I bought an all-terrain pram," he said, eyeing the track's deep ruts doubtfully. "Do you have your cell phone with you, in case you get lost?"

"I do have my cell phone with me," I said, "but I won't need it. According to Emma, the track hugs the northern boundary of your father's property, so I can't possibly get lost."

Emma Harris was not merely a good friend and an accomplished equestrian. She was a master map-reader as well. She'd spotted the disused farm track on an old ordnance survey map, but though she'd told me of her discovery, she hadn't yet explored it. It cheered me to think of Bess and I going boldly where no Emma had gone before.

"Don't walk too far," Bill cautioned.

"Forty minutes out, forty minutes back," I promised. "Unless the track vanishes before our out-time is up, in which case we'll turn around sooner."

"A sensible plan," said Bill, adding under his breath, "if only you'd stick to it . . ." He gave me a kiss and bent low to kiss our sleeping daughter, but as he headed for the humpbacked bridge he couldn't resist calling over his shoulder, "Ring me when you get lost!"

I gave him a dark look as I steered the pram through the opening in the trees and onto the bumpy track. I didn't need Bill to remind me that my map-reading skills were less highly developed than Emma's, but I didn't need map-reading skills to follow the old track's twin ruts. And no map on earth could have warned me—or Emma—of what lay ahead.

None of us could have known that Bess and I were about to enter the strange and mysterious realm of the Summer King.

# Two

I felt almost giddy with freedom as I stepped onto Emma's track. The wild winds and the drenching rains that had kept me indoors throughout March, April, and May had at last given way to soft breezes and shimmering sunshine.

The air was filled with the delicate scents of violets and primroses. Wild strawberries climbed the hedgerows, bluebells carpeted the woods, buttercups gilded the meadows, and birds twittered in the trees. Spring teetered on the edge of summer and I was ready to greet it with open arms.

Inclement weather alone hadn't kept me cooped up in the cottage for weeks on end. A month of strict bed rest culminating in a prolonged and complicated delivery had produced a gratifyingly healthy baby, but it had also put a serious strain on my forty-one-year-old body. In a way, I'd been pleased by my postpartum feebleness, for it had allowed me to spend many guilt-free hours alone with my baby girl.

While a phalanx of friends filled my fridge with casseroles, took care of my household chores, and helped Bill to look after the boys, I tottered from bedroom to nursery and back again, with my daughter in my arms, barely conscious of a world beyond the one I shared with her. She and I weren't completely alone, of course. Bill changed Bess's diapers more often than I did, while Will and Rob, our self-appointed knights errant, kept us fully supplied with cookies, drawings, and dinosaurs.

When our menfolk were away, however, I enjoyed the luxury of having Bess all to myself. My earliest days with the twins had passed in a blur of new-mother panic and blinding fatigue and I didn't want history to repeat itself. Bess would, I knew, be my last child, and I cherished the chance to devote myself to her, body and soul, during the first fleeting weeks of her infancy.

Feeble tottering was not, however, the best way to get back into shape after a difficult pregnancy, a fact that had been made painfully clear to me when I'd tried on my matron of honor gown at a fitting. Amelia's bridesmaids, a quartet of whippet-slim art students who were half my age and who'd never given birth to anything bigger than an idea, had also attended the fitting, and though I wasn't abnormally vain, I couldn't help noticing that, while the seamstress had taken their dresses in, she'd gone to great lengths—literally—to let mine out.

I knew I would never be whippet-thin again, but I had no intention of becoming a too matronly matron of honor. The fitting inspired me to get off my backside before it became any broader. As soon as the weather calmed down, I began to take Bess for long walks through the countryside, exploring the web of pathways and lanes that spread outward in all directions from the village. I was so pleased to be outdoors and so intent on my tiny companion that I sometimes lost track of the time. And the mileage. And my whereabouts.

Once—only once—I'd ended up in an unfamiliar, deserted farmyard, too exhausted to walk any farther. The cell phone had come in handy on that occasion, but Bill had never let me forget the number of farmyards he'd had to search before he'd found his lost wife and his daughter, a full seven miles from home and sound asleep in the shade of a cow barn.

I blamed my farmyard adventure, in part, on the "all-terrain pram" Bill had bought for me when I'd told him of my new exercise program. The pram was an engineering marvel—convertible, collapsible, lightweight, yet sturdy, and so easy to maneuver that it tempted me to outwalk my stamina. Its three oversized wheels were more than a match for the potholes, rocks, and ruts of Emma's track, while its clever suspension and harness systems ensured a smooth, safe ride for Bess. Best of all, the bassinet could face either forward or backward. I preferred the backward position because it allowed me to have face-to-face conversations with Bess, who enjoyed using Bill's pram as much as I did.

I would not, however, allow it to mislead me again.

The moment I lost sight of Bill, I set the alarm on my cell phone to go off in precisely forty minutes. I explained to Bess that we would turn for home at its first beep, then forged ahead, feeling as though I'd saved myself from repeating the error that had given Bill the right to say, "*Six* farmyards! *Six!*" to anyone who would listen.

My fitness regimen wasn't entirely for my own benefit. It seemed to me that a baby born during a blizzard would appreciate the sun's warmth more keenly than most. After so many weeks indoors, I reasoned, the outdoors would stir her senses. She could hear the skylarks, smell the wild thyme, and see a crayon box of colors in the big world beyond the cottage. She might not remember the details of our first walks together, but I hoped they would kindle in her a life-long love of nature.

"On the other hand, you could grow up to be a rock star," I said to her as I pushed the pram carefully over a tangled mass of twisted tree roots that stretched across the track. "Our walks may give you a taste for rocking and rolling."

Bess's eyelids fluttered open at the sound of my voice, then closed again as the pram's bouncing lulled her to sleep. I couldn't yet tell if she was a placid child or a fearless one, but I looked forward to finding out.

I'd been confined to the cottage for so long that I positively reveled in the challenges the old track presented to me. I skirted ruts that resembled crevasses, ducked beneath low-hanging tree branches, splashed through rivulets, and nudged overgrown bushes aside with the same kind of fierce, joyous energy Will and Rob displayed while riding their ponies cross-country. When the old cart track veered to the left, I veered with it, and when the cell phone's alarm sounded, I shut it off and kept walking. I was much too happy to turn back.

Grassy banks gradually rose on either side of the track, but the banks were carpeted with such a profusion of wildflowers that I didn't mind losing the view. Apart from their beauty, the banks also shielded us from a rising breeze that had begun to blow in from the west.

When it came time to change Bess's diaper, I spread her blanket on a flower-strewn bank and went to work, hoping—in vain—that the pleasant scents would cancel out the not so pleasant ones. A little while later, we paused for a snack. Seated in the soft grass with Bess nestled to my breast, I felt as if I'd found paradise. I decided on the spot to reveal Emma's splendid discovery to no one.

"Your brothers have their secret places," I murmured to Bess, "and this place will be ours—yours and mine." I thought for a moment before adding judiciously, "Though we may allow Emma to visit it with us."

I'd planned to turn back after snack time, but curiosity got the better of me. I could see the corner of a stone wall in the distance. One segment of the wall ran parallel to the grassy bank on my right, while the other took off at a right angle and disappeared into a stand of trees. The wall was at least eight feet tall, and it seemed to go on for miles. I wondered whose property it was protecting.

"It's not your grandfather's," I told Bess as we approached the formidable barrier. "Grandpa's walls don't stretch for more than fifty yards from his gates. This one must belong to his neighbor."

As I spoke, I realized with a start that I didn't know who Willis, Sr.'s neighbor was. He'd never mentioned having a neighbor and I'd never imagined him having one. My lack of imagination embarrassed me.

"I hate to break it to you, Bess, but your mother sometimes forgets to use her noggin," I said. "Everyone has neighbors, even Grandpa William, and I was a fool to think otherwise." I pursed my lips thoughtfully. "I wonder why he doesn't talk about them?"

The sound of voices floated over the wall as we strolled and rolled beside it, the high-pitched squeals of excited children, the chatter of teenagers, and the deeper tones of a grown man who shared their elation.

"We have liftoff!" the man shouted.

I lifted my gaze automatically and felt a thrill of delight as six kites rose into the sky in quick succession, each one more fantastic than the last. A red dragon bobbed in the rising breeze beside a skeletal, bat-winged biplane. A goldfish swam sinuously beneath a tall ship with billowing sails. Above them all soared a pair of complex and colorful box kites, breathtaking examples of geometry in motion. I couldn't see who the kite-flyers were, but I was grateful to them for adding such a marvelous spectacle to an already magical day.

If I hadn't been entranced by the kite ballet, I might have avoided the pothole. As it was, I pushed the pram straight into the gnarly cavity, hit its jagged lip at an unfortunate angle, and watched helplessly as the front wheel parted company with its axle and bounced merrily down the track ahead of us.

Bess gave a cry of alarm. To avoid frightening her further, I swallowed my own startled yelp and as a result emitted a sound that wasn't quite human. The jarring bump and the scary noise Mummy made were too much for a baby to bear. Bess opened her rosy mouth and began to wail.

The only thing that kept me from banging my stupid head against the stone wall was my need to comfort my child. I propped the pram's front fork on the left-hand bank, undid Bess's harness, lifted her into my arms, and sat with her beside the broken pram, murmuring soothing and deeply apologetic words to her as I rocked her from side to side. Another snack seemed advisable and as soon as Bess latched on to me, she relaxed.

While my daughter regained her composure, I contemplated our plight. I didn't like the thought of pushing a two-wheeled pram all the way back to civilization, but I liked the thought of telephoning Bill even less.

"The track's too rough for a car, so he'll send a helicopter to rescue us," I said bleakly to Bess. "Everyone in Finch will see it whirling over the village and they'll know before nightfall that I got us into another scrape. Six farmyards *and* a helicopter?" I gave a self-pitying moan. "I'll never hear the end of it."

I was so absorbed in my gloomy thoughts that I paid scant attention to the grunts and the scraping noises coming from the far side of the wall until a deep voice spoke from on high.

"May I be of assistance?"

I looked up and saw a man seated atop the stone wall. His short hair was white, as were his closely clipped beard and mustache, and his gray eyes were surrounded by wrinkles, but he didn't dress like a grizzled old man. His rumpled blue shirt, grass-stained khaki trousers, and soiled sneakers reminded me of the clothes worn by my energetic young sons, but his most striking adornment was a wreath of dried grapevines sprinkled with buttercups and wound around his head like a crown.

The sight of the garlanded figure silhouetted against a sky dotted with dancing kites left me temporarily speechless. While I gazed upward in mute astonishment, the man regarded me politely, as if he routinely clambered up walls to rescue nursing mothers in distress.

"I heard a baby's cry," he continued, "and thought I might help in some way."

"Thanks," I said, trying not to stare at his wreath, "but I'm not sure you can help us." I tipped the pram back with one hand and swung it around to reveal the full extent of the tragedy. "Can you mend it?"

The man studied the pram's empty fork for a moment, then nodded.

"Sit tight," he said with a friendly wink. "Back in a jiffy."

He dropped out of sight before I could ask his name.

I gazed at the spot where the man had been, wondering if I'd conjured him out of thin air. The sound of his voice advising the kite-flyers to "Keep your lines taut!" assured me that he wasn't a figment of my imagination, but I still wasn't sure what to make of him. Could he repair the pram? I asked myself. Would he make it possible for me to walk home on my own two feet, with my head held high?

I exchanged glances with Bess and chose to be optimistic. Though the man's grapevine wreath was a bit peculiar, I wouldn't have cared if he'd reappeared clad in a grass skirt and a bowler hat. If he could spare me the humiliation of calling on Bill for support, I decided, he would be my friend forever.

I propped the pram on the bank again and looked down at Bess.

"Your grandfather's neighbor appears to be related to Bacchus," I said. "Bacchus, for your information, is the god of wine and wild parties. Maybe that's why Grandpa William never talks about him. Wild parties aren't really your grandfather's thing."

Bess was too busy to vouchsafe an opinion, so I sang to her to pass the time. When she'd had her fill of cuddles and comfort food, I returned her to the pram, detached the hooded bassinet from the frame, and placed it gently on the ground.

"I'm preparing the work site," I explained to her as I removed the all-important diaper bag from the frame and set it beside the bassinet. "We don't want our mystery mechanic to think we're entirely useless."

I'd scarcely finished speaking when the white-haired man emerged from a distant opening in the wall, riding an old-fashioned, fat-tire bicycle hitched to a box trailer. He pedaled at a leisurely pace, his blue shirt rippling in the breeze, his buttercup-spangled wreath still firmly in place, seemingly untroubled by the track's rough surface.

"I hope he's better at avoiding potholes than I am," I murmured to Bess.

She gurgled her agreement.

The man paused several times to retrieve the pram's errant wheel as well as what appeared to be bits of axle, then rode on without incident, coming to a halt a few feet away from the pothole that had ambushed me. His wrinkled face and snowy hair had led me to believe that he was in Willis, Sr.'s age bracket, but a closer look suggested that he was younger—in his early sixties, perhaps. He seemed entirely unaware of his unusual headgear and I was reluctant to ask him about it. I didn't want to offend a man who might be able to spare me the ignominy of bumping Bess home in a damaged pram.

"Hello again," I said as he dismounted, wheel in hand. "I'm afraid you left before I could introduce myself. I'm Lori Shepherd, but everyone——"

"Everyone calls you Lori," he interjected with a cheerful nod.

"That's right," I said. "How did you know?"

A tiny frown creased his forehead, as if I'd stumped him with a tough question, but it vanished almost as quickly as it had appeared.

"First impressions," he replied. "You don't strike me as the kind of woman who stands on ceremony, Lori. I don't, either. Stand on ceremony, that is. Hargreaves," he continued, pressing a hand to his chest. "Arthur Hargreaves, but I do hope you'll call me Arthur. You're from Finch, aren't you?"

"I'm beginning to think you read minds, Arthur," I said.

"No, no," he said diffidently. "I merely made an educated guess based upon my knowledge of the local byways. Was I wrong?"

"No," I said. "My family and I live near Finch."

"As I thought." He strolled across the lane to peer into the bassinet. "The newest member of your family, I presume?"

"Right again," I said. "Her name is Bess and she'll be four months old in a couple of weeks."

"Enchanting." He bent low and offered his little finger to Bess, who cooed amiably as she grasped it. "A pleasure to meet you, Bess."

"Do you live . . . there?" I asked, nodding toward the stone wall.

Arthur followed my gaze, reclaimed his finger from Bess, and straightened.

"I do," he replied. "There's been a Hargreaves at Hillfont Abbey for more than a hundred years."

"Is that where we are? Hillfont Abbey?" I asked interestedly. "I've never been down this way before, so I'm not familiar with the landmarks. I believe my father-in-law's property runs alongside yours. His name is William Willis and he owns Fairworth House."

"Ah, yes," said Arthur. "The retired attorney with a passion for orchids. He's getting married, isn't he?"

"He is," I said, smiling. "I didn't realize you knew him."

"I don't," said Arthur. "I've set out to introduce myself to him any number of times, but I've never actually managed to get away."

I blinked at him in confusion.

"If you've never met William," I said slowly, "how do you know that he's a retired attorney who's fond of orchids?"

"How does one come to know anything in the country?" Arthur asked lightly. "One listens."

"I'm a pretty good listener," I said, eyeing him doubtfully, "but I've never heard of you." "You might have, if you lived in Tillcote," he said, naming a village fifteen miles north of Finch. "The lane from Hillfont to Tillcote is paved and in good repair. The lane from Hillfont to Finch is neither. I prefer the safer route."

"I don't blame you," I said ruefully. "The unpaved section is downright dangerous."

"Indeed." Arthur held up the detached wheel. "Shall we proceed?"

"By all means," I said.

Arthur rolled up his sleeves and got to work. He turned the pram frame upside down, ran his hand along the front fork, poked his fingertips into the oily holes that had once housed an axle, and slid the wheel in and out of the fork. He then wiped his oily fingers on his trousers and turned to face me.

"On the plus side," he said, "you didn't damage the fork or the wheel. On the minus side, you shattered the axle."

"I wasn't watching where I was going," I admitted guiltily.

"It's not your fault," Arthur assured me. "The axle was clearly defective. When I'm finished here, I'll get on the blower and advise the manufacturer to issue a recall. You could, of course, sue the company for——"

"No, I couldn't," I interrupted. "My husband and I don't believe in frivolous lawsuits. Bess and I were startled, yes, but there was no real harm done to either of us. As long as the manufacturer issues a recall, we won't take anyone to court."

"Good," said Arthur. "I won't have to preserve the evidence."

"I don't care if you bury the evidence in a deep, dark hole," I told him, "as long as you can fix the axle."

"I'm afraid it's beyond repair," Arthur replied, "but I can replace it with a better one."

"How?" I said, taken aback. "Did you bring a non-defective pram axle with you, just in case?"

Arthur was about to answer when a renewed chorus of shouts and laughter reached us from beyond the stone wall. I glanced up and saw the goldfish chasing the red dragon across the sky.

"Who are the kite-flyers?" I asked.

"A veritable horde of Hargreaveses," Arthur replied, smiling. "Grandchildren, mainly. They've designed and built the kites, so it would be a pity for them to miss launch day."

"Do you throw a party on, er, launch day?" I inquired carefully. "Is that why you're, um, dressed up?"

"Dressed up?" Arthur looked from his rolled shirtsleeves to his grease-and-grass—stained trousers, then peered at me questioningly. "I'm not sure I know what you mean."

"I mean . . ." I pointed at my own head, then at his.

"Oh, I see," he said as enlightenment dawned. "Sorry, I forgot." He touched a finger to his grapevine wreath and smiled sheepishly. "I was crowned just an hour ago."

# Three

I wasn't sure whether Arthur was joking or not, but his twinkling eyes seemed to indicate that he didn't take his title too seriously.

"Are you King Arthur?" I said. "The man who invented the Round Table? Camelot's head honcho?" I allowed myself a small smile. "My goodness, Bess, we're in exalted company today."

"I rule a realm larger than Camelot," Arthur informed me. "I am the Summer King."

"Impressive," I said playfully. "What does a Summer King do, Your Highness?"

"He banishes clouds, promotes sunshine, repairs prams . . ." Arthur shrugged. "The usual."

I laughed out loud.

"It's a family tradition," he continued. "There's always been a Summer King at Hillfont Abbey." He reached up to make a minute adjustment to his crown. "The coronation took place early this year because one of my grandsons will be in Chile on Midsummer's Day. He leaves tomorrow."

"Holiday?" I asked.

"A working holiday," Arthur replied. "He's delivering a paper at an astrophysicists' conference in Santiago, but I'm sure he'll find ways to enjoy himself while he's there."

"Wow," I said, authentically impressed. "Your grandson's an astrophysicist? You must be very proud of him."

"He's a good lad," Arthur said complacently. "He designed and built the biplane kite. He wouldn't dream of missing its first flight."

"Naturally," I said, wondering how many astrophysicists flew kites in their spare time.

Arthur carried the pram's frame across the track and set it down beside the box trailer. I looked in on Bess, saw that she was contentedly playing with her toes, and trotted over to stand beside the frame. I was ready to offer Arthur an extra pair of hands if he needed one, but when he raised the trailer's hinged lid, it occurred to me that he might not need my help. If appearances were anything to go by, Arthur was a pram repair specialist.

The box trailer appeared to be filled to the brim with pram parts. An assortment of wheels and frame components lay in orderly piles at one end, while the smaller parts—screws, nuts, washers, and such— were stored in neatly stacked plastic trays at the other end. Arthur pulled a toolbox from between two of the trays and opened it.

"Good grief," I said, scanning the trailer's contents. "You really did bring a non-defective pram axle with you."

"As a matter of fact, I brought quite a few," he said, selecting a crescent wrench from the toolbox. "I harvest the useful parts from my family's old prams and recycle the rest. I could build an entirely new pram for Bess, but there's no need. A simple axle replacement will do."

A gurgle caught my ear and I dashed back to the bassinet. Bess had decided that her toes were less interesting than what Mummy was doing, so I scooped her up and carried her with me to watch the Summer King save the day. He did so at warp speed. In less than ten minutes, the reassembled pram was upright and rolling as smoothly as ever.

"There you are," said Arthur, snapping the bassinet into place. "Your chariot awaits. For safety's sake, I replaced all three axles. The new ones will stand up to any amount of abuse. I know." He inclined his head toward the wall. "I've tested them."

"Thank you, Arthur," I said, beaming at him. "Thank you very much indeed. If Bess could talk, I'm sure she'd tell you how grateful she is, too."

"Think nothing of it," he said. "It was a very basic repair. Your sons could have managed it, young though they are."

My smile faded slightly as he placed the toolbox and the defective axles in the trailer and closed the lid.

"How do you know my sons are young, Arthur?" I asked. "You can't have heard about them in Tillcote. Bill and I have never been to Tillcote, nor have our sons."

"Another educated guess," he answered readily. "You're much too young yourself to have grown children."

Since I'd spent most of the winter feeling like an elderly hippopotamus, the compliment cheered me immensely. Before I could do more than blush and stutter, however, a new voice joined the conversation.

"Grandad? Sorry to intrude, but you're needed."

I looked up to see a boy in torn blue jeans, a tie-dyed T-shirt, and scruffy sneakers straddling the stone wall. He had shaggy blond hair, his blue eyes were framed by round, wire-rimmed spectacles, and he couldn't have been more than fourteen or fifteen years old. Bess squirmed in my arms and smacked her lips when she heard him, as if she hoped to catch his eye.

"Why am I needed?" Arthur asked the boy.

"Harriet's got kite paste in her hair and she wants to cut it out with her pocketknife," the boy replied. "I've told her to rinse the paste out with water, but she claims it'll take too much time."

"Please tell Harriet to put her knife away," Arthur said calmly, "and ask her to meet me at the spigot in the kitchen garden. I'll be along presently. My grandson Marcus," he added for my benefit. "Marcus? Allow me to introduce Lori Shepherd and her daughter, Bess."

"Pleased to meet you," said Marcus. "I'd hurry, if I were you, Grandad. Harriet's in one of her impetuous moods. She's not likely to listen to me."

The boy twisted around like a gymnast, pushed himself off the wall, and landed with an audible thud on the other side.

Arthur turned to me with a wry smile.

"I'm needed," he said.

"I understand," I assured him. "Paste emergencies are a regular occurrence in my house. I don't know how you'll turn your bike and your trailer around in a hurry, though. The lane's pretty narrow."

"I designed the hitch to function in tight spaces," said Arthur. "It's a yoke, you see. I simply detach it from the bicycle, swing it over the trailer, move the bicycle to the opposite end of the trailer, reattach the hitch, and voilà!"

He matched his actions to his words and by the time he finished his sentence, he was ready to tow the trailer back to the distant opening in the wall.

"Clever," I said admiringly.

"Simplicity itself," he countered, mounting the bicycle. "Good day, Lori. I've enjoyed meeting you and Bess. If you're ever in the neighborhood again, please feel free to pay us a call."

"Thank you, Arthur," I said. "We may take you up on your invitation." I kissed Bess's plump cheek. "I think my daughter has a crush on your grandson."

"What a pity," said Arthur. He stood on the pedals and, with an almighty effort, forced them to rotate. "Marcus leaves for Santiago tomorrow."

"Is his father the astrophysicist?" I asked, giving the trailer a shove to help Arthur on his way.

"No," he called to me as the bicycle picked up speed. "Marcus is."

My jaw dropped. My sons were as bright as buttons, but with the best will in the world I couldn't picture either one of them delivering a paper at an academic conference before they were old enough to drive.

"Well, my dear," I murmured to Bess, "it's good to know you like 'em smart."

I watched Arthur until he disappeared from view, then returned Bess to the pram and began to retrace our steps. I tried to avoid the track's most obvious hazards, but I found it difficult to keep my mind from wandering.

I felt as if I'd stepped through the looking glass into a world where shaggy-haired, kite-flying boys morphed overnight into jet-setting scientists while their grandfathers dissected used prams, invented ingenious trailer hitches, and claimed sovereignty over a season instead of a kingdom.

"Maybe he's a crackpot," I said to Bess. "Maybe Grandpa William heard about his wacky ways and decided not to pursue the acquaintance."

Bess waved her arms in protest.

"You're right," I said. "If Arthur Hargreaves is a crackpot, he's a very nice crackpot. Without him——"

I broke off and came to a standstill as my cell phone rang. It was Bill.

"In case you hadn't noticed," he said with some asperity, "forty minutes came and went over an hour ago. Are you lost *again*? How many farmyards will I have to search *this* time?"

"None," I told him airily. "Bess and I were unavoidably detained, but we're on our way home now."

"What detained you?" Bill asked.

"I'll tell you when I see you," I replied. "The story would be incomplete without arm gestures and facial expressions."

"Must be some story," he said.

"It's a doozy," I confirmed. "We'll be home soon."

"I'm home already," said Bill. "I'll have lunch on the table when you get here."

"You are a prince among men," I said, and after exchanging goodbyes, we ended the call.

I tucked the cell phone into my pocket and resumed my homeward journey, but I couldn't stop thinking about the Summer King. I'd become accustomed to knowing just about everything about everyone in Finch. It was unsettling to realize how little I knew about someone who lived within walking distance of the village.

Who was Arthur Hargreaves? I asked myself. Did he live alone at Hillfont Abbey or did the veritable horde of Hargreaveses live there with him? What would I see if I looked over the tall stone wall?

The story, I decided, was far from over.

Bill was shocked to learn that his fabulous all-terrain pram was defective, but he wasn't shocked enough to file a lawsuit. He *threatened* to file one when he telephoned the manufacturer after hearing my tale of woe, but he didn't have to employ scare tactics to stir the company into action because Arthur Hargreaves had already done the job for him.

According to a corporate minion, Arthur had kept his promise to "get on the blower and advise the manufacturer to issue a recall." Acting solely upon my new friend's recommendations, the company's CEO had immediately dispatched an urgent recall notice, cut ties with the supplier who'd provided the faulty axles, and begun the process of vetting a replacement.

By the time Bill finished regaling me with the results of his phone rant, I was halfway through the fruit smoothie and the veggie-stuffed pita sandwich he'd prepared for me. Long walks always made me peckish. Bess, on the other hand, had turned down a meal in favor of practicing push-ups on her padded floor mat, watched from a distance by Stanley, who'd followed Bill into the kitchen. The sleek black cat seemed to find Bess fascinating, but he wisely kept his long, curling tail far away from her questing fingers.

"Who is Arthur Hargreaves?" Bill asked when he'd finally calmed down enough to sit with me at the kitchen table. "And why does he wield so much clout in the corporate world?"

"I don't know and I don't know," I replied. "I was hoping you could tell me."

"Sorry," said Bill. "I've never met the man, but I'd like to shake his hand. He may have saved our daughter's life."

"Let's not get overdramatic," I mumbled through a mouthful of grilled eggplant. "It's not as if Bess flew out of the pram and landed on her head."

"Even so," said Bill, reaching for his own sandwich, "Mr. Hargreaves did us a great favor. I wish I could think of a way to repay him."

"I don't think he'd accept repayment," I said thoughtfully. "He seems like the kind of guy who helps people because he likes to help people." I finished my sandwich and took another swig of the smoothie before continuing, "I can't believe he's flown under our radar for an entire decade, Bill. He lives next door to your father, for heaven's sake.

You'd think they'd have a nodding acquaintance, but as far as I can tell, they've never set eyes on each other. Don't you find it a bit odd?"

"Not really," said Bill. "Father's estate is fairly large, remember. Hillfont Abbey may be next door to Fairworth House, but it isn't next door in the same sense that Pussywillows is next door to the tearoom. Father can stroll the grounds from dawn to dusk without running into another living soul."

"If I were in William's shoes," I said stubbornly, "I'd make more of an effort to get to know my neighbors."

"Father knows quite a few of his neighbors," Bill pointed out. "I'm pretty sure he knows every villager in Finch, whether he wants to or not. He may be relieved to have at least one neighbor who isn't constantly dunning him for donations or recruiting him to work at the church fête."

"*I* recruited William to work at the church fête," I protested in injured tones. "I thought he enjoyed announcing the raffle winners."

"He does, Lori, but it's not only the church fête, is it?" said Bill. "He reads the lessons at church, plays Joseph in the Nativity play, judges the roses at the flower show, pays for the brass band at the gymkhana, holds the sheep dog trials in his south meadow. . . ." Bill shook his head. "I could go on, but you get the picture. It all adds up. He may be content to let sleeping neighbors lie."

"I suppose so," I said grudgingly.

"You're not, though," said Bill.

"I'm not what?" I asked.

"You're not content to let anything lie," Bill declared, laughing. "You're planning to investigate your new chum, aren't you? You're going to make the rounds at church tomorrow morning in order to dig up whatever gossip you can find about Arthur Hargreaves."

"Why wait until tomorrow morning?" I retorted loftily. "I'm not the only inquisitive soul around here. I can think of someone close at hand who's bound to know more about Arthur than we do. I thought I'd ask her about him after lunch."

"A fine idea," said Bill. He popped the last bite of his sandwich into his mouth, brushed the crumbs from his fingers, and pushed his chair away from the table. "I was hoping to grab some daddy-daughter time with Bess while the boys are at the stables."

"Grab all the daddy-daughter time you want," I told him, getting to my feet. "If you need me, I'll be in the study, chatting with Aunt Dimity."

# *Four*

**H**ardly anyone knew about Aunt Dimity. Bill was one of the scant handful of people who were aware of her existence. I didn't advertise her presence in the cottage because she wasn't a normal house guest. She was, in fact, about as far from normal as it was possible to get.

When I was a little girl, my mother told me stories about a wonderful woman named Aunt Dimity who lived in a magical, faraway place known as England. They were my favorite stories and since none of my friends were familiar with them, I grew up believing that my mother had invented Aunt Dimity for the sole purpose of entertaining me, her only child. Many years passed before I learned that my mother had modeled her fictional creation on a real-life Englishwoman named Dimity Westwood.

Dimity Westwood had been my mother's closest friend. The two women had met in London while serving their respective countries during the Second World War. They'd been very young, very frightened, very brave, and very determined to live life to the fullest despite long work hours, short rations, and the ever-present threat of high-explosive bombs blowing them to kingdom come.

When the war in Europe ended and my mother returned to the States, she and Dimity maintained their friendship by sending hundreds of letters back and forth across the Atlantic. After my father's sudden death, those letters became my mother's refuge, a peaceful haven in which she could find respite from the rigors of teaching full time while raising a rambunctious daughter on her own.

My mother was extremely protective of her refuge. I knew nothing of her close ties with Dimity Westwood until I was almost thirty years old and both she and Dimity were dead. It was only then that I learned through a law firm—Bill's law firm—that the seemingly fictional Aunt Dimity had been a living, breathing woman who'd bequeathed to me a comfortable fortune, the honey-colored cottage in which she'd grown up, the precious correspondence she'd exchanged with my mother, and a curious book filled with blank pages and bound in smooth blue leather.

It was through the blue journal that I came to know the real Aunt Dimity. Whenever I gazed at its blank pages, her handwriting would appear, an old-fashioned copperplate taught in the village school at a time when one-room schoolhouses were commonplace. I nearly jumped out of my skin the first time Aunt Dimity wrote to me, but after I'd calmed down enough to read what she had written, I quickly realized that my mother's best friend had become mine.

I had no idea how Aunt Dimity managed to pass through the barrier between this world and the next, and she wasn't too clear about it, either. I occasionally thought that I might be her unfinished business on earth, an ongoing project she had to complete before she could move on. When I was in a less egocentric frame of mind, however, I suspected her of sticking around simply because she couldn't fathom spending eternity without a daily dose of village gossip. As I had pointed out to Bill, I wasn't the only inquisitive soul in the cottage. And for that, I was profoundly grateful.

I stood in the study's doorway for a moment, listening to Bill commune with his darling daughter, then stepped inside and closed the door behind me. I didn't want the sound of my voice to distract Bess from her father's.

The study was silent, but not entirely still. The breeze that had lifted the Hargreaves horde's kites continued to stir the strands of ivy that crisscrossed the diamond-paned windows above the old oak desk, causing shadows to dance across the floor-to-ceiling bookcases. I lit the lamps on the mantel shelf, then paused again.

"'Afternoon, Reginald," I said.

Reginald was a small, powder-pink flannel rabbit who'd entered my life on the same day I'd entered it. He'd been my confidant and my companion in adventure throughout my childhood and he was still a very good listener. A more mature woman might have put him away when she put away childish things, but I couldn't imagine treating my old friend so shabbily. Instead, Reginald sat in his own special niche in the bookshelves, very near the blue journal, and I rarely entered the study without greeting him.

"Bess and I rubbed elbows with royalty this morning," I continued.

Though Reginald didn't speak his thoughts aloud, I could tell by the gleam in his black button eyes that he was intrigued.

"You and me both, little buddy," I said. "I'm counting on Aunt Dimity to give me a crash course on the Summer King."

I touched a fingertip to the faded grape-juice stain on Reginald's pink flannel snout, then took the blue journal from its shelf and sat with it in one of the pair of tall leather armchairs facing the hearth.

"Dimity?" I said as I opened the journal.

I smiled as the familiar lines of royal-blue ink began to loop and curl gracefully across the page.

*Good afternoon, Lori. How are you, my dear? Feeling better, I hope?*

I suppressed an impatient sigh. During my pregnancy, Aunt

Dimity had fallen into the habit of inquiring after my health and she hadn't yet fallen out of it. I found her concern touching, if a bit outdated.

"I'm as strong as an ox," I assured her.

*And Bess?*

"She's in the kitchen, showing Bill how to do push-ups," I said.

*And her brothers?*

"It's Saturday, Dimity," I reminded her. "Will and Rob are galloping over hill and dale on Thunder and Storm."

*Of course they are. They spend every Saturday with their ponies. What about Bill, then? Is he well?*

"He was when I left him," I said, "but if Bess wins the push-up contest, he might be a bit demoralized."

*And how is everyone else? Have you heard from Bree and Jack lately?*

Bree Pym and Jack MacBride were from New Zealand and Australia, respectively, though they currently resided in Finch. Both were in their early twenties and each had been drawn to the village by the death of a relative. Bree had inherited her great-grandaunts' redbrick house, just as Jack had inherited his uncle's ivy-covered cottage, but while Bree intended to go on living in her inheritance, Jack had put his up for sale.

Bree and Jack were the youngest unmarried couple in Finch by a matter of decades. As such, they'd been subjected to an excruciating degree of scrutiny by their neighbors. The women hazarded endless guesses about when, where, and how they would marry and the men placed bets on when Jack would move in with Bree, whether they were married or not.

While speculation swirled around them, the young couple had decided—quite wisely, in my opinion—to put their fledgling relationship to the test by embarking on a lengthy tour of their home countries. They'd been away for two months already, but they'd kept in touch with me, and as far as I could tell, they were still a couple.

"We received a postcard from them this morning," I said in reply to Aunt Dimity's question. Bree and Jack were gracious enough to acknowledge my lack of computer skills by resorting to quaint, old-fashioned methods of communication, none of which required the use of a keyboard. "They've made it to Uluru, but I don't think Bree will ever love the place as much as Jack does. All she wrote was: 'The flies are horrible and the heat is worse.'"

*Oh, well. They don't have to agree on everything. Few couples do. And Bree adored Sydney and the Great Barrier Reef. You don't suppose Jack will persuade her to stay in Australia, do you?*

"I'll never forgive him if he does," I said fervently. "Finch needs Bree's energy, not to mention her sense of humor. What it doesn't need is another empty house. Two is already too many."

*Three, if you count Pussywillows.*

"Thanks for the reminder," I said gloomily. "But you're right. When Amelia takes her rightful place as the mistress of Fairworth House, Pussywillows will be empty, too. And Finch will be one step closer to becoming a ghost town."

*Are there still no prospective buyers on the horizon?*

"I'm sure there are plenty of prospective buyers on the horizon," I said, "but they don't seem to come any closer. It's weird, Dimity. It's as if Finch is surrounded by a home-buyer-repelling force field."

*I suspect that something other than a force field may be to blame for the situation. The cottages may be overpriced. They may have structural defects of which we are unaware.*

"None of them have structural defects," I said swiftly, though honesty compelled me to add, "At least, they don't have any *visible* defects."

*Exactly so. They could have dry rot or rising damp or cracked foundations or an infestation of deathwatch beetles or any number of invisible defects that would keep a rational home buyer at bay.*

"Impossible," I said. "Jack spent a small fortune refurbishing Ivy Cottage and Amelia wouldn't have bought Pussywillows in the first place if it had been a wreck. And if Rose Cottage was on the verge of collapse, I would have heard about it. Someone in the village would have told me."

*Are you certain? You've been rather busy for the past four months. You may not be as up-to-date with village news as you once were.*

Aunt Dimity's comment hit me like a bucket of cold water because I knew as soon as I read it that it was true. Since Bess's birth, I'd been too preoccupied to dive into the stream of gossip that flowed ceaselessly through the village. For all I knew, Rose Cottage might be filled to the rafters with dry rot, rising damp, and deathwatch beetles.

While I stared in dismay at the journal, Aunt Dimity's handwriting continued.

*Then again, the cottages may not be the problem. Finch may be too small and too isolated for some people. Families with children, for example, might prefer to live closer to a school or to a hospital or to both.*

"Bill and I have children," I said resentfully, "and we don't feel the need to live near a school or a hospital."

*Your children have never had a medical emergency, have they, my dear?*

"No," I conceded grudgingly. "I'm the only member of my family who's seen the inside of an emergency room, but that's beside the point." I could feel my temper flare at the mere thought of outsiders belittling my community. "The point is: People have been raising children in Finch since the year dot and they've gotten along perfectly well without a hospital on their doorstep. And the schools in

Upper Deeping are practically next door. What kind of parents would begrudge spending a few extra minutes in a car if it meant that they could raise their children in a safe and healthy environment?"

*You needn't convince me, Lori. I was born and raised in Finch and I couldn't have had a happier childhood.*

"Nor could Will and Rob," I declared angrily. I glared at the empty hearth, as if it had insulted my village, then muttered gruffly, "Sorry, Dimity. I didn't mean to raise my voice to you."

*No offense taken, my dear. I know how much Finch means to you. If you weren't devoted to the village, you wouldn't worry about its future.*

"I am worried about its future," I acknowledged. "Will and Rob have lots of playmates at the stables, but what if Bess doesn't care for horses? Where will she find friends? Local friends, I mean, children she can play with after school. If I could have my way, Dimity, I'd fill those empty cottages with young couples and babies."

*I doubt that many young couples with babies can afford to own a country cottage, especially if the cottage is overpriced. I can't imagine that any would wish to purchase a property that required an immense investment of time and money to repair.*

"I agree with you, Dimity," I said, "but what can I do about it?"

*What can you do?* Aunt Dimity's handwriting paused and when it began again, it dashed across the page in a flurry of royal-blue ink. *You can set a good example for your daughter. You can stand up and fight for her future as well as Finch's because, as you so rightly indicated, the two are intimately entwined. If you want Bess's childhood to be as happy as mine——as happy as your sons'——I suggest that you stop wasting your time on tantrums and tirades and start using it wisely. I suggest, in short, that you use your resourcefulness, your creativity, and your considerable intelligence to find a solution to Finch's empty-cottage dilemma!*

If ink could yell, my ears would have been ringing. Aunt Dimity had never taken me to task quite so forcefully before, but I felt as though I'd earned a good scolding. I'd been bemoaning Finch's fate as if I were powerless to change it, despite my firm conviction that no creature on earth was more powerful than a mother rising up to defend her young.

"Message received, Dimity," I said, sitting bolt upright and squaring my shoulders. "I'll find out who the estate agents are and whether or not they've priced the houses correctly. If not, I'll have a word with them about local property values and the advantages of a speedy sale."

*Lori.*

I glanced down at the journal and saw my name, but I was on a roll, so I continued, "I'll ask Mr. Barlow about invisible defects. Our peerless handyman has been in and out of every cottage in Finch more times than I can count. If anything's wrong with Rose Cottage, Mr. Barlow will know what it is and how to fix it. I'll pay him with my own money to make sure that the cottage isn't hiding any unpleasant surprises."

*Lori?*

Again, I glanced down at the journal and again, I went on without stopping. It was as if my brain had awakened from a long nap and was raring to go. I couldn't slow it down.

"I'll also speak with the headmistress, the teachers, and the other parents at Morningside School," I said. "I'll speak with Emma's riding school parents, too. Someone is bound to know of someone who's looking for a home in the country." I looked at the clock on the mantel shelf. "It's a bit late in the day to get started and I'd rather not pester people on a Saturday, but——"

I broke off as Aunt Dimity finally managed to command my attention.

*AT EASE, LORI! Stand down! I don't expect you to find three qualified home buyers overnight, my dear, though I'm glad to hear that you intend to find them. You've had four months of private bliss with little Bess. It's time for you to take an interest in the world beyond the cottage. Finch needs you, Lori.*

"Not as much as I need Finch," I stated firmly. "I'm on it, Dimity. Bess and I will find out everything we can and report back to you."

A knock sounded on the study door. I looked over my shoulder and smiled as Bill entered the room, carrying Bess.

"Nearly time to pick up the boys," he said apologetically. "I've changed Bess's diaper, but she insists on having the one thing I can't give her."

"Gotta go, Dimity," I said. "Bess is hungry."

*Kiss her for me, my dear.*

"You know I will," I said, and as the graceful lines of royal-blue ink began to fade from the page, I closed the journal.

Bill and I exchanged book and baby and while Bill returned the journal to its shelf, I readied myself for mealtime.

"I meant to tell you," he said, "Father has invited us to a welcome-to-Fairworth dinner for my aunts next Saturday—a week from to-day." He sat on the arm of my chair and smoothed Bess's wispy curls back from her forehead. "He'd like us to be there by eight. Formal attire, naturally."

I admired my father-in-law's tactics. Willis, Sr., was aware of Bill's antipathy toward Honoria and Charlotte. I suspected he'd delayed the official family gathering for a week in order to give his son a few extra days to gird himself for it. He'd also limited the amount of time Bill would have to spend with the Harpies: A dinner that started at eight o'clock could be politely concluded by ten.

The meal's formality was another clever touch. A casual brunch or a luncheon could be held in the conservatory, on the terrace, or in the rose garden at Fairworth House, but a formal dinner had to take place in the dining room. The dreaded reunion would, I thought, proceed more peacefully if Bill were separated from his aunts by the broad width of Willis, Sr.'s dining room table.

"I hope your aunts won't expect us to bring the boys," I said. "Will and Rob have a hard time remembering to be formal at formal dinners."

"I couldn't care less about my aunts' expectations," said Bill. "I've already made arrangements for the boys. They'll spend the weekend with Emma at Anscombe Manor."

"You've thought of everything," I said, impressed. "We'll bring Bess with us, of course. If she needs forty winks or a feed, she and I will repair decorously to William's nursery."

"I call dibs on diaper changes," Bill said instantly.

"Now, there's a sentence I never thought you'd utter," I said, giggling.

"Needs must," Bill grumbled.

"Will you be at Fairworth House on Monday to welcome your aunts?" I asked, though I thought I knew the answer.

"No can do," he said, shaking his head. "I'll be tied up at the office all week, working on Didier Pinot's revised will."

"Has he revised it again?" I said, surprised. Bill's fractious client had, to my knowledge, revised his will seven times since January.

"I may have suggested that Monsieur Pinot review the section concerning his collection of medieval artifacts," Bill admitted, studying his fingernails. "He was going to leave the skulls to his third niece, but I think they'll be better off with his second nephew."

"What a convenient suggestion," I said, arching an eyebrow.

"I had to do something," he said. "Work is the only excuse the Harpies will accept for my absence." He frowned down at me. "You're not planning to roll out the red carpet for them, are you?"

"I'm not planning on it," I said, "but if Amelia asks me to come over, I will. She hasn't met Charlotte and Honoria before. She may need my support."

"No," Bill declared adamantly, getting to his feet. "I can't let you face those dragons unprotected."

"I won't be unprotected," I said. "Bess will be with me." I caught his hand in mine and gave it a reassuring squeeze. "I'll be fine, Bill, and Amelia will be a lot less nervous without you there, huffing and puffing and muttering death threats under your breath. I could be wrong, but I don't think her wedding plans include a double homicide at Fairworth House."

Bill laughed in spite of himself.

"Let's hope she doesn't ask you to come over," he said. The clock on the mantel shelf chimed softly and he bent to kiss Bess and me. "I'd better be on my way or the boys will start making beds for themselves in the hayloft."

He kissed me a second time, then left the study. He'd closed the front door behind him before it dawned on me that I'd failed to do the one thing I'd set out to do when I'd entered the study. Although I'd been closeted with Aunt Dimity for nearly an hour, I hadn't asked her a single question about Arthur Hargreaves.

"I'll ask the villagers about him after church tomorrow," I murmured complacently. "You don't know it yet, baby girl, but we're surrounded by the most comprehensive spy network on the planet."

Chuckling softly, I settled in to savor another moment of private bliss with Bess.

# Five

A moderately alarming telephone call from my father-in-law's fiancée interrupted our pre-church readiness drill the following morning. I picked up the phone in the kitchen, leaving Bill to run a wet comb through Rob's hair, make sure Will's socks matched, place Bess in her car seat cum carry cot, and replenish the diaper bag's ever-diminishing contents.

"I'm afraid William and I won't attend church today, Lori," Amelia began. "And I'm very sorry to say it, but we've canceled brunch as well."

I blinked in surprise. My father-in-law seldom altered his routines. On Sundays, as regular as clockwork, he attended the morning service at St. George's, then hosted a family brunch at Fairworth House. He seemed to regard each activity as a sacred duty, so it came as something of a shock to hear that he was backing out of both. Since the weather was flawless, I could think of only one reason for his defection.

"Is William ill?" I asked.

"Not in the least," Amelia replied. "He's in fine fettle at the moment, but I think——and he agrees with me——that he should conserve his strength before his sisters arrive tomorrow."

"How right you are," I said feelingly. "William will need all the rest he can get before Honoria and Charlotte invade Fairworth House because he won't get much while they're there. What time do you expect them?"

"Noon or thereabouts," said Amelia. "I plan to be here by nine, to oversee last-minute preparations. Not that there will be much for me to oversee. As you know, Deirdre Donovan is an excellent house-keeper." She hesitated, then went on more quietly, as if she didn't wish to be overheard. "To tell you the truth, Lori, I'm a bit appre-hensive about meeting William's sisters. I gather they can be some-what . . . overwhelming."

"Overwhelming is one way to describe them," I said dryly. "I can think of a few others. But don't worry, Amelia. Bess and I will be there to soften them up for you. We'll go straight to Fairworth House after we drop Will and Rob off at school."

"And Bill?" she asked.

"He's swamped with work," I replied, resisting the temptation to inform Amelia that Bill had swamped himself with work for the ex-press purpose of avoiding his aunts. "He'll be chained to his desk all week—there's no avoiding it—but he and I will come to William's dinner on Saturday."

"Wonderful," said Amelia. "What time should I expect you to-morrow?"

"I'll be with you as fast as I can," I promised.

It crossed my mind to ask Amelia if Willis, Sr., had ever spoken to her about Arthur Hargreaves, but a glance at the kitchen clock told me that I had to cut the call short or risk arriving at church even later than usual.

"I'm sorry, Amelia, but I have to dash," I said. "Give William my love. Tell him his granddaughter can't wait to see him."

"I will," she said. "Please convey our apologies to the vicar."

"Consider it done," I said.

I said a final good-bye, then dropped the phone onto its cradle and ran outside to join Bill, Will, Rob, and Bess, who were waiting for me in our canary-yellow Range Rover.

"Who called?" Bill asked as he backed the Rover out of our gravel driveway and into the lane.

"Amelia," I replied and quickly summarized the conversation.

Bill's grip on the steering wheel tightened when I mentioned Charlotte and Honoria. He knew better than to speak unreservedly in front of the attentive little pitchers in the backseat, but his white knuckles seemed to indicate that he was once again entertaining the notion of strangling his aunts. I rubbed his shoulder soothingly and his fingers gradually relaxed, but I doubted they would stay that way while the Harpies were in town.

We made it to St. George's in ten minutes flat, but we were still the last family to slide into a pew. We were almost always the last family to be seated in church, but instead of receiving a volley of sharp glances and disapproving sniffs from those who invariably arrived on time, we were greeted with nothing but friendly nods and sympathetic smiles. A family with a new baby in tow could get away with just about anything in Finch.

Bess slept through the vicar's sermon, as did her father and several other members of the congregation. The vicar was held in high esteem by everyone who knew him, but his sermons could not be called stimulating. If it hadn't been for Will and Rob, I would have dozed off, too, but they kept me awake with whispered suggestions about what we could do after church, now that brunch at Grandpa's house was off the table.

The first thing they did after church was to play a rousing game of tag in the churchyard. Bill rounded them up and took them to the village green to play tag in a more appropriate setting, but I stayed behind with Bess and the diaper bag to pursue my goal of learning what I could about Arthur Hargreaves. I had no trouble attracting villagers. Bess was the most popular girl in town.

Before I could commence my inquiry, however, I would have to withstand a barrage of child-rearing advice from my well-meaning neighbors. After the twins were born, Bill and I had discovered that everyone in Finch knew how to raise our children better than we did. The situation was much the same after Bess's birth and we reacted to it in much the same way. We listened politely, then did what we thought was right.

Peggy Taxman was the first villager to approach me. Peggy sailed across the churchyard like a battleship, scattering all before her, while Jasper Taxman, her mild-mannered husband, plodded meekly in her wake. I readied myself for combat. I sometimes found it difficult to listen politely to Peggy Taxman.

When Peggy reached me, she looked into the carry cot, regarded me dolefully, and observed in a voice that could be heard ten miles away, "I don't know how you got pregnant before Nell and Cassie."

My friends and neighbors, Nell Anscombe-Smith and Cassie Harris, were half my age, give or take a few years. They'd been the leading contenders in Finch's pregnancy sweepstakes until I'd pipped them at the post by producing Bess. I doubted that Peggy would ever stop moaning about it.

"Don't you?" I said brightly. "It's quite simple, really. When a man and a woman love each other very much——"

"Still giving Bess the breast?" Peggy broke in, glaring at me.

"Both breasts, actually," I replied. "Whenever she wants them. I learned how to do it when I had the twins, but I'm much better at it now. Would you like me to demonstrate?"

Jasper Taxman blushed crimson, spun on his heel, and hastened to join George Wetherhead and Mr. Barlow, who were standing together near the lych-gate. Jasper, like many men of his generation, felt that maternal matters should not be discussed, much less demonstrated, in mixed company.

While Jasper made his escape, Peggy's eyes narrowed dangerously behind her pointy, rhinestone-studded glasses.

"The bottle was good enough for me!" she thundered. "It's common knowledge that breast feeding makes children weak and submissive."

I caught a glimpse of Will and Rob tackling their father on the village green and smiled serenely.

"Common it may be, but it's not knowledge," Sally Cook declared, marching up to stand at Peggy's elbow. Silver-haired, energetic, and grandmother-shaped, Sally looked like a bobbing buoy beside her tall, broad-shouldered rival. "My mother breast-fed my sister and me and we're not weak or submissive."

"Same goes for me and my brothers," said Christine Peacock as she joined our growing circle.

I didn't have to say a word. Sally had already proved her point by sending her husband off to open the tearoom, as had Christine, who'd sent her husband off to open the pub.

"Nothing wrong with breast feeding," Christine continued. "Mother's milk boosts a baby's immune system."

"I'd swaddle her more tightly, though," Sally said, peering down at Bess. "Nothing makes a baby feel more secure than a nice, tight swaddle."

"Swaddling's good for other things, too," bellowed Peggy, who was always reluctant to let Sally—or anyone else—have the last word. "It keeps babies from scratching their faces with their sharp little fingernails."

"I'd put mittens on Bess," Christine opined. "Mittens are the best way to keep a baby from scratching her face."

"Nonsense!" roared Peggy. "Mittens are a well-known choking hazard!"

"My brothers and I didn't choke on *our* mittens," Christine said heatedly.

"My sister and I didn't need mittens because we were properly swaddled," Sally said with a superior air.

Our little group doubled in size with the addition of Selena Buxton, Opal Taylor, Millicent Scroggins, and Elspeth Binney, a quartet of widows and spinsters whom Bill had dubbed "Father's Handmaidens" because of their ill-fated attempts to woo Willis, Sr. They, too, had strong opinions on mittens and swaddling, among many other topics, and they didn't hesitate to express them. I listened politely and hoped they'd run out of steam before Will and Rob ran out of games to play.

A happy gurgle from Bess silenced the debate and I leapt at the opportunity to change the subject.

"I met the most interesting man yesterday," I said. "Do any of you know Arthur Hargreaves?"

"Hargreaves?" said Sally. Her lips tightened. "They're Tillcote folk. We don't have much to do with Tillcote folk."

"Why not?" I asked.

"They're an uppity bunch," said Christine. "A Tillcote chap came into the pub a few years back and spat out a mouthful of Dick's homemade wine. He said it wasn't fit for pigs."

"One of their women told me that, if I wasn't careful, I'd eat up my profits," Sally said huffily. "As if anyone would trust a skinny baker."

Since Dick Peacock's homemade wine could easily be mistaken for paint thinner and since Sally Cook was very far from skinny, I couldn't argue with the Tillcote folks' observations, but I could certainly find fault with their manners.

"They never come to our flower show," said Selena.

"Or our art show," said Elspeth.

"A pair of them came to the jumble sale once, but they didn't buy anything," Opal said indignantly. "They made snippy comments about my seashell lamp, then walked away with their noses in the air."

There was a pause as those of us who'd made our own snippy comments about Opal's lamp averted our eyes, but Millicent Scroggins soon got the ball rolling again.

"They reckon their church is prettier than St. George's," she said.

"They're thieves!" Peggy boomed, clearly intent on trumping the others. "One of their youngsters pinched a packet of crisps from the Emporium a few years ago. I couldn't prove it, but I know it was him." She pursed her lips haughtily. "It's the sort of behavior I've come to expect from Tillcote folk."

"You steer clear of them, Lori," Sally warned me. "Tillcote folk'd steal the pennies off a dead man's eyes. Well," she went on cheerfully, as if she hadn't just denounced an entire village, "I'd best be off. My Henry should have preheated the ovens by now. Lemon poppy-seed cake in an hour for those who want it."

"I'll be off, too," said Christine. "Dick'll need a hand with the beer barrels."

"We should be on our way as well," said Elspeth, and the rest of the Handmaidens nodded their agreement. "We're going to see Mr. Shuttleworth's art exhibit in Upper Deeping this afternoon."

"Well, Jasper and I can't stand around jabbering all day," Peggy thundered. "We have to open the Emporium *and* the greengrocer's shop!"

The women bade a fond farewell to Bess and left the churchyard, taking Jasper Taxman with them. They were replaced almost instantly by Grant Tavistock and Charles Bellingham, who ran an art appraisal and restoration business from their home, Crabtree Cottage. Grant was short and slim, with neatly trimmed salt-and-pepper hair, while Charles was tall, portly, and balding. I enjoyed their company immensely.

"Thank heavens," Charles murmured. "I thought they'd never leave."

He took the carry cot from me and made soft kissing noises at Bess, who tried her best to imitate him.

"What did the ladies tell you to do this time?" Grant asked, gallantly relieving me of the diaper bag. "Stop nursing Bess immediately or keep nursing her until she's old enough to vote?"

"A little of both," I said, laughing.

"The dear ladies of Finch," Charles said with an affectionate sigh. "Is any subject beyond their ken?"

"I may have found one," I told him. "They didn't have a lot to say about a man I met yesterday. His name is Arthur Hargreaves."

Charles snapped to attention and Grant looked as though I'd announced a UFO sighting.

"Arthur Hargreaves!" Charles exclaimed. "The Hermit of Hillfont Abbey? You can't possibly have met *him*!"

# Six

*I* felt as though I'd struck gold. The dear ladies of Finch might not know much about Arthur Hargreaves beyond his connection with the uppity folk in Tillcote, but Grant and Charles evidently did.

"Are you serious, Lori?" said Grant. "Have you really met Arthur Hargreaves?"

"By which we mean to say: Did you, in actual fact, have an up-close, face-to-face encounter with him?" Charles amplified.

I looked past Grant and observed that Bill and the twins had finished roughhousing on the village green and begun strolling up the lane toward St. George's. Bill stopped at the low stone wall surrounding the churchyard, saw that I was engaged in gossip-gathering, and signaled that he would take Rob and Will to the tearoom. I gave him a thumbs-up in return. Our sons were big fans of Sally Cook's lemon poppy-seed cake.

*"Well?"* Charles said impatiently, reclaiming my attention.

"I did, in actual fact, have an up-close, face-to-face encounter with Arthur Hargreaves," I said with mock solemnity, amused by the awestruck glances the pair exchanged.

"When?" Grant asked eagerly. "Where?"

"How?" Charles added.

"Bess and I met Arthur yesterday," I explained. "We were walking near Hillfont Abbey when a wheel on Bess's pram came off. Arthur was kind enough to fix it for us."

*"Arthur?"* Charles goggled at me. "You're on a first-name basis with *Arthur Hargreaves?*"

"I guess so," I said. "He certainly didn't introduce himself as the Hermit of Hillfont Abbey."

"Hermits don't usually introduce themselves," Charles said brusquely. "Anonymity is a hallmark of hermithood."

"What were you doing near Hillfont Abbey?" Grant asked, waving his partner to silence.

"I told you," I said. "I was taking Bess for a walk."

"And Arthur Hargreaves just happened to come along and fix Bess's broken pram," said Grant, as if he had to hear the story twice over before he could bring himself to believe it.

"That's right," I said. "He heard Bess crying and offered to help us. He's a very nice man."

"A very nice man," Grant repeated incredulously.

"He was our knight in shining armor," I stated emphatically. "As a matter of fact, he called himself the Summer King."

"Why?" Charles demanded, gazing avidly at me.

"It's a family tradition, apparently," I said. "The title's been passed down from father to son for as long as there have been Hargreaveses at Hillfont Abbey." I smiled as I recalled Arthur's lighthearted description of a Summer King's duties. "Arthur didn't seem to think it was a big deal. He gave me the impression that it's a kind of game his family plays to celebrate summer."

"Did you meet his family as well?" Grant asked faintly.

"Only his grandson Marcus," I replied, "the teenaged astrophysicist."

Grant gaped at me, then sat abruptly on the late Joseph Cringle's table tomb, as if his legs had given way.

"Are you all right?" I asked, eyeing him with concern.

"He's bowled over," said Charles.

"Completely bowled over," Grant confirmed, putting a hand to his forehead.

Charles rested Bess's carry cot on the tomb, but the secure grip he maintained on the handle met with my approval.

"I must confess that I'm bowled over as well," Charles said. "We know of Arthur Hargreaves, of course, but we've never had the privilege of meeting him or his grandson. We didn't even know he had a grandson, let alone a teenaged astrophysicist grandson. You've joined an extremely exclusive club, Lori."

I took a step closer to the tomb and the three of us automatically tilted our heads forward and lowered our voices, as one did when sharing confidential information in Finch.

"I've told you mine," I said. "Now you tell me yours. Come on, boys, spill it. What do you know about Arthur Hargreaves?"

"We know that the villagers don't think much of him," said Charles. "It has something to do with an ancient feud between Finch and Tillcote. Peggy Taxman had a fit when we mentioned his name. We've avoided the subject ever since."

"You don't have to avoid it with me," I said. "I'm all ears."

"We don't *know* anything," Grant said, but when I looked daggers at him, he hastened to add, "We've *heard* a few tidbits, though."

"Rumor has it," said Charles, "that he's madly wealthy and— some say—ever so slightly mad."

"According to a reliable source," said Grant, "he has a history of making anonymous bids at high-end art auctions."

"Bids that are invariably successful," Charles put in.

"Who is this reliable source?" I asked.

"Florence Urquhart," Charles replied readily. "Flo's an old chum of ours. She was working the phones at a well-known art auction house when the bids came in. Flo would lose her job—and her pension—if she revealed the bidder's identity, but she couldn't keep herself from dropping a few leaden hints over wine and cheese at a gallery opening last winter."

"If Arthur Hargreaves is indeed the man behind the anonymous bids," Grant said, "he has exquisite taste and *fantastically* deep pockets. I'd give a big toe or two to own the da Vinci sketch he purchased a month ago." He winked broadly at me as he added, "*Allegedly.*"

"How did Arthur become madly wealthy?" I asked.

"Inheritance, followed by clever investments, or so we've heard," said Grant. "I've never heard it said that he *works* for a living."

"Nor have I," said Charles.

"But you have heard it said that he's mad," I reminded them.

"Ever so slightly mad," Charles corrected me. "He has an absolute mania about privacy. He doesn't give interviews. He doesn't make public appearances. He doesn't leave the abbey, if he can help it. He's the very definition of a recluse. Hence, his soubriquet: the Hermit of Hillfont Abbey."

"Yet he's tremendously influential," Grant chimed in.

"We've always pictured him as a spider sitting at the center of a web," said Charles. "He has only to twang a silk thread to make things happen."

I remembered Bill's telephone call to the pram manufacturer and his subsequent comments about the clout Arthur appeared to wield in the corporate world.

"Would he have a direct line to the CEO of a big company?" I asked.

"My guess is that Arthur Hargreaves has many direct lines to many CEOs of many big companies," said Grant.

I'd been keeping an eye on Bess, but she'd shown no signs of feeling neglected. She'd followed our conversation with rapt attention, inserting an occasional stream of baby babble that had been adoringly mimicked by Charles, despite his keen interest in the subject under discussion. He would, I thought, have made a wonderful father.

"You can imagine our surprise," Grant continued, "when you told us that Arthur Hargreaves fixed Bess's pram. It doesn't seem like the sort of thing a high-powered mystery mogul would do."

"Maybe not," I said, "but the Arthur Hargreaves Bess and I met is nothing like the man you've described. He wasn't standoffish or intimidating, and there was nothing spider-like about him. The man we met was warm, funny, and down-to-earth."

"Perhaps he has a soft spot for children," Charles suggested. He turned to Bess and said in his talking-to-infants voice, "Who wouldn't have a soft spot for you, my little angel?"

"We must, of course, defer to your better judgment, Lori," said Grant. "Unlike you, Charles and I are not on a first-name basis with Mr. Hargreaves."

"Bess is on a first-name basis with him, too," I said proudly. "She may not be able to say Arthur's name yet, but if she could, I'm sure he would allow it."

"Who could refuse you anything?" Charles asked Bess. "You're *irresistible*."

A pair of dimples appeared in Bess's plump cheeks and three hearts melted simultaneously.

"Do *not* tell me it's gas," Charles commanded, with a stern look in my direction. "I know a smile when I see one."

"It's not gas," I said obediently, but as a familiar aroma rose from the carry cot, I was forced to add, "It is, however, time for a diaper change."

The speed with which Charles passed the carry cot to me gave me second thoughts about his fitness for fatherhood.

"Forgive us," he said as he backed away from the scene of the crime. "We've kept you talking too long."

Grant seemed to be making a valiant attempt not to grimace as he retreated alongside his partner.

"You will give Mr. Hargreaves our number, won't you?" he said from a safe distance. "You'll tell him we're right here in Finch? Charles and I would be honored to clean, restore, and/or appraise any work of art in his collection."

"If I see him, I'll tell him," I promised. "If you see Bill, will you tell him that Bess and I are in St. George's?"

"Will do," Charles called. "Until we meet again, little angel."

He kissed his fingers to Bess and followed Grant out of the churchyard.

It would have been disrespectful to use Joseph Cringle's tomb as a changing table, but I knew the vicar wouldn't object to me using a church pew. There wouldn't be another service until Evensong, and as he'd said himself, the mess in a child's nappy was nothing compared to the mess left behind in St. George's after the beast blessing.

I chose the pew my family and I had recently vacated, swapped Bess's dirty diaper for a clean one, and gathered her up for a cuddle. The humble old church's serene atmosphere seemed to seep into us and we remained blessedly undisturbed until a footstep sounded in the south porch.

# Seven

The iron-banded oak door swung inward and after a moment's pause, Mr. Barlow entered the church. Mr. Barlow was a compact but powerfully built man with grizzled hair and a strong work ethic. When he wasn't busy looking after the church and the churchyard, he looked after the village at large.

I thought of him as Finch's own Mr. Fix-It. If the Range Rover refused to start, I called Mr. Barlow. If one of the twins batted a cricket ball through the kitchen window, I called Mr. Barlow. If the Summer King hadn't repaired Bess's all-terrain pram, I would have called Mr. Barlow. Everyone in Finch called on Mr. Barlow for help because he was the rarest of entities: an honest, reliable, highly skilled handyman.

I was always pleased to see him, but my promise to Aunt Dimity made me even happier than usual to catch him on his own. I was certain that he'd be able to answer the questions she'd posed about Rose Cottage's structural integrity.

Mr. Barlow had already changed out of his Sunday best and into his everyday work attire—a short-sleeved cotton shirt, twill trousers, and well-worn leather work boots. The slight delay in his entry was explained by the fact that he strode into St. George's carrying a stepladder under his left arm and a toolbox in his right hand.

"Hello, Mr. Barlow," I said.

I spoke softly to avoid startling him, but I might as well have screeched. He took one look at Bess and me, blushed to his roots, and would have executed an abrupt about-face if the ladder hadn't hindered him. He seemed to be under the impression that I was engaged in a maternal activity he didn't wish to witness.

"Sorry, Lori," he said, staring stolidly at his feet. "Came to mend the ceiling lamp in the vestry. Didn't see you there. I can come back later."

"Diaper change, Mr. Barlow!" I called, to put him at ease. "Not . . . the other. And I'm done with the diaper. We're both perfectly decent, I promise you."

Mr. Barlow slowly raised his head to peek at us.

"Please don't go," I said. I returned Bess to her carry cot and tucked a blanket around her to ward off lurking drafts. "If you can spare a minute, I'd like to have a word with you."

Mr. Barlow leaned the ladder against the wall, placed the toolbox on the floor, and crossed to sit in the pew in front of ours, half-turned, with his arm draped over the back. He looked down at Bess and chuckled ruefully.

"You must think I'm as old-fashioned as a butter churn," he said.

"So what if you are?" I retorted. "I'd rather you were old-fashioned and polite than modern and rude."

"How's the little one coming along?" he asked. "I didn't have a chance to look in on her after church, what with the ladies crowding round you like a flock of old biddies."

"Bess is healthy, happy, and as sweet as honey," I replied. "I'm a lucky mum."

"That you are," he said, gazing tenderly at Bess.

"Would you like to hold her?" I asked.

"No, thanks," he said, recoiling in alarm. "I'm better with shovels than babies, Lori. I'd only make Bess cry. Or drop her. Or worse."

"You wouldn't do anything of the sort," I said. "If you can mend a light fixture, you can hold a baby."

"That's as may be," said Mr. Barlow. "But I'd rather not risk it." He cleared his throat and got down to business. "What can I do for you, Lori? Will and Rob break another window?"

"Not yet," I said with a wry smile, "but it's only a matter of time. No, Mr. Barlow, there's nothing wrong with *my* cottage. I want to know if there's something wrong with Rose Cottage."

"Like what?" he asked, frowning slightly.

I remembered the litany of ills Aunt Dimity had cited the previous evening and used it in my reply.

"A problem that isn't easy to see from the outside," I explained, "like a cracked foundation or rising damp or an infestation of death-watch beetles."

"Rose Cottage is as sound as a bell," Mr. Barlow stated firmly. "Mr. and Mrs. Blanding took good care of it before they moved up north to be near their son. I had to replace a few slates on the roof, patch a flagstone in the hearth, and rehang a sash window in the back bedroom for them, but those are routine maintenance jobs, not major overhauls." His eyes narrowed. "Why? What have you heard? If Peggy Taxman has been spreading nasty rumors about——"

"She hasn't," I broke in. "Not within my hearing, anyway. I'm simply trying to figure out why Rose Cottage and Ivy Cottage have been sitting around, unsold, for the past five months."

"It has nothing to do with their condition," Mr. Barlow said stoutly. "Jack MacBride spent a small fortune updating Ivy Cottage before he and Bree took off on their trip. He left the place in tip-top shape." Mr. Barlow glanced at me. "Have you heard from them lately, Jack and Bree?"

"Postcard on Saturday," I said. "They're still in Australia and having a mostly wonderful time."

"Hope they come back," Mr. Barlow said with a worried frown.

"I'm sure they will," I said with more confidence than I felt. "Bree's attached to her great-grandaunts' house and Jack's attached to Bree, so I can't imagine them living anywhere else after they're married."

"Are they to be wed?" Mr. Barlow leaned toward me attentively, demonstrating that no one in Finch, not even our down-to-earth handyman, was immune to the gossip bug.

"They haven't picked a date yet," I told him, "but I'll be utterly amazed if they don't pick one as soon as they get back." I paused to munch on a foot Bess had kicked free from her blanket, then covered her up again and continued, "Why would Peggy Taxman spread nasty rumors about Rose Cottage?"

"Because she's greedy," he replied. "Enough is never enough for Peggy. She always wants more. She's already got the Emporium and the greengrocer's shop, and she tried to snatch the tearoom from Sally Cook last year. She must be licking her chops over Rose Cottage and Ivy Cottage. I reckon she'd rent them out as holiday homes for part-timers. You know, weekenders and such, like that woman who had Pussywillows before Amelia Thistle." He clucked his tongue in disgust. "Glad to see the back of that woman. Slept here, that's all she did. Didn't even come to the church fête."

"If Peggy wants to buy the cottages," I said, bypassing the conversational detour, "why hasn't she gone ahead and bought them? Why would she waste time inventing rumors about them?"

"To drive the price down, of course," said Mr. Barlow, as if it were the most obvious conclusion one could draw. "If she makes the places look bad, she'll scare away the competition and Marigold Edwards will have to lower the prices."

Bess was absorbed in a second attempt to free her foot, so I switched three-quarters of my attention to Mr. Barlow. I had a feeling that I was about to strike gold again.

"Who is Marigold Edwards?" I asked.

"She's an estate agent," said Mr. Barlow. "*The* estate agent, really. Marigold married into the business, but her husband's agency, the Edwards Estate Agency, has handled property in Finch for as long as I can remember. Old man Edwards—Marigold's father-in-law—he's retired now, but he found my house for me, just like Marigold found Pussywillows for Amelia Thistle."

Since I'd inherited the cottage from Aunt Dimity, and since the inheritance had been handled by a law firm well versed in English property law, I hadn't had to deal with a real estate agent when I'd moved to Finch, but I had a vague recollection of seeing one show Pussywillows to Amelia.

"Petite woman?" I said tentatively. "Blond? Well dressed? Not quite as young as she'd like to be?"

"That's Marigold," said Mr. Barlow, nodding.

"You wouldn't happen to have her phone number with you, would you?" I asked.

"Have it right here," said Mr. Barlow, tapping the side of his head, "but I'll write it down for you, if you like."

"Please," I said.

Mr. Barlow took a small notebook and a carpenter's pencil from his shirt pocket, wrote the phone number on one of the notebook's pages, tore the page out, and handed it to me.

"Her office is in Upper Deeping," he said. He looked down at his roughened hands, then raised his eyes to look straight into mine as he asked, "You and Bill aren't thinking of selling your cottage, are you?"

"Definitely not," I replied, as I tucked the scrap of paper into the diaper bag. "I asked for Marigold's number so I can have it on hand if I run into someone who's in the market for a country cottage." I hesitated, then said, "I don't mean to pry, Mr. Barlow, but . . . why do you know Marigold's phone number by heart?"

"I work for the Edwards agency," he said. "Marigold pays me good money to look after Ivy Cottage and Rose Cottage. I look in on Bree's house, too, but I don't have to be paid to do that."

I peered at him curiously. "When you say you 'look after' the cottages, what do you mean, exactly?"

"I air them, check the roofs and the windows for leaks, keep the gardens from running wild, make sure the plumbing's in good working order, that sort of thing," Mr. Barlow replied. "I expect I'll do the same for Pussywillows, once Amelia Thistle becomes Mrs. Willis and moves into Fairworth House." He pursed his lips thoughtfully. "Houses like to be lived in, Lori. They go to rack and ruin if they're left on their own for too long."

"I suppose they do," I said. "It sounds as though Marigold Edwards knows her business."

"She does," said Mr. Barlow. "Some people think she's flighty, but she isn't. She has a good head on her shoulders, does Marigold. If Peggy Taxman is up to her old tricks again, Marigold will put a spoke in her wheel. I hope she will, anyway." His brow furrowed and a shadow seemed to cross his face. "Finch is a small place, Lori. Folk who choose to live here have to do their bit or nothing will get done. Holiday-makers like to watch the sheep dog trials, but they don't want to get their hands dirty, setting up the hurdles. They take, but they don't give back."

"They give money," I reminded him. "They buy groceries at the Emporium. They have meals at the pub and the tearoom. A few of them even buy the pamphlets Lilian Bunting wrote about St. George's."

"It's not enough," Mr. Barlow insisted. "I want those cottages to go to people who are willing to do the real work of the village, not to tourists who think it all happens by magic." He ducked his head suddenly and grinned sheepishly at me. "Sorry about the sermon, Lori."

"What better place to give it?" I said, raising a hand to indicate our surroundings. "But you're preaching to the choir, Mr. Barlow. I'm already on your side. Residents have a stake in the community, visitors don't, and I know which ones I'd prefer to have as neighbors."

Mr. Barlow stood.

"I've enjoyed our little chat," he said, "but I'd best be on my way. I promised the vicar that I'd have the vestry lamp working by Evensong."

"I should be going, too," I said. "Bill will think I've fallen asleep in here. He and the boys must be eating their way through Sally Cook's entire stock of pastries."

"They could do worse." Mr. Barlow smiled down at Bess. "Goodbye for now, young lady."

He caught her flailing foot in his hand and gave it a gentle shake, then retrieved his ladder and his toolbox and carried them into the vestry.

"Interesting," I murmured when he was out of earshot. "I wonder if everyone thinks Marigold Edwards is the bee's knees? I don't think Mr. Barlow would allow a paycheck to influence his opinion of her, but you never know. I believe we'll have to meet Marigold for ourselves, Bess, and make our own judgment."

Bess flexed her toes and cooed, which I took to be a clear sign of agreement. I pulled the blanket over her foot again, then checked my immediate surroundings for stray socks, toys, tubes of ointment, and other baby-related detritus. I put those I found into the diaper bag, slung the bag over my shoulder, picked up the carry cot, and left the church through the south porch.

My eyes were still adjusting to the sunlight when I noticed that I was not alone in the churchyard. Lilian Bunting was standing at the foot of the newest grave, unaccompanied by her husband, the Reverend Mr. Theodore Bunting. I could scarcely believe my luck.

Lilian Bunting was a scholar and a local historian, but above all, she was an exemplary vicar's wife. While Mr. Bunting viewed his parishioners through a benign haze, Lilian saw them clearly and managed them cleverly, for the good of St. George's. She could bring order to a tempestuous parish meeting without offending anyone in attendance; she knew better than to pair Peggy Taxman with Sally Cook in the church's flower-arranging rota; and she was aware of the chaos that would ensue if she asked bashful, soft-spoken George Wetherhead to make public announcements during the church fête.

The vicar might live with his head in the clouds, but Lilian had her sensibly shod feet planted firmly on the ground. If I asked her what she thought of Marigold Edwards, she'd tell me the unvarnished truth, though she would phrase it diplomatically.

"It looks as though we'll make one more stop," I murmured to Bess, "before we round up our missing menfolk."

I'd just finished speaking when Lilian looked toward me and smiled.

"Lori," she called. "Do you have a moment?"

"I do," I responded, and wove my way between tilted headstones and lichen-speckled tombs to join her.

# Eight

T he vicar's slender, gray-haired wife was dressed in the crisp, cream-colored linen blazer and skirt she wore on warm summer Sundays. The look suited her, but it wouldn't have worked for me. After five minutes in close proximity to Bess, crisp, cream-colored linen would no longer have been crisp or cream-colored.

Lilian nodded pleasantly to me as I drew near.

"I promised Jack MacBride that I'd put fresh flowers on his uncle's grave while he and Bree were traveling," she explained, gesturing to the headstone. "A needless promise, as it happens, because there are always fresh flowers on Mr. Huggins's grave. The dear man may be gone, but he's certainly not forgotten, not by the villagers, at any rate."

"Before I forget," I said, "William and Amelia send their apologies for missing church today. They're getting Fairworth House ready for a family visit."

"So I've heard," said Lilian. "Millicent Scroggins imparted the news to me before church this morning. She also described the food, the drink, and the table setting William and Amelia have chosen for next Saturday's grand dinner."

"How thorough of her," I said, rolling my eyes.

Though I spoke flippantly, it stung a bit to learn that Millicent Scroggins, who worked twice a week as a charwoman at Fairworth House, knew more about Saturday's dinner than I did. Aunt Dimity had warned me that I might not be as up-to-date with village news as I had been before Bess's arrival, but it hadn't occurred to me that I might be behindhand with family news as well.

"Millicent spends more time listening at keyholes than cleaning them," I went on. "She's an expert eavesdropper."

"Aren't we all?" Lilian laughed. "Please tell William and Amelia that their apologies are accepted, but unnecessary. Teddy and I are well aware of how disruptive visitors can be. We spent a fortnight readying the vicarage for the bishop's visit, and he spent only two days with us. I shudder to think of the preparation required for a three-week visit. The meal planning alone would shatter me." She tilted her head slightly to peer over my shoulder. "Are Bill and the twins still in the church? Or were you on your way to meet them elsewhere?"

"Bill and the twins are stuffing their faces at the tearoom," I replied. "I was on my way there, but I'd rather stay here with you than watch my sugared-up sons bounce off the tearoom's walls. When they want me, they know where to find me."

"Good." Lilian gestured toward a stone bench beneath a cedar of Lebanon that shaded the churchyard. "Shall we sit?"

"*We* shall," I said, "but I think Bess would prefer to sprawl."

I spread a blanket on the soft bed of needle-like leaves the tree had shed over many years and freed Bess from the carry cot. It took her a few seconds to get used to the springiness of the leaf layer beneath the blanket, but she soon began her daily round of push-ups.

"Will she be safe, lying on her stomach?" Lilian asked as I took my place beside her on the bench.

"*Et tu*, Lilian?" I said, rounding on her. "I thought you'd turned down a membership in the we-know-better-than-you club."

"Sorry," she said meekly.

"I forgive you," I said. "As a matter of fact, it's good for Bess to spend time on her belly. She's strengthening the muscles she'll need to sit up, crawl, stand, walk, wind surf, boogie, and climb Mount Everest." I patted Lilian's knee reassuringly. "And she'll do so safely, because you and I are here to keep an eye on her."

"What a splendid child she is," Lilian said, as if to make amends for her faux pas. "Teddy still talks about how cheerful she was at her christening. He's more accustomed to infants who find the experience either terrifying or annoying." Lilian folded her hands in her lap and turned to face me. "I'm glad I caught you, Lori. I meant to speak with you earlier, but I lost track of you after church." She paused to survey me from head to toe. "You're looking very trim, I must say, and Bess, of course, looks as though she could conquer the world."

Lilian Bunting evidently expected me to chatter happily about my daughter and my fitness program, but I had other fish to fry.

"Bess and I are flourishing, thank you, which is more than I can say for Finch," I said. "Mr. Barlow tells me that Marigold Edwards handles property sales in the village. How well do you know her?"

"How well do I know Marigold Edwards?" Lilian repeated, sounding surprised and faintly puzzled. "Not well at all, I'm afraid. Teddy and I don't use estate agents because our housing is provided by the church. The vicarage and St. George's are a package deal, you see. One comes with the other and both are owned by the diocese."

"Have you met Marigold?" I asked.

"I've run into her occasionally," said Lilian. "She likes to bring her clients to St. George's to see our wall paintings."

The church's medieval wall paintings—the largest of which depicted a blotchy St. George battling a snaky-looking dragon—were Lilian's pride and joy. One of her husband's Victorian predecessors had "modernized" St. George's by concealing the primitive images beneath layers of whitewash, but Lilian had been instrumental in rediscovering and uncovering them.

I didn't care for the paintings. Had I been an estate agent, I wouldn't have gone out of my way to show them to prospective home buyers, but I didn't dare say so to Lilian. In her mind—and in the minds of quite a few medieval scholars—they were inestimable treasures.

"I didn't realize that Marigold had shown the cottages to *any* clients," I said.

"Oh, yes," said Lilian. "I've met quite a few. Let's see . . ." She drummed her fingers on the bench as she searched her memory. "I've spoken with a pair of young lawyers, an advertising executive and his wife, a surgeon, a banker, an Oxford don, a man who has something to do with economics, an architect . . ." Her voice trailed off and she shook her head. "I'm certain I've forgotten someone, but it's difficult to remember them all when there have been so many."

"If you've met Marigold as often as that," I said reasonably, "you must have spoken with her."

"I've answered her clients' questions about the church and its history," said Lilian, "but I've never had a meaningful conversation with Marigold. We exchange pleasantries and move on."

"You're good at reading people," I persisted. "You may not be Marigold's best friend, but you must have formed an opinion about her character. Do you think she's honest, for example?"

"What an extraordinary question," said Lilian. "Do you suspect Marigold Edwards of shady dealings?"

"I don't suspect her of anything," I replied less than honestly. "I'd just like to know what sort of person she is."

"I would say that Marigold Edwards is as honest as an estate agent can be," Lilian temporized. "They do tend to embroider the truth for the sake of a sale, but as far as I know, Marigold keeps her embroidery within acceptable bounds." Lilian directed a searching look at me. "Why are you quizzing me about our local estate agent? Are you and Bill contemplating a change of address?"

"Absolutely not," I said. "You and the vicar are stuck with us, Lilian. We're not going anywhere."

"I'm pleased to hear it," said Lilian.

Bess's gymnastic display had tired her, so I turned her onto her back, gobbled her tummy, and gave her a teething ring to gum. She promptly tossed the ring aside and chewed on her toes.

"I don't know why I bring toys with me," I said as I resumed my seat. "Bess would much rather play with her hands and feet."

"She's remarkably flexible," Lilian observed. She watched Bess in fascinated silence for a moment, then returned to the subject at hand. "If you and Bill intend to remain in your cottage, what has piqued your interest in Marigold Edwards?"

"Rose Cottage and Ivy Cottage," I replied. "And pretty soon, Pussywillows."

"I see," said Lilian. "You're concerned about the two vacant cottages and the cottage that will be vacant after Amelia's wedding."

"I'm very concerned about them," I said. "It sounds as though plenty of prospective buyers have seen Rose Cottage and Ivy Cottage. If Marigold Edwards is doing her job properly, why are they still vacant? Doesn't it make you question her competence or doubt her trustworthiness?"

"No, it doesn't," said Lilian. "The situation isn't as dire as you seem to think it is, Lori, and it's certainly not unusual. Cottages in Finch don't come on the market often, but when they do, they tend to stay there for a while. The greengrocer's shop went quickly because Peggy Taxman leapt on it, but Pussywillows was untenanted for six months before Amelia's arrival."

"Six months?" I said, frowning doubtfully. "Are you sure? It didn't seem like six months to me."

"I'm not surprised," said Lilian. "Pussywillows' previous owner—Miss Ponsonby? Was that her name?—was virtually invisible. She kept her drapes drawn at all times, she couldn't be bothered to plant flowers in her window boxes, and she rebuffed every friendly advance."

"Dervla Ponsonby," I said, nodding slowly. "A memorable name for an unmemorable woman. The only thing I can recall about Dervla Ponsonby, apart from her name, is the stir she created when she rejected the casseroles."

No one who'd lived in Finch at the time would ever forget the stir. Precisely three days after the elusive Miss Ponsonby had taken possession of Pussywillows, Millicent Scroggins, Opal Taylor, Elspeth Binney, and Selena Buxton had attempted to present her with a quartet of tasty, filling, and easily reheated casseroles, as a neighborly way of welcoming her to the village.

When Miss Ponsonby spurned their well-intentioned offerings, they'd acted as though she'd insulted their mothers, hurled rocks at their houses, and stabbed them through the lungs with a hot poker. The casserole incident had provided Finch with a solid month's worth of outraged gossip.

"It was the first and last stir Miss Ponsonby created," Lilian remarked. "Pussywillows appeared to be vacant even when she was living in it."

"She didn't make the slightest effort to get to know us," I said wistfully.

"I'm sure she's much happier in London," said Lilian. "Village life didn't suit her."

"I'm beginning to think it doesn't suit anyone who doesn't live here already," I expostulated. "I don't get it, Lilian. Why is it so hard to sell a house in Finch?"

"I expect it's because Finch lacks the amenities most people require nowadays," she replied, unconsciously echoing Aunt Dimity's sentiments.

"Like a school or a hospital," I grumbled.

"Or a library or a cinema or a leisure center," Lilian put in. "Or a petrol station."

"We have lots of other things," I protested. "Like peace and quiet and . . . and . . . *nature.*"

"Of course we do," said Lilian. "But not everyone values peace and quiet and nature as much as you and I do."

Bess emitted a tiny squawk and began to drool spectacularly.

"Snack time," I announced. "In the nick of time, too. I was about to treat you to a lengthy diatribe about numbskulls who prefer petrol stations to bluebell glades, but nursing Bess always calms me down."

"Bless you, Bess," said Lilian, pretending to mop her brow. "I feel as if I've had a lucky escape."

Once Bess was nestled against me, my crankiness dissolved. Lilian seemed content to listen to the birds and to watch butterflies flutter among the headstones while I recovered my good humor.

"Why were you looking for me earlier?" I asked, after my temper had cooled. "Was it just to say hello or did you have something in particular to say to me?"

"The latter," she said, as if she were grateful for the reminder. "I'm not as proficient at eavesdropping as Millicent Scroggins, but I couldn't help overhearing the first part of your conversation with

Grant and Charles. I believe I heard Charles mention the name Arthur Hargreaves."

"Mention it?" I said, laughing. "He practically shouted it at me. Jack and Bree could have heard him, and they're in Australia."

"Why did Charles shout Arthur Hargreaves's name at you?" Lilian asked.

"I surprised him," I said, "when I told him that I'd met Arthur Hargreaves."

Lilian leaned toward me, her face alive with interest.

"Were you pulling Charles's leg?" she asked.

"No," I said. "I was telling him the truth. Bess and I met Arthur yesterday."

Lilian took a deep breath and expelled it in one explosive puff. I had the distinct impression that she was restraining an impulse to shout.

"Remarkable," she said. "And brave."

"Brave?" I said.

"The villagers aren't fond of Arthur Hargreaves," said Lilian. "I don't know why, but they seem to harbor a grudge against him."

"Would I be right to assume you haven't met him?" I asked.

"You would," said Lilian. "I don't know if he's a churchgoer, but if he is, he'll attend services at All Saints Church in Tillcote rather than St. George's." She shifted her position to face me directly. "What's he like?"

Bess had fallen into a milky trance, so I moved her to my diaper-draped shoulder and made myself presentable while I turned Lilian's question over in my mind. I'd told Grant and Charles that Arthur Hargreaves was a knight in shining armor, but Lilian deserved a less clichéd response.

"Arthur Hargreaves," I said finally, "didn't offer me one word of

child-rearing advice. Not one. He said Bess was enchanting. Period."
I smiled broadly. "I can't tell you how refreshing it was."

"He must be a real gentleman," Lilian said approvingly. "How did
you come to meet him?"

"Are you familiar with the old, disused farm track that runs along
the northern boundary of William's estate?" I asked.

"I'm aware of it," Lilian replied, "but it floods so easily that I've
never had the courage to explore it."

"It *floods*?" I said, aghast. The rivulets Bess and I had crossed came
to mind, along with the appalling image of me clawing my way up
the flower-strewn banks with Bess cradled in one arm and the rising
waters lapping at my heels.

"It turns into a raging stream every time it rains," Lilian confirmed.

"That would explain the ruts," I said, making a vivid mental note
to avoid the farm track in wet weather. "Be that as it may . . ."

As I recounted my tale of the old farm track, the gnarly pothole,
and the defective pram axle, I felt a renewed sense of gratitude to the
man who'd spared me the humiliation of being rescued—again—by
Bill. Lilian, however, was clearly more impressed by Arthur's eccen-
tricity than by his gallantry.

"He called himself the *Summer King*?" she said. "And he wore a
*crown*?"

"It's a family thing," I said, dismissing her amazed reaction with a
flick of my hand. "A bit of fun. He didn't wave a sword around or
order me to curtsy. He's not bonkers, Lilian. He's just . . . nice. He
invited me to drop in on him the next time I'm near Hillfont Abbey."

"Oh, do take him up on it," Lilian pleaded with unexpected fer-
vor. "I'd give a great deal to hear an eyewitness description of Hillfont
Abbey. It would be one of the most notable landmarks in the county
if its gates weren't shut to visitors."

"What's notable about it?" I asked.

"In the first place," said Lilian, "it isn't an abbey."

She was about to expand on her intriguing prologue when a double-throated shout smote our ears.

"Mummy!" bellowed Will and Rob.

My sons raced through the lych-gate and ran toward us, dodging headstones and leaping over graves like a pair of exuberant lambs.

"Don't run in the churchyard!" Bill hollered as he entered the sanctified grounds at a more seemly pace.

Will and Rob skidded to a side-by-side halt, spraying the blanket's Bess-shaped indentation with a shower of dirt and dried leaves, then sprinted forward to rub their sister's back vigorously and to give me two powerful hugs.

"Hi, Mummy. Hi, Bessy," they chorused breathlessly. "Hello, Mrs. Bunting."

"Good morning, boys," said Lilian. She rose to greet Bill, then excused herself, saying, "I must remind Teddy that lunchtime is approaching. If I don't, he'll forget to eat."

"Good to see you, Lilian, however briefly," said Bill.

"And you, Bill," she responded.

Lilian ruffled the twins' windblown hair affectionately and headed for the vicarage. I passed Bess to Bill and repacked the diaper bag, then sat on the stone bench to take stock of our sons. Their boisterousness filled me with trepidation.

"How many slices of lemon poppy-seed cake have you had?" I asked them, giving Bill a dark, sidelong glance.

"One apiece," Rob replied.

"And a glass of milk each," Will added.

Bill confirmed the veracity of their statements as well as the unfairness of my unspoken accusation with a haughty nod.

"You must have eaten very slowly," I said to the boys. "You've been at the tearoom for ages."

"We weren't eating the whole time," Will said, tossing his head scornfully.

"Mr. Cook was teaching us to juggle," Rob explained, his eyes shining.

Henry Cook, a former cruise ship entertainer, possessed a wealth of talents guaranteed to dazzle a pair of nine-year-old boys. Although I appreciated his willingness to introduce Will and Rob to the performing arts, I couldn't help thinking that a tearoom was not an ideal venue for juggling lessons.

"What did you juggle?" I asked, picturing Sally Cook's floor strewn with smashed cups and saucers.

"Bread rolls," said Will.

"Without butter," Rob amplified.

I heaved a sigh of relief.

"But we're done with juggling," said Will.

"We're going to the Cotswold Farm Park!" Rob exclaimed.

"Are we?" I asked, looking at Bill.

"The vote was unanimous," he informed me solemnly.

"Mrs. Cook packed us a picnic lunch," said Will. "It's *huge*."

"It's already in the Rover," said Rob.

"Boys?" said Bill. "Please walk—*do not run*—to the car and wait for us there. Mummy, Bess, and I will be along in a moment."

"Righty-ho, Daddy!" they chorused.

Watching Will and Rob trying to walk was like watching a pair of colts trying not to kick up their heels. Their self-control filled me with pride.

"Righty-ho?" I said wonderingly, when the boys were safely out of earshot. "Where did that come from?"

"Don't ask me," said Bill as he placed Bess in her carry cot. "They must have picked it up at the stables. Is the Cotswold Farm Park all right?"

"Children, animals, and a *huge* picnic lunch?" I said, grabbing the diaper bag. "Sounds like a winning formula to me."

Bill took the diaper bag from me and slung it over his own shoulder, then picked up the carry cot.

"I've been collecting information," he said mysteriously.

Bill wouldn't demean himself by gossiping, but he saw nothing wrong with "collecting information." If there was a difference between the two, I couldn't see it.

"Have I got a story to tell you," he added.

"Could you save it for later?" I asked. "I need some Mummy time with Will and Rob."

"Righty-ho!" he said.

I laughed, and while he did the heavy lifting, I thrust Marigold Edwards and Arthur Hargreaves out of my thoughts to make room for my boys.

# Nine

Despite a skinned knee, a broken shoelace, and a close encounter with an irate goose, our outing was a resounding success. Will and Rob introduced Bess to polka-dotted pigs, long-horned oxen, and stately shire horses; fed park-approved treats to the little white goats that had the run of the main enclosure; and went with Bill to watch the sheep-shearing demonstration while Bess and I took our afternoon naps in the Rover.

Sally Cook's picnic lunch was so huge that soup and sandwiches sufficed for dinner. Story time followed bath time and by half past seven, Bess and the boys were in bed and asleep. I'd just finished loading the dishwasher when Emma Harris dropped by to return a book Will had left at the stables. I invited her to join Bill and me under the apple tree in the back garden and the three of us headed outdoors to enjoy the lingering warmth of the long summer's day. Stanley followed us out, waited patiently for Bill to take a seat, then jumped into Bill's lap and began to purr.

Bill placed the baby monitor on the teak table between his lawn chair and mine, and Emma sat in a third lawn chair, facing ours. Slightly built, with blue-gray eyes and graying, dishwater blond hair, Emma Harris was the sort of person who found it irksome to sit still. She preferred to be engaged in one activity or another, whether it was knitting, gardening, trying new recipes, writing computer programs, training horses, caring for horses, or teaching students of all ages to ride. She couldn't even take an evening stroll without bringing a compass along with her to practice her map-reading skills.

As someone who cherished every moment I spent sitting still, I welcomed the sight of her lying back in her chair, with a glass of chilled rose hip tea at her elbow, doing nothing that could possibly be construed as productive.

"Emma," I said, "did you and Derek work with Marigold Edwards when you bought Anscombe Manor?"

"No," she said. "We dealt directly with the previous owner's solicitor. Why do you ask?"

"I don't understand why she hasn't found buyers for Rose Cottage and Ivy Cottage," I said. "I'd like to know more about her."

"I've heard nothing but good things about her from the villagers," said Emma.

"Same here," I said. "Thanks, by the way, for returning the book. And thanks in advance for letting the boys stay with you over the weekend."

"Will and Rob can stay with me anytime they like," said Emma. "They're as horse-crazy as I am. As for the book . . ." She sat up to sip her tea, then leaned back in her chair, cradling the glistening glass in her hands. "To be perfectly honest, I had an ulterior motive for coming over here tonight."

"Out with it," I commanded, though I was too relaxed to put much oomph into my words.

"I heard that you tackled the disused farm track I found on the old ordnance survey map," she said.

I hadn't yet told Emma about my adventure, but I wasn't shocked to learn that someone had. News drifted through our small community like wisps of gossamer, though with considerably more speed.

"I might hike it myself next weekend," she continued. "I'd like to hear your take on it."

I looked down at my drink. Though I'd told Bess that I might allow Emma to visit our secret place, I felt a sudden, childish impulse to keep it to myself for the time being. Almost without thinking, I decided to downplay the track's undeniable beauty by emphasizing its less attractive aspects.

"The verges are pretty," I said indifferently, "but the track itself is a disaster—nothing but roots, rocks, and ruts."

"And potholes," Bill put in.

"And potholes," I repeated with an emphatic nod. "Lots and lots of deep, dark, nasty potholes."

"I could explore it on horseback," Emma proposed. "Peg's good at negotiating rough trails."

"You'd be knocked out of the saddle," I told her. "I had to duck under branches and I wasn't riding a fifteen-hand chestnut mare like your Pegasus. And let's not forget the track's least endearing feature: According to Lilian Bunting, a drop of rain turns it into a torrent. You might want to annotate your map to that effect, to keep future ramblers from drowning in flash floods."

"That must be why the track was abandoned," Emma said thoughtfully. "Farmers aren't stupid. They won't go to the trouble and the expense of maintaining a cart track that washes out every time it rains." She sighed. "Maybe I'll give it a miss."

"I would if I were you," I said. "You wouldn't want Peg to break a leg."

"I wouldn't want to break my own leg, either," Emma said.

I should have been thoroughly ashamed of myself for misleading my friend, but I felt only a half-ashamed sense of relief. The old track would remain my secret place, I thought, until I was ready to share its secrets with others.

Bill was clearly ready to change the subject.

"Emma," he said, "what do you know about the Finch-Tillcote feud?"

Emma and I exchanged bewildered looks, then stared at Bill questioningly.

"What brought the Finch-Tillcote feud to mind?" I inquired.

"The information I collected at the tearoom this morning," he replied. "You don't think I spent all of my time there watching Will and Rob throw bread rolls at each other, do you?" Turning to Emma, he explained, "Lori put the cat among the pigeons after church by uttering the name of a family associated with Tillcote."

"The Hargreaves family," Emma said, nodding. "I heard." She wagged a finger at me. "It was a silly thing to do, Lori."

"Why?" I asked, roused from my lethargy. "Do you know the Hargreaveses?"

"No," said Emma, "but if I did, I wouldn't admit it to anyone in Finch, not unless I wanted to get the stink-eye every time I walked into the Emporium, the pub, and the tearoom."

"Why would the villagers give you the stink-eye?" I asked.

"Because the Hargreaves family is on the wrong side of the great divide that separates the decent people of Finch from Tillcote mafia," said Emma.

"The Tillcote *mafia*?" I said with a snort of laughter. "You've got to be kidding."

"Derek's word, not mine," said Emma, referring to her eminently sensible husband. "He thinks the feud is ridiculous and he jokes about it when we're alone, but he steers clear of Tillcote nevertheless. He doesn't want to be accused of consorting with the enemy."

"Good grief," I said. "You make it sound like *West Side Story*."

"If a Tillcote girl dated a Finch boy, or the other way around," said Emma, "it would be exactly like *West Side Story*. Except for the singing. And the dancing. And, I would hope, the murders."

"You would hope?" I echoed, gaping at her. "How serious is this feud?"

"It's serious." Emma set her glass aside and sat upright, folding her legs beneath her like a Girl Scout perched beside a campfire. "Derek and I found out about it a couple of weeks after we moved into Anscombe Manor. We'd spent a day driving around, as you do when you're new to an area—"

"Bill and I did our share of aimless driving when we first moved to Finch," I broke in, "but we never made it to Tillcote." I glanced at Bill. "I'm not sure why."

"There's no direct route between the two villages," Emma reminded me. "You have to make an effort to reach Tillcote, or stumble across it by accident, which is what happened to Derek and me."

"Is it anything like Finch?" I asked.

"It's bigger than Finch," said Emma, "thanks to the council housing built there in the fifties. It's hemmed in by two major roadways as well. Derek and I didn't think much of it."

"Emma," said Bill, "what happened on the day you and Derek spent driving around?"

"Oh, right," said Emma. "Back to the story." She paused for a moment, then picked up where she'd left off. "On the way home from our drive, we stopped at the Emporium to buy a few groceries."

"Did Peggy Taxman offer you a warm welcome to Finch?" Bill asked. "She must have been pleased to meet two new local customers."

"Peggy Taxman was Peggy Kitchen then," said Emma, "and she

was nice enough to us until we made the mistake of telling her that we'd visited All Saints Church in Tillcote."

"What did she do?" I asked.

"She gave us the stink-eye," said Emma. "If we hadn't been newcomers, I think she would have shown us the door. Thankfully, she made allowances for our ignorance and did her best to educate us. She explained that, if Derek and I wished to be on friendly terms with our neighbors in Finch, we wouldn't have anything to do with Tillcote."

"Scary," I said. "Her voice alone must have rattled you. I've seen it rattle the windows in the Emporium."

Emma laughed.

"Did you ask Peggy why Tillcote was off-limits?" Bill inquired.

"Derek did," said Emma. "She gave him a list of reasons as long as her arm. Tillcote folk, as she called them, were arrogant, deceitful, dishonest, lazy, greedy, ill-mannered . . ." She raised her hands in a helpless gesture, as if words had failed her. "Basically, she told us that they were the spawn of Satan and that we would be tarred by the same brush if we spent too much time with them."

"If I know Derek," Bill said shrewdly, "he ignored Peggy's advice."

"He went straight back to Tillcote the next day," Emma confirmed. "And he was treated to an encore performance by the woman who ran their general store, only in reverse. Her speech about Finch folk was almost exactly the same as Peggy's speech about Tillcote folk. In the end, we decided to give Tillcote a wide berth." She shrugged. "Derek and I didn't wish to be at odds with our new neighbors."

I squinted at her incredulously.

"Your decision wasn't based solely on the ravings of a pair of competing shopkeepers, was it?" I asked.

"Of course it wasn't," said Emma. "Derek threw out feelers to every villager he came across and the response was always the same. It still is."

"It certainly is," said Bill. "The tearoom was buzzing with resentful chatter this morning. Christine Peacock told me——"

He broke off and Stanley raised his gleaming black head as the baby monitor lit up.

"It's okay," I said, recognizing the sounds emerging from the small speaker. "She's talking to herself."

Stanley went back to sleep.

"Is Bess talking already?" Emma asked, her eyes widening.

"Yes," said Bill, without cracking a smile. "She's scheduled to deliver a lecture on semantics at the Bodleian Library on Friday morning."

"He's teasing you," I said to Emma. My friend sometimes misunderstood my husband's puckish sense of humor. "The only language Bess speaks at the moment is baby."

"True," said Bill, "but she speaks it fluently."

"Go on about the tearoom," I said to him. "Sally Cook told me that Tillcote folk would steal the coins off a dead man's eyes. What did Christine Peacock say about them?"

"She told me that Teddy Bunting can't stand Tillcote's rector," said Bill.

My eyebrows rose. "I thought the vicar liked everyone."

"He does," said Bill, "with one exception. He feels that Mr. Gunninger is more concerned with showmanship than he is with pastoral care. Or, as Christine put it . . ." Bill launched into a passable imitation of Christine Peacock's West Midlands accent. "'Mr. Gunninger is one of those hellfire and damnation types, the sort of preacher who likes the sound of his own voice and the rustle of pound notes in the collection plate.'"

"Ouch," I said, wincing. "Not a glowing review."

"It gets worse," said Bill. "Mr. Gunninger charges a small fee to open his church for anyone, including his own parishioners, between services."

My jaw dropped. Theodore Bunting allowed his parishioners to slip in and out of St. George's whenever they pleased. In Finch, the church was regarded as a place for worship and contemplation, not as a profit-making venture.

"I'm with Teddy Bunting," I said stoutly. "Mr. Gunninger sounds like a very disagreeable man."

"Oddly enough," said Bill, "Mr. Gunninger is the only Tillcote resident Christine or anyone else in the tearoom could name. They grumbled about 'this bloke' or 'those ladies' or 'that lad' from Tillcote, but the offenders were otherwise anonymous. Our neighbors seem to regard Tillcote folk as generic demons rather than real human beings."

"The ladies in the churchyard recognized Arthur Hargreaves's name," I pointed out, "though they didn't seem to know much about him."

"They don't seem to know much about *anyone* in Tillcote," said Bill, "but they think the worst of them all the same."

"Derek sees it as a case of small-town rivalry run amok," said Emma. "No one remembers how the feud started, but everyone feels compelled to keep it going. It's the same old story, isn't it? An us-versus-them mentality. Some people need to have an enemy in order to feel good about themselves."

"Arthur Hargreaves isn't my enemy," I said stubbornly. "And I don't care who knows it."

"You will," said Emma, "once you start getting the stink-eye." She straightened her legs and stretched luxuriously. "Time for me to go,

I think. If I leave now, I should be able to finish my evening chores before it gets too dark to see the water troughs."

"One more question?" Bill asked.

"Go ahead," said Emma.

"Lori and I have lived here for ten years, but we didn't find out about the feud until today," he said. "Why hasn't anyone educated us?"

"More to the point," I chimed in, "why didn't *you* educate us?"

Emma ducked her head sheepishly.

"To tell you the truth, I'd forgotten about the feud," she said.

"How could you forget about it?" I demanded. "It's *West Side Story* in the Cotswolds!"

"Avoiding Tillcote has become second nature to me," Emma replied. "It's as automatic as breathing. You wouldn't expect me to explain breathing to you, would you?"

"I guess not," I conceded.

"What about the rest of our neighbors?" Bill asked. "Why haven't they drilled it into us?"

"The villagers don't talk about Tillcote if they can help it," Emma explained. "I suppose it's another way of demonstrating their superiority. Why waste your breath on a place that's beneath your notice?" She pointed at me. "If you hadn't forced the issue by bandying the Hargreaves name about, you'd still be living in blissful ignorance."

"I'm all for blissful ignorance," I said, "but not if it gets us into trouble. Is there anything else we should know about the feud?"

"Nothing springs to mind," said Emma. "If something does, I'll give you a call."

"Please do," I said. "I'd rather be educated by you than by Peggy Taxman."

"Who wouldn't?" Emma said. She got to her feet. "Now it really is time for me to go. Thanks for the tea and the trail review."

"Thanks for returning the boys' book," said Bill, "and for filling us in on the feud."

"Better late than never, eh?" she said ruefully.

Bill, Stanley, and I walked Emma to the door, then split up. Stanley padded into the living room to colonize Bill's favorite armchair, and Bill and I went on toy patrol, our name for the daily round of hit-or-miss tidying that brought a semblance of order to the cottage.

Job done, we went upstairs, looked in on the children, and retreated to the sanctuary of the master bedroom. Though it wasn't yet nine o'clock, we were ready to call it a day and went straight to bed. I was halfway to dreamland when the baby monitor indicated that Bess was awake.

"I'll go," Bill offered drowsily.

"Stay put," I murmured. "She's hungry."

Bill smiled sweetly. "It looks as though Bess isn't the only one who speaks baby fluently."

"I wish I spoke Finch half as well," I said and sleepwalked my way to the nursery.

# *Ten*

**B**ess had a natural aptitude for sleeping. She'd slept through the night ever since Bill and I had brought her home from the hospital. It had worried us at first, but after a few sleepless nights of our own we'd realized——with profound joy and gratitude——that we could stop tiptoeing into the nursery every five seconds to make sure that she hadn't stopped breathing.

Bess was still our Sleeping Beauty. If she requested a nighttime feed, it was almost always because she'd had a particularly stimulating day. Since our day at the Cotswold Farm Park had been nothing if not stimulating, I wasn't taken aback to find myself in the big rocking chair in the nursery, soothing Bess's jangled nerves, while the rest of my family slept.

It didn't take long for Sleeping Beauty to live up to her name, but by the time I resettled her in her crib, I'd regained something approximating full consciousness. I would have lain awake staring at the ceiling if I'd gone back to bed, so I went downstairs to the study instead.

The study was as dark as a tomb, brightened only by the baby monitor's dim glow. I lit the mantel lamps, said hello to Reginald, took the blue journal from its place on the bookshelves, and sat with it in one of the tall leather armchairs that faced the hearth. I didn't bother to light a fire. I didn't think I'd be up long enough to need a fire's warmth or its companionship.

"Dimity?" I said, opening the journal. "I'm pretty pooped, but I think I can stay upright long enough to fill you in on a few things."

The familiar handwriting appeared at once, scrolling across the blank page in graceful loops and curves of royal-blue ink.

*In that case, we'll do our very best to stick to the highlights, my dear. Did you ask Mr. Barlow about Rose Cottage?*

"I did," I said. "He says that Rose Cottage is as sound as a bell. Ditto for Ivy Cottage, but we already knew how much work Jack put into rehabbing his late uncle's place."

*And we know why Jack MacBride was so exacting in his refurbishment of Ivy Cottage.*

"We do indeed," I agreed. "He used the rehab as an excuse to stay in Finch while he was courting Bree." I smiled reminiscently. "I caught him using a cotton swab to polish the bathroom tiles one day."

*He was—and is—very much in love. Happily, his persistence was rewarded. I believe Bree is as much in love with him as he is with her.*

Although I enjoyed discussing young love as much as the next woman, I was also aware that my second wind wouldn't last all night. Experience had taught me that fatigue was hovering in the wings, ready to pounce.

"Can we get back to Mr. Barlow for a minute?" I requested.

*I'm sorry, Lori. I thought we'd finished with him.*

"Not yet," I said. "Mr. Barlow is afraid that Peggy Taxman will buy the empty cottages and turn them into vacation rentals."

*Heaven forfend! Has Peggy expressed an interest in expanding her empire?*

"I don't think so," I said, "but I don't know for sure." I sighed heavily. "You were right, Dimity. I am out of touch with the villagers."

*I have no doubt that you'll get back in touch with them the next time you're in Finch. You can't help being inquisitive, Lori. You'll soon find out whether Mr. Barlow's fears are baseless or well-founded.*

"I'll give it my best shot," I said. "I do know one thing for sure, though. The cottages aren't vacant because they're in bad shape. Deathwatch beetles aren't scaring away buyers, but Marigold Edwards might be."

*Who is Marigold Edwards?*

"An estate agent," I said. "She's handling the sales of Rose Cottage and Ivy Cottage. She also sold Pussywillows to Amelia Thistle and it looks as though she'll sell it to the next owner, if she ever finds one."

*Marigold Edwards doesn't, by any chance, work for the Edwards Estate Agency, does she?*

"She married into the family firm," I replied. "Why? Are you familiar with the Edwards agency?"

*I was. It was an old and respectable firm in my day, but I had no idea that it was still in existence.*

"It's alive and well and doing business in Upper Deeping," I said. "Finch is on Marigold's turf, so to speak. She seems to be responsible for most of the property transactions that take place here. Mr. Barlow and Lilian Bunting didn't have a bad word to say about her." I frowned. "If you ask me, they've gotten so used to Marigold's way of doing business that they've missed the obvious."

*What is "the obvious"?*

"It's obvious, isn't it?" I said. "Marigold Edwards is either the world's most inept estate agent or she's up to no good."

*I imagine you think her inept because she hasn't yet sold a pair of cottages that are as sound as a bell.*

"Rose Cottage and Ivy Cottage are just the tip of the iceberg," I said. "Lilian told me, quite casually, that properties in Finch routinely sit empty for months and months before they're sold. The only exception she could cite was Peggy's lightning-fast purchase of the greengrocer's shop."

*I believe we've discussed Finch's limitations, Lori.*

"I'm aware of Finch's limitations," I said testily. "My question is: Why add to them? Why go out of your way to discourage people from moving here?"

*Has Marigold Edwards gone out of her way to discourage people from moving to Finch?*

"Seems like it to me," I said. "Why else would she bring them to see the wall paintings in St. George's?"

*The church's medieval wall paintings are of great historical value, Lori.*

"They're creepy," I said flatly. "They give me the heebie-jeebies. If Will and Rob weren't in love with all things ghoulish, St. George and his creepy dragon would give them nightmares. An estate agent with Finch's best interests at heart would steer her clients away from the wall paintings." I looked up from the journal and spoke half to myself as a fresh thought occurred to me. "Maybe Marigold tells her clients about the feud as well. She could make it seem as though the village is a hotbed of seething hostility."

*I'm afraid you'll have to be a little less cryptic, my dear. Are you referring to the state of war that exists between Sally Cook and Peggy Taxman? If so, I can assure you that such rivalries are not unique to Finch. They exist in every community.*

I looked down at the journal and smiled grimly.

"Wrong feud," I said. "I'm referring to the state of war that exists between Finch and Tillcote."

*Good grief. I thought the Finch-Tillcote feud ended years ago.*

I gaped at the journal.

"Y-you knew about it?" I stammered. "And you didn't tell me?"

*Of course I knew about it. I grew up with it, though it started long before I was born.*

"You might have mentioned it," I said reproachfully.

*I would have, had I known that the villagers were still engaged in it. I may have grown up in Finch, Lori, but I spent most of my adult life in London. After my mother and father died, I lost touch with my old neighbors. I retained ownership of my family's cottage, but I rarely visited it. When I did return, no one spoke of the feud to me. I assumed, quite naturally, that it had faded into obscurity.*

Aunt Dimity's final comment reminded me of something Emma Harris had said to Bill and me beneath the apple tree: *"Why waste your breath on a place that's beneath your notice?"*

"The villagers don't talk about it," I said as understanding glimmered. "Not often, anyway."

*I rest my case. How does the jury find? Is the defendant guilty or not guilty?*

"Not guilty," I said penitently. "I'm sure you would have warned me about the feud if you'd thought I'd be dragged into it."

*Have you been dragged into it?*

"To be honest, I sort of dragged myself into it," I replied. "I came close to inciting a riot after church when I asked Peggy Taxman and the rest of the ladies if they knew Arthur Hargreaves. My innocent inquiry triggered a full-on tirade about Tillcote folk, who have, at various times, insulted Dick Peacock's homemade wine, made fun of Sally Cook's spreading waistline, looked down their noses at St. George's, and ridiculed the horrible lamp Opal Taylor takes home from the jumble sale every year because she can't persuade anyone to buy it."

*Everyone in Finch ridicules Opal's lamp.*

"Not to her face," I said pointedly.

*Oh. I see.*

"Finally," I continued, "Peggy claimed that a Tillcote lad had stolen a bag of potato chips from the Emporium, and Sally topped her by declaring that Tillcote folk would steal the coins from a dead man's eyes. Oh, and Bill found out later that Teddy Bunting can't stand Tillcote's money-grubbing rector." I shook my head. "What a kerfuffle! Honestly, Dimity, if I'd known about the feud, I wouldn't have asked the ladies about Arthur Hargreaves."

*Why did you ask the ladies about Arthur Hargreaves?*

I stared blankly at Aunt Dimity's question, then raised a fist and thumped myself on the forehead.

"Stupid me," I said. "I keep forgetting to tell you: Bess and I met Arthur yesterday."

To save time, I attempted to distill the broken-pram saga into a few brief sentences, but I couldn't bring myself to leave out the marvelous kites or the fat-tired bicycle or the cart filled with pram parts or the Santiago-bound grandson or the paste in Harriet's hair or a host of other details that had made my first meeting with Arthur so memorable.

The mantel clock was chiming half past ten as I approached the end of my tale, and my hopes of returning to dreamland at a reasonable hour went down the drain. I had no regrets, though. I felt as if I'd done justice to Arthur. The portrait I'd drawn for Aunt Dimity was, to my mind, more complete and more accurate than the distorted image Grant and Charles had presented to me.

"He was as nice as nice can be," I concluded. "To Grant Tavistock and Charles Bellingham, Arthur Hargreaves is the Hermit of Hillfont Abbey, a wealthy recluse who collects art anonymously and manipulates powerful businessmen from the jealously guarded confines of his hilltop lair, but to me . . ." My voice trailed off as I envisioned Arthur as I'd first seen him, perched atop the tall stone wall, clad in his rumpled shirt and his grass-stained trousers, with the grapevine wreath encircling his head. "To me, he's the man who heard my baby cry and ran to help her."

Aunt Dimity didn't respond at once. I couldn't blame her. I'd given her a lot to think about and I wasn't done yet.

"I wish I'd been able to get a word in edgewise this morning," I said. "If I'd told Peggy and Sally and the others about my encounter with Arthur, I'm sure they would have changed their minds about the Hargreaves family."

*I doubt it.*

"Why?" I asked.

*They probably hold the Hargreaves family responsible for starting the Finch-Tillcote feud. My mother and father did.*

"Did your parents know the Hargreaveses?" I asked.

*Certainly not. They would have been shunned by their neighbors had they befriended a member of the Hargreaves family. My parents knew only what their parents had told them and they passed their knowledge on to me. I presume they did so to keep me from falling into the same quagmire you fell into this morning.*

"What knowledge did they pass on to you?" I asked, fascinated.

*Let me see . . . According to my mother, the original Hargreaveses weren't proper aristocrats. They were parvenus who'd made their money in trade. Hillfont Abbey*

"Lilian Bunting claims that it isn't an abbey," I put in swiftly.

*She's quite right. Hillfont Abbey was built by Arthur's great-great-grandfather, Quentin Hargreaves, a Victorian manufacturer who wanted something to show for his hard work. Newly affluent Victorians saw it as the height of fashion to build whimsical country houses loosely based on historical mod-els. I imagine Quentin Hargreaves equated his mythical abbey with stability and success, but the villagers referred to it as Quentin's Folly. They thought it was outlandish and they regarded him as nothing more than an uncouth tradesman, flaunting his wealth.*

"Snobs," I muttered.

*England's class system was more rigid in those days. People at both ends of the social spectrum looked down on self-made men. If Quentin Hargreaves had built a less flamboyant home, the villagers might have warmed to him—eventually—but his faux abbey put him beyond the pale.*

"Okay," I said. "The villagers sneered at Hillfont Abbey. They probably made snippy comments about it, too, but I don't see how a fancy house could ignite a feud between Finch and Tillcote."

*Hillfont Abbey didn't ignite the feud. I'm simply setting the scene for what happened next.*

"What happened next?" I asked reflexively.

*Quentin sided with Tillcote in a dispute that arose between the two vil-lages. My mother couldn't recall the exact nature of the dispute, but my father believed that it had something to do with three stolen pigs. Whatever the cause, it seems certain that a dispute took place.*

"Did Quentin accuse someone in Finch of stealing the pigs?" I asked.

*Not directly, but the implication was there for all to see. Quentin Harg-reaves wasn't a popular figure in Finch before the dispute. Once he aligned himself with Tillcote's notorious pig thieves, Finch turned its back on him and his family. The cart track that ran between Finch and Hillfont Abbey was al-lowed to deteriorate and the Hargreaves name was dropped from polite conver-sation.*

"Whoops," I said, wincing.

*You couldn't have known.*

"What did you make of the feud when you first heard about it?" I asked. "Did you feel duty-bound to continue it?"

*I didn't hear about it all at once, Lori, as you've done just now. I grew up with it. It permeated the atmosphere in Finch, like a poisonous gas. Strange things don't seem strange when one grows up with them.*

"The feud should seem strange to Peggy and Sally and Christine and the Handmaidens," I said. "None of them grew up here. Most of them were approaching middle age when they moved to Finch."

*If you'll recall, some of them were billeted in Finch when they were children. Young children are very impressionable. They may have absorbed their host families' prejudices. As for the others . . . Those new to a community often adopt its foibles. It's not uncommon to find incomers resurrecting traditions the native-born have allowed to lapse, as a way of declaring their allegiance to their new home.*

"And the, er, Tillcote folk haven't exactly declared a truce," I said.

*They have been rather combative.*

"It still seems odd to me," I said. "I mean, it's ancient history, isn't it? Why would a Victorian spat continue to affect people today?"

*I believe the strong feelings provoked by the American Civil War continue to affect people today. I'm not, of course, comparing the petty bickering of two small villages to a great and terrible civil war. I'm simply pointing out that the past has a way of intruding on the present, whether we're conscious of it or not.*

"Derek Harris thinks it's a case of village rivalry run amok," I said. "He thinks it's ridiculous, but he goes along with it anyway."

*He goes along to get along, as my mother used to say.*

"I wonder if Arthur is aware of the feud?" I said. "He didn't make any wisecracks about Finch while I was with him. He didn't treat me or Bess badly because we live in Finch. If the track between Finch and Hillfont were paved, I suspect he'd show his face more often in Finch."

*I'm not convinced that Quentin Hargreaves was aware of the resentment he'd stirred up among the villagers. He may have sided with Tillcote once, but he never did so again. Neither he nor his descendants participated in village life, either in Finch or in Tillcote. They kept themselves very much to themselves.*

"They avoided the poisonous gas that permeated the atmosphere in Finch," I said reflectively. "It's a disturbing image, Dimity. Marigold Edwards could use it or something like it to drive off prospective buyers."

*Why would she do such a thing, Lori? How would it benefit her?*

"I haven't the faintest idea," I said, "but I intend to find out. I'd confront her tomorrow if I hadn't already promised myself to Amelia."

*Why did you promise yourself to Amelia?*

"Bill's aunts," I said bleakly.

*Oh, dear. I'd forgotten about Honoria and Charlotte. They'll be here tomorrow, won't they?*

"Amelia expects them to arrive at Fairworth House around noon," I said. "I promised to get her through the ordeal."

*Who will get you through the ordeal, my dear?*

"Bess," I replied.

*I should have guessed. Good gracious, Lori, what are you doing down here at this late hour? You should be upstairs and asleep. You'll need all of your strength if you're to face your aunts-in-law tomorrow.*

"I'm on my way, Dimity," I said. "Thanks for the history lesson."

*You're quite welcome, my dear. Now, scoot!*

I waited until the elegant lines of fine copperplate script had faded from the page, then closed the blue journal and returned it to its shelf.

"I don't care about village rivalries or multigenerational hissy fits," I said to Reginald. "I won't turn my back on Arthur Hargreaves."

My pink bunny's black button eyes gleamed softly in the lamplight, as if he'd given me his blessing to pursue my budding friendship with the Summer King.

# Eleven

I felt surprisingly chipper when Bess roused me from slumber at the crack of dawn on Monday. Even so, I didn't hesitate to accept Bill's offer to drive the boys to school in his Mercedes and to pick them up at the end of the day. While his agenda contained nothing more pressing than the busywork he'd invented to avoid spending time with his aunts, mine was chock-full of vital tasks, the first of which I accomplished before leaving the cottage.

After downing a few hurried mouthfuls of breakfast, I waved Bill, Will, and Rob on their way, put a load of presoaked diapers into the washer, ate a proper breakfast, straightened the kitchen, and brought Bess and her workout mat into the study with me, so I could keep an eye on her while I called the number written on the page from Mr. Barlow's notebook.

As normal business hours had not yet commenced, I thought I would have to leave a recorded message for Marigold Edwards. I was pleasantly surprised, therefore, when my call was answered by a courteous human voice telling me that I'd reached the offices of the Edwards Estate Agency. Marigold might not be a go-getter, but Mrs. Dinsdale—the firm's office manager—evidently was.

Mrs. Dinsdale informed me that Mrs. Edwards would be happy to meet with me at ten o'clock on Friday morning. I would have preferred to come to grips with my quarry sooner, but I was in no position to argue with Mrs. Dinsdale's apologetic but firm assertion that Mrs. Edwards would be fully engaged until then.

I confirmed the date and time of the appointment, thanked Mrs. Dinsdale for her assistance, and ended the call, muttering, "I'll bet Marigold Edwards isn't fully engaged in finding buyers for *our* cottages."

By then, Bess needed a diaper change.

I sorted her out and left her in her playpen, shaking a rainbow-striped toucan rattle, while I put the clean diapers into the dryer and the one she'd recently dirtied into the presoak bin. The clean-dirty diaper cycle was never-ending.

I loaded the all-terrain pram into the Range Rover in case Willis, Sr., wished to take his granddaughter for a stroll, but I didn't bother to dress Bess in a special meet-the-grandaunts outfit because the one she had on would almost certainly have to be changed before Charlotte and Honoria made their grand entrance.

Since Bess was a drooling, pooping, upchucking clotheshorse, however, I packed the usual assortment of extra outfits in the diaper bag and hoped that her great-grandaunts would approve of the one she was wearing when they met her. It was a wan hope, admittedly, but when it came to dealing with Bill's aunts, a wan hope was the only kind of hope I could manage.

I had no hope whatsoever of escaping criticism aimed at my own attire, regardless of what I wore. I could have been depressed by the thought, but I chose to regard it as liberating. It freed me to wear sneakers instead of heels and a utilitarian nursing top instead of a fancy blouse. I even felt a small rush of pride when I pulled on a pair of blue jeans I couldn't have squeezed myself into six weeks earlier.

By nine o'clock, Bess, the diaper bag, and I were in the Range Rover and on our way to Fairworth House. It was another splendid summer morning, warm but not too warm and still without being stuffy. The sun shone in a cloudless sky and a myriad of small birds fluttered in and out of the hedgerows that lined the lane. I told Bess about Anscombe Manor and Bree Pym's redbrick house as we drove past them, and announced our arrival when we reached the entrance to her grandfather's estate.

Most of my friends had garage-door openers hooked to their car visors. I had a wrought-iron-gate opener hooked to mine. I pressed it and the gates guarding Willis, Sr.'s tree-lined drive swung inward. As I passed between them, I glanced upward, half expecting to see Amelia perched on a tree branch, polishing leaves. The Donovans wouldn't have left her much else to do.

Deirdre and Declan Donovan lived in the self-contained apartment Willis, Sr., had carved out of the attics in Fairworth House. They were in their early thirties and they were the only full-time staff members my father-in-law employed. Declan worked outdoors, tending to the estate's gardens, meadows, and woods and occasionally serving as Willis, Sr.'s chauffeur, while Deirdre filled the dual indoor roles of cook and housekeeper. They were both very good at their jobs. What's more, they were good people. Bill and I slept more soundly at night, knowing that Willis, Sr., had such a competent, compassionate couple looking after him.

The Donovans thought themselves lucky to live and work in such a beautiful place, and when Fairworth House came into view, I couldn't help but agree with them. There was nothing outlandish or flamboyant about my father-in-law's home. It was a solid, respectable Georgian mansion—classical, restrained, and relatively modest in size. Its limestone walls glowed like old gold in the morning light, its tall windows sparkled, and its white trim work gleamed. Fairworth was, like its owner, elegant, understated, and well groomed.

I spotted Declan Donovan in the rose garden as I pulled onto the graveled apron in front of the house. Declan, a short, stocky, red-headed Irishman, was dressed in his gardening gear—a loose-fitting short-sleeved shirt, scruffy Wellington boots, and black nylon trousers with padded knees and a variety of pockets. When he saw me, he shoved his secateurs into a leg pocket and came over to lend me a hand with the diaper bag while I released Bess's carry cot/car seat from the Rover.

"How's our Bess this fine morning?" he inquired.

"Blooming," I replied. "How's our Amelia?"

"You'll see for yourself in a min—"

Declan broke off as Amelia flung the front door open and all but flew down the front steps.

"Oh, dear," I said under my breath.

"Yep," Declan murmured succinctly.

"You're here!" Amelia exclaimed, enveloping me and the freed carry cot in a hug. She planted a quick kiss on Bess's forehead, snatched the diaper bag from Declan, and tugged me up the stairs and into the high-ceilinged entrance hall.

Amelia Thistle was a petite, pleasantly plump widow in her early sixties. She was also a world-renowned watercolorist. She found inspiration in nature and spent much of her time tramping through the countryside, clad in a bulky pullover, a ratty rain jacket, and corduroy trousers, with her painting gear crammed into a grubby old day pack. Her complexion was ruddy and she wore her gray hair in a perpetually tousled knot at the back of her head, but though she preferred to dress down, she knew how to dress up.

She'd clearly made an effort to put her best foot forward for her prospective sisters-in-law. Her flowing, knee-length silk gown looked as though she had painted it herself, then dipped it in water to make the pastel colors run together. It was striking, but not showy, and its soft violet shades played off the amethyst in her antique engagement ring.

"Come into the morning room," she said, pulling me across the entrance hall. "We're saving the drawing room for later."

I assumed that "later" meant "when Charlotte and Honoria arrive," and that Amelia wished to make a good impression on them by ushering them into a room that was marginally more formal than the morning room. They would, no doubt, find the morning room insipid.

I thought it was lovely. The walls were a delicate shade of apricot, the windows were hung with gold brocade drapes, and the furnishings were light and feminine, with slender cabriolet legs and embroidered upholstery. Porcelain figurines graced the white marble mantel shelf, and the silver filigree desk set on the rosewood writing table was so finely wrought it could have been made of lace. Willis, Sr., had put the finishing touch on the morning room when he'd replaced its oil paintings with a selection of his fiancée's superb watercolors.

Amelia had added an unexpected splash of color to the decor by placing a bright-red bouncy chair in the middle of the room. The chair looked slightly out of place on the Aubusson carpet, but when Bess saw it, she gave a squeaky chortle and began to kick like mad. She was very fond of the bouncy chair.

Amelia dropped the diaper bag on the settee near the windows, then prowled the room like a caged lioness while I placed Bess in her favorite piece of furniture. I secured the safety restraints, to keep my rock 'n' roll girl from launching herself into the stratosphere, then sat back on my heels and looked up at Amelia.

I intended to put our time together to good use. Having made an appointment to see Marigold Edwards, I was ready to tackle the second item on my agenda: soliciting Amelia's opinion of her.

"Are you sure you haven't pulled those straps too tight?" Amelia asked, peering at the bouncy chair. "We wouldn't want to cut off Bess's circulation."

"Bess is fine," I said through gritted teeth. "Where's William?"

"Oh, he'll be along as soon as he finds out that Bess is here," Amelia said fretfully. "He's been shut up in his study all morning. He called it his hurricane shelter. I haven't the least idea what he meant by it."

I grinned knowingly, got to my feet, and seated myself on a non-bouncy Regency armchair near Bess.

"It's a little joke he picked up from his son," I explained. "Bill called me Hurricane Lori when I arranged William's housewarming party. You must be Hurricane Amelia."

Amelia drew an indignant breath, then sank onto the settee and began to laugh.

"I have been behaving like a lunatic," she admitted. "I feel as if I should be *doing* something, but everything's been done, so I keep walking in circles, moving things that don't need to be moved, then moving them back to where they were in the first place. Hurricane Amelia, indeed." She shook her head and chuckled. "Poor William. I *drove* him into his study."

"You've got stage fright," I said. "Who wouldn't? It's easier to meet future in-laws than it is to contemplate meeting them. You'll be fine once the show gets under way. In the meantime, let's talk about anything *but* Charlotte and Honoria."

"Oh, yes, let's," she said imploringly. "If I touch another ornament, Deirdre will lock me in the cloakroom and throw away the key."

"We can't have that," I said, smiling. "I'm a little parched, though. May I have a glass of water?"

"Good Lord," said Amelia, jumping up from the settee. "I've officially lost my mind. Forgive me, Lori. I forgot that nursing makes you thirsty. I should have had a pitcher of water waiting for you. I'll be right back."

She'd scarcely taken two steps away from the settee when the door to the dining room opened and Deirdre Donovan entered the morning room, carrying a silver tray that held a Waterford pitcher filled with ice water, two Waterford tumblers, and a plateful of madeleines.

Deirdre was almost a full head taller than her husband and her refined English accent bore no trace of the years they'd spent together in his homeland. She was an exotic beauty, shapely and graceful, with a swanlike neck and a creamy complexion. During working hours, her "uniform" consisted of a full-skirted white shirt dress, a crisp black apron, black pumps, and a demure black snood—she was the only woman I knew who owned a snood—into which she bundled her luxuriant chestnut hair.

"Thank you, Deirdre," said Amelia, resuming her seat. "I may have forgotten my manners, but you haven't forgotten yours."

"Don't be so hard on yourself, Amelia," said Deirdre. "You're under more pressure than I am." She placed the silver tray on the occasional table at my elbow. "Shall I pour?"

"I think I can manage," I said. "But thanks."

"Will there be anything else?" Deirdre asked.

"Not at the moment," said Amelia.

Deirdre motioned to the buzzer concealed beneath the mantel shelf.

"Ring if you need me," she said. "I'll be in the kitchen. Hello, Bess," she added, smiling down at my bouncy daughter. "Your grandfather will be with you shortly."

She bent low to caress Bess's wispy curls, then left the morning room. Amelia waved away the glass of water I offered to her, so I drank it down greedily, refilled the glass, and drank half of it before setting it aside.

"I thought Deirdre would have a child of her own by now," said Amelia, lowering her voice.

"So did I," I said.

Amelia peered worriedly at the dining room door. "I hope she and Declan realize that William has no objection to—"

"Hold on," I interrupted. "Would you mind skipping over the Donovans for now? I'd like to pick your brain about someone else."

"Who?" Amelia asked.

"Marigold Edwards," I replied. "What's your take on her?"

"What's my take on Marigold Edwards?" Amelia gave me a piercing look, then said cautiously, "I think she's an excellent estate agent. My experience with her was completely satisfactory. I'd recommend her to anyone, apart from you and Bill, because you'd break William's heart if you—"

"We're not moving," I stated firmly. "I'm just curious about Marigold. What is it, exactly, that makes her an excellent estate agent?"

My reassuring words seemed to enable Amelia to speak more freely and with more enthusiasm about the woman I would meet on Friday morning.

"Having Marigold as my agent was like having a friend in Finch," she said. "She was thoroughly professional, of course, but she was also . . ." Amelia's voice trailed off and she began again. "The first time I came to Finch to see Pussywillows, Marigold didn't merely show me the cottage. She took me to the tearoom, the Emporium, the pub, the old schoolhouse, and the church."

"Did she show you the wall paintings?" I asked.

"Naturally," said Amelia. "They're among Finch's finest treasures and I would have missed them if Marigold hadn't pointed them out to me. She drew my attention to all sorts of little details and she introduced me to everyone we met." Amelia looked down at her hands.

# Twelve

**M**y father-in-law wasn't physically imposing, but he had impeccable manners, patrician good looks, and a flawless sense of style. His gleaming black leather shoes and his black three-piece suit fit him as though they'd been made for him, which they had, and his white shirt wasn't blindingly white, but a more subtle shade that complimented his snowy hair perfectly.

His gray silk tie and pocket square were familiar accent pieces, but the forget-me-not in his buttonhole was a relatively new touch. He'd worn a fresh flower in his lapel ever since Amelia had tucked an anemone into his breast pocket during one of their long country rambles. It was his way of wearing his heart on his sleeve.

Bess went bananas as soon as Willis, Sr., entered the room. She kicked like a mule, waved her fists in the air, squeaked, gurgled, giggled, and favored him with a broad, gummy smile. His handsome face lit up when he saw her and when he spoke, he spoke as much to her as to me.

"Please forgive me for neglecting you so shamefully," he said. "I had no idea that you were here. I have just this moment returned from paying my respects to Augusta Fairworthy."

Augusta Fairworthy, who was distantly related to Deirdre Donovan, had grown up in Fairworth House. When she'd died, Willis, Sr., had honored her request to be buried on the estate, within view of the house, beneath an oak tree she'd climbed many times as a child.

"As you know, Lori, I had my own reasons for purchasing Pussywillows, but Marigold gave me new reasons, fresh reasons, reasons that would never have occurred to me."

"Such as?" I asked.

"Colorful characters," Amelia said promptly. "Candid conversations. Concern for one's neighbors. Pride in one's village. And more else besides."

I leaned toward her. "Did she tell you about the Finch-Tillcote feud?"

"Oh, yes," said Amelia. "Marigold made it quite clear that the two villages did not get on. It put me off, rather." Amelia frowned. "I felt as if I'd glimpsed the dark side of village life and I didn't like it one bit. If I hadn't had a very special reason to move to Finch, I might have chosen to live elsewhere." A slow smile curved her lips as she stroked her engagement ring with her thumb. "Which would have been a grave mistake on my part."

"I'm sure William would agree with you," I said. "You weren't looking for love when you came to Finch, but you found it anyway."

"Life," she said, her smile widening, "is full of surprises."

The most wonderful surprise in Amelia's life chose that moment to walk into the morning room.

"I hope you, too, will forgive my absence," he continued, approaching Amelia.

"You were wise to absent yourself," she said ruefully. "You're safe now, though. The hurricane warning has been lifted."

Willis, Sr., caught my eye and smiled, then raised his fiancée's hand to his lips.

"Your desire to be helpful is wholly admirable, my dear," he said, straightening, "if occasionally misplaced." He held his arms out to Bess and looked questioningly at me. "May I?"

"You don't have to ask, William," I said, exasperated. "I'm pretty sure I've mentioned it to you a few thousand times already, but for the thousand and oneth time: You don't need my permission to hold your granddaughter."

To spare Willis, Sr.'s back, I lifted Bess from the bouncy chair. To spare his exquisite suit, I draped a clean diaper over his shoulder before handing her to him.

"My granddaughter has gained weight," he commented.

I headed him off before he could rile me by asking if I was feeding Bess properly.

"I know," I said brightly. "It's great, isn't it? According to Dr. Finisterre, Bess is exactly the right weight for her age."

"Dr. Finisterre is a fine physician," Willis, Sr., said, nodding his approval.

He carried his granddaughter to the windows to show her the view, but she was more interested in grabbing his nose, poking him in the eye, and putting her fingers into his mouth. There was no such thing as dignity where Bess was concerned.

"We've been discussing Marigold Edwards," said Amelia.

Willis, Sr., turned to face me.

"We're not moving," I said doggedly, in answer to his unspoken question. "We're not even thinking about moving. Bill and I are as happy as clams in the cottage."

"Why, then, were you and Amelia discussing Mrs. Edwards?" he inquired.

"I've taken an interest in her," I replied. "Did you deal with her when you bought Fairworth House?"

"I did not," he said. "I dealt directly with the previous owner. He was eighty-four years old at the time, and living in Singapore. He wished to rid himself of an inherited estate that had become an encumbrance. I had no difficulty conducting the transaction without the aid of a local estate agent."

With Bess gripping his chin and patting his lips, Willis, Sr., was unable to enunciate his words with his usual precision, but he managed to make himself understood.

"Although I have not yet met Mrs. Edwards," he went on, "I will, of course, be eternally grateful to her for facilitating Amelia's purchase of Pussywillows." He bestowed a tender glance on his beloved.

I was about to move on to the third item on my agenda when Deirdre Donovan returned, bringing with her a second pitcher of ice water and a single Waterford tumbler, presumably for Willis, Sr.'s use. She placed the pitcher and the tumbler on the salver, then sniffed the air.

"Unless I'm mistaken," she said, "someone needs a fresh nappy."

Willis, Sr., sniffed his granddaughter delicately, then nodded.

"My olfactory receptors are not as acute as yours," he said, "but I believe you are correct."

"Sorry, William," I said, standing. "I must be getting used to it."

"Please, allow me," said Deirdre, taking Bess from Willis, Sr. "You don't mind if I do the honors, do you, Lori?"

"Have I ever kept you from changing Bess's diapers?" I said, sinking back into my chair. "Knock yourself out!"

Bess was familiar with Deirdre and went with her willingly. A moment later, the sound of the elevator Willis, Sr., had installed in the entrance hall told us that they were on their way to the top-floor nursery. Willis, Sr., divested himself of his suit protector and Amelia tucked it into the diaper bag, looking thoughtful.

"Perhaps she's practicing," Amelia proposed, as Willis, Sr., seated himself beside her on the settee, "for when she has to change her own baby's nappies." She turned to him. "Has Deirdre said anything to you about starting a family, William? Has Declan?"

"They have not," said Willis, Sr. "I would not expect the Donovans to discuss such a personal matter with me and I would urge you to refrain from discussing it. They may not wish to have children, they may wish to postpone having them, or they may be unable to have them. It is entirely their own affair. Speculation by a third party would be disrespectful, intrusive, and potentially hurtful."

"You're right, of course," said Amelia, but her fiancé's comprehensive critique of idle gossip didn't prevent her from adding, "What a tragedy it would be if they were infertile."

"Shall we change the subject?" Willis, Sr., requested with a swift glance in my direction.

Willis, Sr., knew that I'd once harbored doubts about my own ability to start a family. He seemed to think that Amelia's musings might revive memories I did not wish to recall. I could have told him that those memories no longer troubled me. I could have said that each of my children had been well worth the wait. Instead, I shamelessly exploited his concern for me by pouncing on the chance to change the subject.

"Arthur Hargreaves," I said abruptly, putting a triumphant mental check mark next to the third item on my agenda. "What can you tell me about him, William?"

"Why do you wish to know about Arthur Hargreaves?" Willis, Sr., asked, looking bemused. "Have you taken an interest in him as well?"

"Bess and I met him on Saturday," I said. "I was a little surprised when he told me he'd never met you."

"Who is Arthur Hargreaves?" Amelia asked.

"He's William's next-door neighbor," I replied. "He lives in a place called Hillfont Abbey."

"The Hargreaves estate is adjacent to mine," Willis, Sr., clarified. "Technically, Mr. Hargreaves is my neighbor, but he and I do not interact in what most people would describe as a neighborly fashion."

"Why not?" Amelia and I asked simultaneously. She sounded astonished, but I simply wanted to hear Willis, Sr.'s side of the story.

"I cannot speak for Mr. Hargreaves," he said, "but it is an old habit of mine to respect a person's privacy until he or she invites me to do otherwise. I have received no such invitation from Mr. Hargreaves."

Amelia tossed her head impatiently.

"William," she said, "for an intelligent man, you can be remarkably obtuse at times. What if poor Mr. Hargreaves is waiting for *you* to invite *him* to invade *your* precious privacy?"

"If such is the case," said Willis, Sr., "I fear that we shall remain strangers."

"You haven't avoided him intentionally, have you?" I asked. "Because of the Finch-Tillcote feud?"

Willis, Sr., appeared to be faintly puzzled.

"Are the two villages engaged in a feud?" he asked.

"Of course they are," Amelia expostulated. "You must know about the feud, William. It's been going on for ages. Marigold Edwards told me all about it when I first came to Finch."

"I am not acquainted with Mrs. Edwards," Willis, Sr., reminded her.

"Nor am I," I said. "William and I are in the same boat, Amelia. Neither of us used an estate agent when we moved to Finch. No one told me about the feud until yesterday, but you're right—it's been going on for a long time."

"How long?" Willis, Sr., inquired.

"Victoria was still on the throne when it started," I said, recalling Aunt Dimity's history lesson. "Local lore has it that Arthur's great-great-grandfather, Quentin Hargreaves, sided with Tillcote in a quarrel about three stolen pigs."

"Did Quentin Hargreaves blame the theft on a person or persons residing in Finch?" Willis, Sr., asked.

"Quentin didn't point a finger at anyone," I said, "but he chose Tillcote over Finch, so he must have believed that the guilty party lived in Finch."

"Implications can sometimes do more damage than outright accusations," Willis, Sr., observed. "One can defend oneself against an accusation. An implication is more difficult to refute."

"Quentin's implication outraged Finch's law-abiding residents," I said. "They shunned the Hargreaves family because of it and they've been shunning them ever since. That's why I thought you might . . ." My voice faded as Willis, Sr., gave me a withering look.

"I think he's outraged by your implication," Amelia said in a deliberately comical stage whisper.

Willis, Sr.'s frosty expression thawed.

"I beg your pardon, Lori," he said contritely. "I was taken aback by your suggestion that an ancient quarrel might influence my choice of friends. I can assure you that such is not the case, nor would it ever be the case. I have seen petty vendettas tear families apart far too often. I refuse to participate in one."

Before his retirement, Willis, Sr., had been an international attorney who'd specialized in estate planning for the fabulously wealthy. He had firsthand knowledge of the spite, bile, and malice that shaped many last wills and testaments.

"It was a long shot," I acknowledged, "but I had to be sure. Everyone else in Finch seems to be caught up in the feud."

"William isn't everyone," Amelia said proudly, putting her hand on his.

"No, he isn't," I agreed. I leaned back in my chair, feeling disappointed. "Are you certain you can't tell me anything about Arthur Hargreaves, William?"

"Our paths have not crossed," he replied. "I have seen bright lights in the sky above Hillfont Abbey from time to time and I have heard the occasional explosion, but apart from that—"

"Bright lights?" Amelia exclaimed.

"Explosions?" I said, sitting upright.

Deirdre Donovan's reputation for good timing took a serious hit when she chose that precise moment to return to the morning room with Bess. I saw immediately that she hadn't merely changed my daughter's diaper. She'd exchanged Bess's simple white jumpsuit for an unfamiliar gray onesie topped with an equally unfamiliar but adorable coral cardigan.

"Do you like them?" she asked me, plucking anxiously at the onesie's collar and smoothing the cardigan before passing Bess to me. "They caught my eye the last time I was in Upper Deeping and I couldn't resist buying them. I've been dying to try them on Bess."

"They're wonderful," I said. "The color combination is very sophisticated. I wouldn't have thought of pairing coral with gray, but they look great together. Thank you, Deirdre."

Deirdre looked so relieved that I didn't have the heart to tell her that all baby clothes, no matter how sophisticated, were doomed to a life that was damp, sticky, and short. She acknowledged my thanks with a beaming smile, filled the three tumblers with water, and took the empty pitcher with her as she left the room.

Bess should have been ready to chow down, but she was too excited to think about eating, so I put her back in the bouncy chair before turning my gimlet gaze on Willis, Sr.

"Bright lights in the sky?" I said. "Explosions? What the heck are you talking about, William?"

"Yes, William," Amelia chimed in. "What in heaven's name are you talking about?"

"I assume Mr. Hargreaves enjoys fireworks," said Willis, Sr. "I have never had a reason to test my assumption. The pyrotechnics I have witnessed have had no deleterious effects on my property."

Amelia and I exchanged looks of helpless disbelief.

"If I heard explosions coming from my neighbor's house," I said, "I'd mosey over to have a little chat with him."

"So would I," Amelia said feelingly. "Where is Hillfont Abbey?"

"The abbey itself lies slightly to the northeast of Fairworth House," said Willis, Sr., "but the Hargreaves estate shares my estate's northern border."

"You could *walk* there," Amelia said, staring at him.

"I have no desire to trespass on a stranger's property," said Willis, Sr. "It is true, however, that a five-minute stroll through the orchid wood would bring me to a side entrance in the wall that surrounds the abbey." He peered at me inquisitively. "Where did you happen upon Mr. Hargreaves?"

"He happened upon us," I said. "Bess and I were exploring a long-forgotten farm track Emma Harris had told me about, when——"

"Are you referring to the disused cart track that runs parallel to my property line?" Willis, Sr., interjected, looking alarmed.

"Yep," I said. "And before you accuse me of risking Bess's life, let me say in my own defense that I wouldn't have taken her down the old track if I'd known it was prone to flash floods."

"Good heavens," Amelia breathed.

"When did you become aware of the danger?" Willis, Sr., asked.

"Yesterday," I said. "Lilian Bunting alerted me to it."

Willis, Sr., heaved a brief but heartfelt sigh of relief.

"I will express my profound gratitude to Mrs. Bunting when next we meet," he said.

"Go on with your story," Amelia urged me. "Tell us how Arthur Hargreaves happened upon you."

I opened my mouth, but closed it again when Bess emitted a fussy squeak. I glanced down at her, expecting her gaze to be fixed firmly on my chest, but she'd turned her head toward the windows. As I looked to see what had caught her attention, Deirdre strode into the morning room.

"Battle stations," she announced. "Our guests have arrived."

# Thirteen

*A*melia jumped to her feet as if propelled from a cannon. The color drained from her face as she wheeled around to peer through the windows at the classic, silver-gray Bentley that had appeared on the drive's graveled apron. Willis, Sr., rose in a more leisurely fashion, but he put a reassuring hand on her back as he, too, turned to observe the Bentley. Deirdre went into the entrance hall and prepared herself to open the front door for Charlotte and Honoria.

I had scarcely any time at all to decide on my own course of action. Would I support Amelia in her hour of need? Or would I show my true colors and flee? I dithered for less than a nanosecond, then chose the coward's way out.

"Bess needs a feed," I said. "Back in a minute."

I scooped Bess up from the bouncy chair and ran for the elevator. I left the diaper bag behind in my haste, but I didn't go back to collect it because I wouldn't need it. The nursery was fully stocked with maternal necessities.

I flung myself into the elevator as Deirdre opened the front door. I caught a glimpse of a uniformed chauffeur burdened with pristine leather luggage before I closed the elevator's door and allowed myself and my child to be whisked to the third floor. I was fairly certain that Bill's aunts wouldn't follow me. They weren't overly fond of infants.

The late Augusta Fairworthy had once lived in the room that had become the nursery. Willis, Sr., had left a few of her prized possessions in place as a tribute to her memory. Bess wanted to taste the Murano paperweights, the enameled snuffboxes, and the silver, sheep-shaped salt and pepper shakers that twinkled so invitingly from the locked display cabinet in the corner, but she eventually calmed down enough to avail herself of a more nutritious meal.

"I'm not proud of myself for running out on Amelia," I told her gravely after we'd settled ourselves in the rocking chair. "When you grow up, I hope you'll be braver than I am. If your great-aunts are still around then, though, you may understand why we're here now."

I cut my soliloquy short when the nursery door opened and Deirdre appeared, carrying a tray set with three covered dishes, silverware, a linen napkin, a tumbler, and a small cut-glass pitcher of ice water. Her mouth was set in a thin line and her nostrils flared slightly as she spoke.

"Mrs. Steele and Mrs. Wilberforce don't want the lunch I spent all morning preparing for them," she said, "but I thought you might."

I seldom used Charlotte's and Honoria's last names, but even if I'd never heard them before, I would have known who'd rubbed Deirdre the wrong way.

She placed the tray on a low table and removed the dishes' covers.

"Tomato bisque, tarragon chicken salad, and mixed wild greens," she announced. "I left the bitter herbs out of your portions, so you don't have to worry about them flavoring your milk."

"Thank you, Deirdre," I said. "I'm sure I'll enjoy every bite."

"They're having tea in the drawing room," she informed me icily. "Tea in the drawing room instead of lunch in the dining room."

"Try not to take it personally," I said, putting a placatory hand out to her. "Charlotte and Honoria hardly ever eat lunch. They think midday meals are plebeian."

"I wish I'd known it sooner," Deirdre said tersely.

"I'm sorry," I said. "I should have done more to prepare you and Amelia for the calamity that was about to befall you. I've been so wrapped up in Bess that I—"

"A mother should be wrapped up in her child," Deirdre interrupted. "You're here now, though. Tell me about the calamity."

"William's not the most reliable source of information about his sisters," I explained. "They're his kid sisters, the only girls in a family that included five boys before two of them died. Bill claims that two of his uncles moved to California in order to get away from his aunts, but your boss has a soft spot for them."

"What else should I know?" Deirdre asked, folding her arms.

"Where to begin?" I said, gazing heavenward. "Nothing you do will satisfy them, but keep trying anyway. Surprise them by being the same consummate professional you've always been. When they push you to your limit, remind yourself that they'll be gone in less than a month."

Deirdre drummed her fingers on her biceps for a moment, then unfolded her arms and lifted her chin.

"I accept the challenge," she said and left the nursery.

Bess finished her über-plebeian midday meal a few minutes later. She was mellower than she had been when she first entered the nursery and so was I. I tidied us both, scarfed down the meal Deirdre had left for me, took a deep breath, and went downstairs to introduce my drowsy baby to her grandaunts.

The sense of tranquility that had enveloped me in the nursery evaporated when I entered the drawing room. The mere sound of Honoria's familiar nasal drawl set my teeth on edge. She and Charlotte sat in a pair of Chippendale armchairs facing Amelia, who was seated in a Chippendale side chair, with the tea table at her knee.

Willis, Sr., stood near the white marble fireplace, gazing benevolently at his sisters, but Amelia looked slightly shell-shocked. I wondered how many cunningly disguised insults Charlotte and Honoria had hurled at her in the past half hour. If my experience was anything to go by, they would have thrown quite a few.

"Lori!" Amelia exclaimed, with a note of desperation in her voice. "I'm so pleased to see you. I'll fetch Bess's bouncy chair."

She left the room as quickly as her short legs could carry her. I didn't expect her back anytime soon. Her rapid departure made me feel a little less guilty about my own.

"Hello, Aunt Honoria. Hello, Aunt Charlotte," I said with as much enthusiasm as I could muster. "Welcome to England."

Willis, Sr.'s sisters could have been twins. They were, by choice, thin to the point of emaciation. They wore their silvery hair in short, rigidly coifed styles and dressed in vintage Chanel suits and shoes. Though they limited their makeup to the merest touch of powder and lipstick, they drenched themselves in their favorite Chanel perfume. Bill had once referred to them as "a sweet-smelling pair of vultures."

Since neither woman rose to greet me, I bent awkwardly to kiss their papery cheeks while holding Bess to my shoulder.

"Is this our great-niece?" Honoria asked, scanning her chic, boxy blazer to make sure her great-niece hadn't drooled on it.

"Yes," I said, straightening. "This is Bess."

"Bess," said Charlotte. "What a charming soubriquet. I'm almost tempted to call William 'Billy' and myself 'Char.'"

Honoria tittered gaily.

"You call your nephew 'Bill,'" I said stiffly.

"So we do," Charlotte agreed smoothly. "I meant no offense, dear, and I hope none was taken."

I forced a smile and sat on the Regency chaise longue in front of the windows. Bess nuzzled her head into my neck and went to sleep.

"It's a pleasure to see you looking so well," said Honoria. "Child-bearing at an advanced age can wreak havoc on a woman's body."

"I understand why you had to dress down," said Charlotte, taking in my non-designer attire. "I, too, had a terrible time finding nice things to wear when I was shedding my baby weight. Don't let it trouble you." She pointed a beautifully manicured, bony finger at me. "With a little effort on your part, you'll soon have your figure back."

Bess whimpered softly in her sleep and I tightened my hold on her to assure her that I was still there.

"She won't sleep through the night if you allow her to sleep during the day," said Honoria.

"Bess almost always sleeps through the night," I said. "Why do you think I have so much energy?"

"If I lived here, I'd have no energy at all," said Charlotte, gazing languidly around the room. "There's quiet and there's comatose. I've had only a glimpse of Finch, but it seems to fall into the latter category."

"I noticed two houses for sale," said Honoria. "The signs looked ancient."

"Are you implying that no one in his right mind would buy a cottage in Finch?" said Charlotte. "You amaze me."

"I wouldn't care to live there year-round," said Honoria, "but it might do as a summer retreat."

"Do you remember the little knot of senior citizens who stared at us as we drove by?" said Charlotte. "I imagine they're living on fixed incomes."

"They're not trust fund babies," Honoria said archly.

"A clever developer would have no trouble persuading them to sell out," said Charlotte.

"They'd grab the money and run," said Honoria.

"If the developer modernized the cottages and marketed them properly," Charlotte went on, "he could sell them as summer homes. He might even turn a profit. After all, property prices are sky-high in England, even in rural areas."

"The villagers might not wish to sell their homes," Willis, Sr., pointed out gently.

"They might have no choice," said Charlotte.

"Fixed incomes are *such* a nuisance," said Honoria.

Bess whimpered again. I checked her diaper surreptitiously, but it was dry. I didn't know what was bugging her, so I rubbed her back as my mother had rubbed mine when I was a child. It seemed to work. Bess's eyelids fluttered, then closed as she drifted back to sleep.

"Is it true that you have no nanny?" Honoria inquired, looking askance at her great-niece.

"It's true," I replied. "I needed all the help I could get when Will and Rob were babies, but one child is less of a handful than twins."

"And you've had Bill to help you, of course," said Honoria. "Such a dear, thoughtful man."

"Honoria and I were delighted to hear that he went into the office today," said Charlotte. "He's spent so much time at home with you and the children that we were beginning to think he'd retired."

"Bill's a wonderful husband and father," I said stoically. "I don't know how I would have managed if he hadn't taken time off from work after Bess was born."

"You could have hired a nanny," Honoria said brightly. "But I suppose a fully qualified nanny might object to working in such a remote location. Where on earth would she go on her day off? There's nothing for miles around except fields and sheep."

Bess shifted her head restlessly, but relaxed when she heard her grandfather's voice.

"Finch is not as remote as it might seem," he said. "Oxford is nearby and the local market town of Upper Deeping is no more than twenty minutes away."

"I believe we passed through Upper Deeping on our way here," said Honoria, adding dismissively, "It seemed like a quaint little town." She turned toward the entrance hall. "What can be keeping Amelia? Does your fiancée always leave you alone when you entertain guests, William?"

"Perhaps she's lost," Charlotte suggested. "Fairworth House must seem like a maze to her after her cottage."

"Amelia has not always lived in a cottage," Willis, Sr., informed her. "Her previous home was twice the size of Fairworth House."

"Was she compelled to sell it?" Honoria asked, feigning sympathy. "Artists are so often the victims of their own excesses."

"They are," Charlotte said in a sorrowful tone of voice that was equally bogus. "An eminent psychiatrist told me that creative people are prone to alcoholism, drug addiction, and a whole host of mental illnesses."

I glanced at Willis, Sr., hoping he'd seen through their act, but he appeared to take their barbed comments at face value.

"Amelia is guilty of no excesses," he said. "She came to Finch because her former home no longer suited her."

Charlotte and Honoria looked thunderstruck.

"She moved to Finch *voluntarily*?" Charlotte said.

Before Willis, Sr., could respond, Amelia returned to the drawing room, carrying the bouncy chair.

"Forgive me," she said, nodding apologetically to each of us. "I was detained by a telephone call. William? A messenger delivered the papers you were expecting. They're on your desk in the study."

"Please excuse me," Willis, Sr., said to his sisters. "Although I have retired, a few of my clients still rely upon me."

"Business before pleasure," said Charlotte, "is our family motto."

"A motto your son would do well to remember," said Honoria, with a sly, sidelong glance in my direction.

"Run along, William," said Charlotte. "Take as much time as you need. We'll indulge in a little girl-talk while you're gone."

Willis, Sr., left for the study and the sisters fixed their poisonous gazes on Amelia.

Amelia looked as though she'd collected her wits as well as the bouncy chair. She placed one at my feet and used the other to start a conversation about gardening. She must have thought that no one could attack her on such a neutral subject, but she'd scarcely begun to speak when Charlotte cut her off.

"Did you really come to Finch of your own volition?" Charlotte asked.

"Y-yes," Amelia stammered, thrown off her stride. "After my husband died, my old house felt like a mausoleum. I wanted a cozier home and I found one in Finch."

I knew that Amelia had come to Finch to hunt for something other than a cozy home, but I would have undergone oral surgery without anesthetic before I revealed her secrets to the Harpies.

"But there's nothing to *do* here," Honoria expostulated.

"A common misconception," said Amelia. "Finch is, in fact, a hive of activity. We have the harvest festival, the Nativity play, the flower show, jumble sales, sheep dog trials——"

"The full country calendar," Charlotte interrupted sarcastically. "I'm sure you find ways to keep busy, Amelia, but you can hardly compare a flower show to the opera or a harvest festival to the symphony."

"I wasn't comparing——" Amelia began, but again she was cut off.

"You're being unfair, Charlotte," said Honoria. "You can't expect to find the same level of sophistication here as you do in Boston. Operas and symphonies would be wasted on the local inhabitants. One would be casting pearls before swine."

"Very true," said Charlotte. "I'm sure the villagers are content with their jumble sales and their sheep dog trials. Simple pleasures for the simpleminded."

Bess pulled her head out of the crook of my neck and let loose a wail a banshee would have envied. The sound seemed to pierce Amelia's heart, but the sisters were more concerned about their eardrums.

"What's *wrong* with the child?" Honoria demanded, cupping her hands over her ears.

"Can't you *do* something?" Charlotte pleaded, following suit.

"I certainly can," I said. I stood and addressed Amelia, raising my voice to be heard above the din. "I'll take Bess for a walk. That usually does the trick." I winced as Bess upped the volume. "We may be gone for a while."

If Willis, Sr., had been present, Amelia probably would have come with me, but she evidently felt obliged to remain with his guests. I felt no such obligation. Although I was sorry to abandon Amelia for a second time, Bess and I left the sisters behind without a second glance.

Deirdre met me in the entrance hall.

"Is there anything I can do?" she asked as Bess's wails rebounded from the white marble walls.

"Bess needs a breath of untainted air," I explained. "Her pram's in the Rover."

"Right," said Deirdre. "I'll fetch the diaper bag and meet you there. Look after Bess. Let me deal with the pram."

In less than ten minutes, Bess and I were moving briskly across a verdant meadow on one of Willis, Sr.'s well-maintained gravel paths. Soothed by the change of scenery and by the all-terrain pram's familiar vibrations, Bess quickly regained her composure.

I, on the other hand, was ready to spit tacks.

# Fourteen

"*T*rust fund babies," I muttered furiously. "Pearls before swine. Simpleminded pleasures. *Childbearing at an advanced age?*" If I'd been a dragon, I would have breathed fire.

"Your daddy knows his aunts much better than I do, Bess," I went on. "He *knew* they'd try to undermine Amelia. Alcoholism, drug addiction, and mental illness, my foot!"

I walked so rapidly I scattered gravel in my wake. I didn't bask in the sunshine or revel in the loveliness of the flower-sprinkled meadow. I charged ahead like a rampaging rhinoceros. I didn't care where we were going, as long as it was away from the Harpies.

"Later on, Bess, when you're old enough to learn about good and evil," I continued, "I'll show you a photograph of your grandfather and a photograph of the grandaunts you met today and explain to you which is which." I kicked an inoffensive twig and sent it flying into the undergrowth. "Why can't Grandpa William see it?"

Cool air, dappled shade, and the faint scent of moist earth suggested that we were no longer in the sunny meadow. I stopped to look around.

"The orchid wood," I whispered. A shiver went down my spine as Willis, Sr.'s words came back to me. "A five-minute stroll through the orchid wood . . ." I tucked a blanket over Bess's bare legs. "I wonder if the side entrance to the Summer King's estate is locked? Let's find out, shall we? He did invite us to drop in."

I was pretty sure the side entrance Willis, Sr., had mentioned would be locked or rusted shut, but it didn't matter. The mere thought of seeing Arthur Hargreaves again brought my anger with Bill's aunts down to a manageable level.

"He should be at home," I said to Bess. "Remember what Grant and Charles told us? The Hermit of Hillfont Abbey doesn't leave home, if he can help it. Then again, Grant and Charles could be wrong." I pursed my lips and said thoughtfully, "Everyone could be wrong about Arthur."

I jiggled the pram to keep Bess amused while I reviewed the information I'd gathered about Arthur Hargreaves. According to the villagers, he was as mean-spirited and uppity as the rest of the Tillcote folk. According to Grant Tavistock and Charles Bellingham, he was a slightly mad, wholly secretive power broker. According to Willis, Sr., he was a fireworks aficionado, and according to Aunt Dimity, he was the innocent victim of an inherited feud.

"But none of them—not even Aunt Dimity—has met Arthur," I said aloud. "Their impressions of him are based on rumor, hearsay, innuendo, and a story that's been passed down from one generation to the next." I stopped jiggling the pram and gazed steadily into Bess's brown eyes. "This could be our chance to find out if the rumors are true, baby girl. Interested? I knew you would be. Let's go!"

It took some time to locate the correct path among the many crisscrossing, branching trails in the orchid wood, but I eventually found myself standing before a formidable wrought-iron gate set into the boundary wall that had piqued my curiosity and drawn me farther along the old cart track than I'd intended to go. The wall itself was concealed by banks of massed rhododendrons and the gate was around the corner from the section Arthur had climbed.

"We couldn't see the gate from the cart track," I explained to Bess, "because it was hidden in a stand of trees. If your mummy had a better sense of direction, she would have known it was the orchid wood. Emma would have recognized it straightaway." I rolled my eyes. "All that map reading . . ."

Bess sighed sympathetically.

"I can see Arthur's house," I told her excitedly, stepping past the pram. "It's over there."

I peered eagerly through the wrought-iron gate and across a broad expanse of open meadow to the low rise upon which Quentin Hargreaves had built his faux abbey. Aunt Dimity's Victorian ancestors had poured scorn upon "Quentin's Folly," but it filled me with delight.

"Oh, Bess," I whispered. "It's *wonderful*."

From a distance, Hillfont Abbey looked more like a fanciful fortress than a sober monastery. Its basic layout was quite simple—a square tower flanked by a pair of three-story wings—but the magic was in the details.

The central tower was crenellated and pierced by lancet windows. The three-story wings were festooned with spires, turrets, chimney clusters, stepped gables, projecting bays, and slender corner towers with conical caps. The building seemed to possess every shade of Cotswold stone—gray roofs, golden turrets, cream-colored embrasures, butterscotch walls—and it was surrounded by a crazy quilt of courtyards and gardens enclosed by another stone wall.

A flag hung from a pole atop the central tower. When it fluttered in a passing breeze, I caught a glimpse of a multicolored emblem centered on a sky-blue ground. I was too far away to decipher the emblem, but I was willing to swear that it wasn't a Union Jack.

"Quentin Hargreaves probably designed his own flag, too," I said to Bess. "Should I ask your brothers to design a flag for our family? I'll bet your grandaunts would have a lot to say about a family flag emblazoned with ponies, cookies, and dinosaurs."

I began to chuckle but fell silent when a strange buzzing noise reached my ears. It sounded as if someone had crossed a lawnmower with a sewing machine, then tossed a hornets' nest into the mix for good measure. Stranger still, the noise seemed to be coming from the sky.

I tilted my head back to see if the Summer King or one of his grandchildren had launched a marvelous, motorized kite into the air, but the buzzing noise didn't come from a kite. It came from a tiny aircraft that looked as though it had been cobbled together from a lawn chair, spare pram wheels, and leftover kite fabric.

The craft's single, lime-green wing and its tail wings looked marginally reliable, but they were attached to a frame that appeared to be made out of duct tape and plastic pipes. It had no fuselage, no windshield, no doors, no protective shell of any kind, and its buzzing engine sat directly above the pilot's bare head.

My mouth fell open as the flimsy airplane circled once, twice, three times around the abbey, then swooped low to land in the meadow. I held my breath as it touched down and didn't breathe again until it had rolled to within twenty yards of the wrought-iron gate. When it finally came to a full stop, I saw that its pilot had white hair and a short, neatly trimmed beard.

"Arthur may be slightly mad, Bess," I conceded, pressing a hand to my heaving chest, "but we can't fault his courage."

Arthur Hargreaves switched off the engine and unbuckled a shoulder harness and a seat belt. He stashed his goggles and his bulbous ear protectors beneath his seat, then climbed out of the lawn chair and stretched his arms above his head, as if they were stiff. He was dressed in a loose-fitting Hawaiian shirt, khaki cargo shorts, and the same soiled sneakers he'd worn when I'd first met him, but his grapevine crown was missing.

"He must have left it at home so it wouldn't blow away," I whispered to Bess. "If the Summer King had abdicated, it would be raining."

I watched in silence as Arthur secured the little plane, tethering it to stakes he drove into the ground by the simple expedient of stomping on them. He stood back to survey his handiwork, then began to make his way to the abbey.

"Arthur?" I called through the gate. I plucked a clean diaper from the diaper bag and waved it to get his attention. "Arthur! Over here!"

He swung around and looked toward me. A broad grin split his bearded face when he spotted the flapping diaper.

"Lori!" he shouted back. "Good to see you!"

I returned the diaper to the diaper bag and waited expectantly as the Summer King ambled toward me. When he reached the gate, I meant to say, "Hello again, Arthur. I hope Bess and I aren't intruding." Instead, the first thing that came into my head popped out of my mouth.

"That is the coolest thing I've ever seen in my life," I gushed, sounding—even to my own ears—like a starstruck twelve-year-old. "Absolutely the coolest." I slipped my arm through the gate to point at the tiny aircraft. "Did you make it yourself?"

"The ultralight?" he said, glancing over his shoulder. "No, I didn't make it. I merely tweaked a few engine parts for its owner. He'll be along later to pick it up. I think he'll be happy with my improvements." He cocked his head toward me. "Would you like to come in? Or were you merely passing by?"

"No one could pass your gate accidentally, Arthur," I said, grinning. "Of course I want to come in. Unless"—I looked down, feeling suddenly shy—"unless Bess and I are intruding."

"How could you intrude?" he asked. "I invited you."

He tugged on the gate and it swung aside soundlessly.

"It's not locked," I said. "I thought it might be."

"Why would I lock it?" Arthur asked. "Your father-in-law is a decent chap. Or so I've heard."

"William is decent," I said, as I wheeled Bess past him, "but he mystifies me. Come to think of it, so do you. The pair of you live next door to each other, with an unlocked gate between you, yet you haven't exchanged so much as a how-do-you-do." I looked up at Arthur, perplexed. "Is it a guy thing?"

"Yes, Lori," he said, closing the gate behind me. "It's a guy thing. Hello, princess." He bent to stroke Bess's cheek with his knuckles, then squatted to study the pram. "My repairs seem to be holding up."

"So far, so good," I said. "Thank you for calling the company's CEO."

"It was no trouble," said Arthur. "He said himself that he'd rather hear the bad news about the axle from me than from a mother whose child had been injured because of it."

"I wouldn't have known how to get ahold of him," I said, recalling Grant Tavistock's comments about Arthur's mysterious corporate connections. "Is he a friend of yours?"

"A former student," Arthur replied.

His answer seemed to demolish Charles Bellingham's repeated assertions that the infamous Mr. Hargreaves was profoundly antisocial. I doubted that a recluse would feel comfortable in a classroom.

"Are you a teacher?" I asked.

"Everyone's a teacher," he said, standing. "I could do with a cup of tea after my test flight. What about you?"

"I'd love one," I replied.

"Please, allow me," he said, holding his hand out toward the pram. "You probably don't get many chances to walk with your hands free."

"Not lately," I agreed, wondering if I'd ever met a more perfect gentleman. No one who knew Arthur Hargreaves, I thought, could regard him as mean-spirited or uppity.

He took control of the pram and we strode side by side across the broad meadow. Bess was entranced by her new companion. She smacked her lips, cooed, and gurgled, as if she were engaging him in conversation. When he responded with soft noises of his own, she kicked so enthusiastically that her blanket slithered to the ground. I picked it up, shook it out, and put it in the diaper bag. "How's Marcus doing in Santiago?" I asked.

"He's having a ball," Arthur replied. "He's climbed a couple of *cerros*, eaten *pastel de choclo* in a barrio, shouted himself hoarse at a football game, and made lots of new friends."

"Didn't he go there to attend a conference?" I asked uncertainly.

"Oh, yes," said Arthur, as if the conference were an afterthought. "His paper was very well received."

"Good for Marcus," I said. "Are the rest of your grandchildren still here?"

"Just the little ones," he replied, "and Harriet. Her summer hols started last week."

"Harriet's the one who got kite paste in her hair, isn't she?" I asked and Arthur nodded. "Do your grandchildren stay with you often?"

"As often as they please," he said. "They seem to like it here."

"I can see why," I said, gazing admiringly at the abbey. "Hillfont Abbey is——"

"Absurd," Arthur put in. "It's utterly ridiculous." He eyed his home ruefully. "Silly houses were all the rage when my great-great-grandfather built Hillfont. His name was Quentin Hargreaves and he had a taste for medieval kitsch. I'm thankful that he never toured India. If he had, I might be living in a scaled-down version of the Brighton Pavilion."

"I like Hillfont Abbey," I said. "I guess I share your great-great-grandfather's taste for medieval kitsch."

"It's better than the Brighton Pavilion," Arthur conceded. "I can't bear Indo-Gothic architecture. Much too busy. It would be like living inside a kaleidoscope."

I did my best to conceal it, but I was shocked to hear Arthur speak so disparagingly about his family home. If he'd been around when Hillfont Abbey had been built, he would have sided with the Victorian villagers who'd dismissed it as an overdone eyesore. Did he realize that his opinion echoed theirs? I asked myself. Was he aware of the hostility his great-great-grandfather had roused in them?

"I suppose Hillfont Abbey wasn't to everyone's taste when it was built," I said cautiously. "What did your great-great—"

"Please, call him Quentin," Arthur interrupted. "It'll save time."

"Okay," I said. "What did Quentin's neighbors think of his abbey?"

"I wasn't alive at the time," Arthur said, with a wry, sidelong glance, "but my grandfather intimated to me that the abbey wasn't a big hit with the locals. I imagine they preferred your father-in-law's house."

"Fairworth is a little less, um, whimsical than Hillfont," I allowed.

"Fairworth is older than Hillfont," said Arthur, "but it's no less whimsical. Georgian architects looked to ancient Rome for inspiration. Building a Roman house in the English countryside is about as whimsical as it gets."

"Roman kitsch instead of medieval kitsch?" I said, smiling at the thought of what Willis, Sr., would say if I told him that his gracious home was kitschy.

"Exactly," said Arthur. "But people got used to seeing Corinthian columns and Palladian pediments in England. Hillfont was loathed because it was new, not because it was ridiculous."

"Do you really think your home is ridiculous?" I asked.

"I think it's bonkers," said Arthur, "which is why I love it so dearly." He grinned. "Who wouldn't want to live in a mad abbey? It's such fun! Here we are," he went on. "Stay within shouting distance, won't you? If you wander off, we'll have to mount a search party for you. You'll understand what I mean in a minute. It's a bit of a maze."

We'd reached an arched opening in the wall surrounding the welter of courtyards and gardens I'd seen from afar. I tried to look everywhere at once as I followed Arthur through a small apple orchard, a berry garden, an herb garden, a burgeoning vegetable garden, and three or four minor courtyards.

What I saw saddened me.

It seemed to me that a man who could afford to purchase fine works of art—such as the da Vinci sketch Grant Tavistock coveted—should have been rich enough to keep his property in good order, but I saw little evidence of it. Though the gardens were moderately tidy, the courtyards were littered with broken statuary and loose stones that had fallen from dilapidated walls. Two possibilities crossed my mind as I steered the pram around the detritus: Either Arthur had suffered a financial setback or he wasn't as wealthy as Grant and Charles believed him to be.

We saw no one apart from each other and Bess until we entered a sunny, rectangular courtyard paved with large flagstones. It was bordered on three sides by a colonnaded arcade and on the fourth by the abbey's west wing.

"The fountain court," said Arthur, coming to a halt. "We tend to congregate here."

The fountain court wasn't quite as decrepit as the courtyards I'd already seen, but it, too, showed signs of neglect. The stumpy remains of a curved wall served as its centerpiece, piles of twisted metal lay rusting beneath the arcade, and several flagstones were missing entirely. It seemed like an odd place to congregate, but three children called "Hi, Grandad!" to Arthur when we entered it. They couldn't have been more than six or seven years old.

Two rosy-cheeked boys sat at opposite ends of a long wooden table in the arcade's shadowy recesses. I couldn't see what they were doing, but a small girl in a wide-brimmed straw hat knelt on the patch of bare dirt where the flagstones had been, digging industriously with a trowel.

"Is she starting her own little garden?" I asked, smiling at the girl.

"Emily isn't planting seeds," said Arthur. "She's exhuming a corpse."

# *Fifteen*

I was sure—almost sure—that Arthur was joking, but I couldn't detect a trace of humor in his face. To judge by his expression, exhumations were a normal playtime activity for preschool-age Hargreaveses.

"A corpse?" I said faintly. "Whose corpse?"

"I'm not certain," said Arthur. "I'm afraid I didn't ask her name before we ate her."

"You *ate* her?" I said, horrified.

"It's a reasonable thing to do with a chicken," said Arthur, "unless you're a vegetarian. Harriet is a vegetarian, but Emily isn't. Not yet, at any rate. Most of the children go through a vegetarian phase, but—"

"Stop," I interrupted, raising a hand to silence him. "Are you telling me that Emily is digging up a *chicken* carcass?"

"I am," said Arthur. "She buried it yesterday, after dinner. I expect she wants to find out what it looks like now." His blue eyes began to twinkle as he explained in gentle tones, "Emily's mother and father are archaeologists."

"Of course they are," I said, feeling gullible as well as relieved. "You were having a little fun with me."

"A very little," he admitted. "Hillfont's atmosphere creates certain expectations. One wouldn't expect to find a grave robber at Fairworth House, but here"—he made a sweeping gesture—"anything's possible!"

Bess squawked insistently. Arthur lifted her into his arms and let her tug at his beard while he swayed gently from side to side. There was no doubting his experience with babies.

"Hillfont does have a certain air about it," I said. I looked at the piles of twisted metal beneath the arcade. "It seems neat and tidy from a distance, but up close it's a bit"—I cudgeled my brains for an adjective that would be both accurate and polite—"rustic."

"I believe 'rusty' is the word you're searching for," Arthur said good-naturedly, following my gaze. "The unsightly stockpiles belong to my wife. She uses found objects in her art."

"I didn't know that your wife was an artist," I said.

"Elaine is a structural engineer," he said, "but in her spare time, she creates metal sculptures. Welding clears her mind. I'd introduce you to her, but she's on an oil rig in the North Sea at present."

"Too bad she's not a stonemason," I said without thinking, "because some of your courtyards are"—I teetered on the verge of bluntness, but hauled myself back with the same lifeline—"rustic, too."

I winced and wished I'd kept my big mouth shut, but Arthur took my implied criticism in stride.

"Hillfont was designed to fray at the edges," he informed me. "Quentin may not have invented planned obsolescence, but he built the concept into his plans for practical as well as aesthetic reasons. Tumbledown walls make Hillfont look authentically antique, but they also make it cheaper to maintain. He didn't want his extravagant masterpiece to become a burden on his descendants."

"Quentin was a very clever man," I said. "Cleverness seems to run in your family." I peered at the long wooden table beneath the arcade. "What are the boys up to?"

"Stephen is constructing a remote-control Meccano digger, to help Emily with her excavations," said Arthur. "He shares his grandmother's interest in engineering. Colin is dismantling my wife's carriage clock in an attempt to make it run backwards. We're not sure whether he's interested in mechanics or in practical jokes."

I looked at him doubtfully. "Is the carriage clock valuable?"

"Not as valuable as the knowledge Colin will gain by pulling it apart," said Arthur. "Let me show you a ruin Quentin didn't create."

The busy children took no notice of us as we crossed to the stumpy, curved wall in the center of the courtyard. Bess surveyed the scene alertly over Arthur's shoulder while I pushed the pram behind him and made faces at her.

We were still a few steps away from the wall when I heard the sound of gurgling water. When I leaned over the weathered stones, a rush of cool air brushed my face. The soft, upwelling breeze rose from the openings in an iron grate bolted over the mouth of a well shaft.

"If you drop down about ten feet or so, you'll find a natural spring bubbling up from the earth," said Arthur. "The spring inspired a Roman family to build a modest villa here in the fourth century. The well wall is all that remains of the villa. Quentin preserved the wall and named his home after the spring."

"Font," I said, smiling. "Font as in fountain, as in fountain court, as in Hillfont. What happened to the rest of the villa?"

"After the Romans departed," said Arthur, "the locals used its dressed stones in their own building projects. Contrary to popular belief, recycling is not a new concept."

I continued to smile. I'd been in a red-hot rage when I left Fairworth House, but I'd cooled off considerably since then. Arthur's world, with its ultralights, chicken bones, and Roman villas, was the perfect antidote to Bill's toxic aunts.

"What happened to your crown?" I asked. "There hasn't been a coup, has there?"

"No, indeed," he said. "Another granddaughter, Alanna, is replacing the wilted buttercups with fresh ones."

"Don't tell me," I said. "She has a keen interest in millinery."

Arthur laughed. "How did you—"

"Grandad!"

A pair of French doors in the abbey's west wing had opened and a girl had stepped into the sunlight. She wore a striped red-and-white T-shirt, blue-jean shorts, and sandals, and it looked as though someone—an impetuous someone—had chopped a chunk out of her dark hair with a pocketknife. She was older than Colin, Stephen, and Emily—about ten, I thought—and after one hesitating step, she stood motionless, staring at us like a startled rabbit.

"Is that a *baby*, Grandad?" she asked wonderingly. "Where did you get a baby?" She ran across the courtyard to peer eagerly at Bess. "We haven't had a baby in the house since Emily." She looked from Arthur to me. "Is it a boy or a girl?"

"Bess is my daughter," I said. "I'm Lori Shepherd and you"—I surveyed her roughly chopped hair—"must be Harriet."

"I am Harriet," she confirmed. "May I hold Bess? You can trust me. I'm good with babies."

"You can show Lori how good you are with babies by changing Bess's nappy," said Arthur. "Let's go inside. I promised Lori a cup of tea."

Arthur didn't thrust Bess at me, as Charles Bellingham had done in the churchyard. He simply picked up the diaper bag and walked toward the French doors, with Harriet racing ahead of him and me trailing behind with the pram. I parked the pram next to the doors and followed Arthur and Harriet into one of the most appealing rooms I'd ever entered.

It was a library, a real library, a library that was used every day as opposed to an untouched, highly polished showpiece. The concave plaster ceiling was striped with slender oak ribs that curved down to form pilasters dividing one bookshelf from the next. The oak shelves were crammed with books as well as a jumble of odds and ends that included silver inkstands, bronze busts, building blocks, and baby dolls. Framed maps, technical drawings, and inky little hand prints hung from walls covered with a gorgeous, acanthus leaf–patterned wallpaper.

The fireplace's muted green tiles were framed by an exquisitely simple oak mantel and the room's well-worn furnishings looked as though they'd come straight out of William Morris's nineteenth-century workshop. I detected the hand of a master craftsman in each table, chair, lamp, and rug.

While I gawked like a tourist, Arthur used his cell phone to ring for tea and stood over Harriet while she took care of Bess. I was clearly the only person in the room who was startled to see a sofa upholstered in what appeared to be original William Morris fabric used as a changing table. It then occurred to me that the designer would have been unfazed by the sight. He had, I reminded myself, believed in combining beauty with utility.

" 'Have nothing in your home that you do not know to be useful or believe to be beautiful,' " I said, quoting Morris.

"Ah," said Arthur, "you're familiar with the Arts and Crafts movement."

"I'm a big fan of Arts and Crafts design," I acknowledged. "I didn't expect to find so many examples of it here. I thought Hillfont would be furnished with heavy, overdone Victorian pieces."

"William Morris was a Victorian," Arthur pointed out, "but he and others like him rebelled against the Victorian norm. My great-great-grandfather was also a big fan of Arts and Crafts design, which is more than a bit ironic."

"How is it ironic?" I asked.

"Quentin Hargreaves was a manufacturer," said Arthur. "His fortune was based on industrialization and mass production, yet he filled his home with objects that were handmade by individual craftsmen in small workshops."

"I'm glad Bess isn't a boy," said Harriet. "Boys are squirty."

My snort of laughter was echoed by Arthur's. Leave it to a tenyear-old, I thought, to bring a lofty conversation crashing back to ground level.

"They certainly are," I agreed. "I had to do a lot of ducking and dodging when I changed my sons' nappies."

"It was the same for me when Colin was little," said Harriet, as if she'd spent half of her young life tending babies. She finished repacking the diaper bag and looked up at me imploringly. "May I hold her now?"

"Of course you may," I said. "If you talk softly to her, she may fall asleep. She's had a hectic day."

Harriet sat back on the sofa and Arthur placed Bess in her arms. Harriet didn't even look up when a burly, middle-aged woman entered the library with the tea.

The tea set wasn't exactly a set. The chubby blue teapot, the glass sugar bowl, and the china creamer looked as though they'd been picked up for a song at a thrift store, as did the three mismatched teacups and the plate piled high with pinwheel cookies.

"Chamomile," the woman announced, "as you requested, Mr. Hargreaves."

"Thank you, Mrs. Ellicott," said Arthur.

Mrs. Ellicott placed the tea tray on a library table and left the room without saying another word.

"Mrs. Ellicott isn't talkative," said Arthur, "but she's a superlative cook."

"I made the biscuits," Harriet announced. "I'm experimenting with cacao beans."

"They're safe to eat," Arthur said, offering the plate of cookies to me.

"They're delicious," I said, after I'd tried one. "Your experiment was successful, Harriet."

"Still a bit grainy," Harriet said, observing the plate reflectively. "I'll try a finer grind next time."

Harriet was too absorbed in Bess to drink her cup of tea, but Arthur sipped his and I guzzled mine thirstily while he gave me a tour of the library. Though I loved books, I was drawn to the framed technical drawings of catapults, water wheels, and primitive flying machines.

"Quentin did most of the drawings," Arthur told me. "He was a skilled draftsman and an inventor. He would imagine a structure, draw it, then build experimental models. He bought a large estate so he could pursue his dreams in peace."

My ears pricked up.

"Do you like to conduct experiments?" I asked. "My father-in-law has seen bright lights in the sky above Hillfont. He's heard explosions, too. He thinks you're a fireworks fanatic."

"I'm fond of fireworks," Arthur acknowledged, "but I believe your father-in-law may have experienced the side effects of my son's experiments in rocketry. They're quite safe," he added. "Phillip is a cautious and conscientious young man. The European Space Agency is lucky to have him."

"How old is he?" I asked. "Twelve?"

"Phillip is thirty-two," Arthur said, smiling.

"A senior citizen," I said, rolling my eyes. "Honestly, Arthur, I'm beginning to think that every member of your family is a genius."

"All children are geniuses," he said, "given half a chance."

I thought he was underestimating his progeny. Bill and I gave Will and Rob as many chances as we could grab for them, but I doubted that anyone, including me, would classify them as geniuses.

"Who's the map collector?" I asked, moving on to a section of wall covered with a wide array of framed maps, some of which appeared to be quite old.

"I am," said Arthur.

"You'd get along with my friend Emma Harris," I said.

"Ah, yes," he said, nodding, "the other American."

I looked at him in surprise.

"Do you know Emma?" I asked.

"I've never met her," said Arthur, "but I've heard of her riding school. I believe she's the only American riding instructor in the entire county. Her fame precedes her."

"She's good with horses," I said. I allowed my gaze to rove over maps of places I'd never been—Stockholm, Albuquerque, Moscow, Tokyo, Mexico City—then pointed at one that seemed familiar. "Is that Boston Harbor?"

"Well spotted," said Arthur. "It's a Revolutionary War map drawn in 1775. A colleague presented it to me after I gave a series of lectures at MIT. It was a gag gift, from a resident American to a departing Englishman."

"Good joke," I said. I was impressed by the colleague's generosity. His gag gift had probably cost an arm and a leg. "What were your lectures about?"

"I delivered them so long ago that I can hardly remember," Arthur replied, "but I think they had something to do with science. They were terribly tedious."

"Tedious?" I said, raising my eyebrows. "I seriously doubt it. You're the least tedious person I've ever met." I bent to examine a faded, yellowing, hand-drawn map that hung low on the wall. "Is that . . . Finch?"

"Indeed," said Arthur. "It's from the fifteenth century—1485, to be precise." He patted an oak portfolio cabinet. "I have a map of every village within a fifty-mile radius of Hillfont Abbey."

"Finch hasn't changed much," I said.

"I'm glad to hear it," said Arthur. "I haven't been there in years."

"Why not?" I asked, straightening. "I realize that the cart track is rough and likely to flood if you burst into tears while you're on it, but if Bess and I could handle it, you could."

"I seldom leave Hillfont," he said.

"You go to Tillcote," I countered.

"I don't go there often." He sighed tiredly as he looked from one map to the next. "I gave lectures in each of those cities and many more, Lori. Traveling taught me to appreciate the comforts of home."

We'd reached the fireplace. A heraldic shield held pride of place above the mantel shelf. The shield's design was unlike any I'd seen before. Yellow bars divided its sky-blue ground into three equal sections, and each section was emblazoned with a different creature: a bulldog, a bee, and a unicorn.

"That's our coat of arms," Harriet said, speaking for the first time since Bess had fallen asleep in her arms. "My great-great-great-great-grandfather made it up because he couldn't be bothered with inherited knighthoods and peerages. He believed that we each of us make our own way in the world, based on our talents and our hard work. The coat of arms is on our flag, too."

"Tell me about it," I said.

"The bulldog stands for tenacity, the honeybee stands for hard work, and the unicorn represents the power of the imagination," she explained, as if she'd learned the words by heart. "Ideas start up here"—she tapped the side of her head—"but they won't go anywhere if you don't work hard to make them real. And you need to stick with them until you do make them real or until you find out they won't work. That's where the tenacity comes in."

I had a hunch that Harriet was more of a bulldog than a unicorn, but since she was a Hargreaves, I expected her to surprise me.

"Athletes may dream of winning an Olympic medal," Arthur said, carrying on where his granddaughter had left off, "but they won't win medals by dreaming. They have to put in the hard yards."

"Hard work and tenacity," said Harriet, nodding decisively. "That's how a dream becomes real. Grandad, would you hold Bess?"

"I'd love to," he said, adding in an aside to me, "Harriet's not the only one who misses having a baby in the house."

He took Bess from Harriet and Harriet ran from the room, using the same door Mrs. Ellicott had used. Bess nestled into Arthur's arms without waking. I would have taken the opportunity to survey the library's books if I hadn't glanced at the tall case clock in the corner. It reminded me that Bill would be picking the boys up from school in an hour.

"Arthur," I said, turning to face him, "I now know why you're the Summer King. I was in desperate need of a little warmth when I got here and you gave me a big bucketful."

"Dare I ask what chilled you?" he inquired.

I gazed at him in silence for a moment, then asked, "Do you believe blood's thicker than water?"

"Blood's messier," said Arthur. "Its relative density depends on whether it has coagulated or not."

"I'm not talking about real blood, Arthur," I said gently. "I'm talking about family loyalty."

"Oh, I see," he said, as if he'd genuinely misunderstood me. "No, I've never subscribed to that particular maxim. I love and admire most of my relations, but there are one or two I'd like to drop-kick across the Channel. My eldest nephew, for example—a shifty lad. He went into finance, of course. He's creative, yes, but not in a good way." He raised his eyebrows. "Are you having second thoughts about a member of your family?"

"I'd like to drop-kick my husband's aunts across the Atlantic," I said. "They're proper ladies—well-born, well-dressed, and never a hair out of place. They like to remind me that I'm not the well-bred debutante they had in mind for their nephew." I heaved a discouraged sigh. "Let's just say that I'm not looking forward to dining with them at Fairworth on Saturday."

"Until then," Arthur said, "I suggest you dismiss them from your mind."

"I wish I could," I said, "but they'll be here for the next three weeks, taking polite potshots at me. William loves them, so I can't shoot back and I can't let Bill defend me, either." I shook my head. "It's going to be a long three weeks."

"Come here when you can," said Arthur. "Let us cheer you up."

"You already have," I said, "and I'm grateful, but it's time for me to go. The rest of my family will be home soon and I have to get dinner on the table for them."

"I understand," he said, "but I hope you'll stay for just a few more minutes. Harriet will want to say good-bye to Bess."

"Bess will want to say good-bye to Harriet, too," I assured him. "Or she would, if she were awake."

Arthur walked up and down the library, crooning softly to my sleeping daughter, while I searched the sofa and the floor space around it for stray diaper bag supplies. I found a rattle wedged between the cushions and had just added it to the bag when Harriet returned, clutching something in her hands. I thought she would run straight to Bess, but instead she ran to me.

"For Bess," she said, and she presented me with a stuffed animal.

It was a unicorn. Its delicate horn was made of a shiny, smooth, golden fabric and its mane and tale were as fine and fluffy as thistledown. Its shiny black eyes reminded me of Reginald's, but its necklace of crocheted buttercups would always remind me of Arthur.

"Her name is Bianca because she's pure white," said Harriet. "Bianca's how you say 'white' in Latin. And I made her necklace. It's like Grandad's crown."

"It's lovely," I said. "Bianca's lovely, too." I stroked Harriet's inexpertly trimmed hair. "Thank you, Harriet. Bess will thank you herself as soon as she learns to speak English."

"What I want Bess to learn," Harriet said solemnly, "is that everything—*everything*—starts with the imagination."

# *Sixteen*

*A*rthur guided me back through the maze of courtyards and gardens and waved good-bye to me from the arched opening in the outermost inner wall. Bess and I crossed the broad meadow where the ultralight stood and left the Summer King's realm through the wrought-iron gate.

After I closed the gate behind me, I paused to take a last look at Hillfont Abbey, half expecting it to vanish in a puff of glittering stardust. I felt slightly dazed, as if I were awakening from a dream. I ran my fingers lightly through Bianca's fluffy mane to remind myself that Hillfont wasn't a marvelous mirage, but a real place filled with remarkable, but real, people.

Bess and I were still in the orchid wood when she woke. She should have been hungry, but she was content to watch the world pass by as we followed the path back to Fairworth House. Declan Donovan was sweeping the front stairs when we arrived. He spotted us, set his broom aside, and trotted over to lift the pram into the Range Rover while I put Bess into her car seat.

"Taking off, are you?" he asked. "Can't say that I blame you. William's sisters are a right old pair of tartars, aren't they? Amelia hightailed it to Pussywillows as soon as they retired to their rooms to sleep off their jet lag. She had what my wife calls a strategic headache."

"Trust me," I said. "It was a real headache." I eyed the house warily.

"If I'd spent another minute with those two, my head would have exploded. I don't know how Deirdre is going to cope with them."

"Don't you worry about Deirdre," said Declan. "She's tough as nails, my wife."

"She'll have to be," I said. "Would you please tell William that Bess and I have gone home, Declan? I don't want to risk running into the tartars."

"I'll let him know," Declan said.

I thanked him, climbed into the Rover, and cruised slowly down Willis, Sr.'s graveled drive. Part of me was focused on the roadway, but the rest of me was still lost in a dream.

"Lori?" said Bill. "Can you hear me?"

"What?" I said, blinking vaguely at him.

We were in the living room. I was sitting on the couch, folding clean diapers, and Bill was ensconced in his favorite armchair, with Stanley purring blissfully in his lap. Will, Rob, and Bess were, presumably, upstairs and asleep. I had no clear recollection of anything that had happened since Bill had brought the boys home from school.

"You've been on another planet all evening," said Bill.

"Have I?" I said, coming out of my reverie. "I'm sorry."

"It's not your fault," he said. "You're in shock. My aunts have driven you to distraction." He pursed his lips grimly. "I *knew* I should have gone there with you this morning."

"It's not their fault, either," I said. "To tell you the truth, I'd forgotten about them. You were right, by the way. They're gunning for Amelia."

"Of course I was right," said Bill. He peered heavenward. "*Please let them insult Amelia openly, in front of Father.*" He lowered his gaze to meet mine. "If you haven't been reliving a Charlotte-and-Honoria-induced nightmare, where have you been? Because you certainly haven't been here."

"I guess I've been at Hillfont Abbey," I said. "Bess and I spent a couple of hours there this afternoon, with Arthur Hargreaves, and I can't get it out of my mind. It's the most extraordinary place, Bill, and the people who live there are beyond extraordinary."

"Is that where Bess's unicorn came from?" Bill asked. "I noticed it in the nursery. I thought Father had given it to her."

"No," I said. "Bianca was a parting gift from an impetuous little girl named Harriet. . . ."

Bill listened without interrupting while I told him about my visit to Hillfont Abbey. When I finished, he tented his hands over Stanley and scrutinized me.

"You're not in shock," he said. "You're in love."

"No, I'm not," I protested. "I think Arthur's amazing, but he's not—"

"I'm not talking about Arthur," Bill broke in. "You've fallen in love with the whole Hargreaves family, from Great-Great-Grandpa Quentin to little Emily with her chicken bones."

"Am I in love with them?" I folded the last diaper, added it to the stack, and leaned back on the couch to consider Bill's proposition. "I'm intrigued by them, awed by them, enchanted by them—I may even have been seduced by them—but I'm not sure I'm in love with them. They're a little intimidating."

"Overachievers usually are," said Bill. "Will you go back?"

"If your aunts continue to be as horrible to me as they were today," I said, "I'll have to go back. Otherwise, I'll be the one committing a double homicide. And I'd hate to spoil your father's wedding."

Bill's laughter was cut short by a yawn.

"I'm going to bed," he said. "Are you coming?"

"Not yet," I said. "I have some catching up to do."

"Yes, indeed," said Bill. "Dimity will want to hear all about Hill-font Abbey."

Stanley jumped from his lap as he stood, and padded after him as he took the stack of folded diapers upstairs. I sat for a moment, collecting my thoughts, then walked up the hall to the study.

The book-lined room triggered memories of Hillfont's splendid library.

"Reginald," I said, as I turned on the mantel shelf lamps, "I've had a strangely satisfying day. It got off to a terrible start, but boy oh boy, did it get better!"

My pink bunny was all ears as I took the blue journal from its shelf and sat with it in one of the tall leather armchairs that faced the hearth.

"Dimity?" I said as I opened the journal. "I have so much to tell you that I don't know where to begin."

I smiled as Aunt Dimity's elegant handwriting appeared, looping and curling gracefully across the blank page.

*May I suggest a starting point?*

"It might help," I said.

*Marigold Edwards.*

"Marigold Edwards?" It felt as though a thousand years had passed since I'd spoken with the estate agent's office manager, but after a moment's thought, the main point of our conversation came back to me. "I have an appointment to see her on Friday."

*Very good. Were you able to ascertain Amelia's opinion of her?*

"I was," I said. "As it turns out, Amelia's opinion of Marigold Edwards jibes with Mr. Barlow's and Lilian Bunting's. In their view, Marigold is pure gold, but in mine, she's pure tarnish."

*You were never one to mince words, Lori. Have you discovered a gold mine of evidence that supports your view?*

I glanced at the baby monitor, then leaned back in my chair. I didn't have a scrap of hard evidence to lay before Aunt Dimity, but the anecdotal evidence I'd amassed had bolstered my belief that there was something distinctly dodgy about Marigold Edwards.

"Marigold's actions support my view," I replied firmly. "When Amelia came to Finch to look at Pussywillows, Marigold didn't just show her the cottage. She took her on a grand tour of the village and introduced her to Peggy Taxman and Sally Cook and anyone else they bumped into."

*It sounds like a sensible thing to do. One doesn't simply move into a cottage. One moves into a community.*

"It *is* a sensible thing to do," I agreed, "if you're trying to scare off potential home buyers."

*I'm afraid I don't follow you, my dear.*

"The villagers made a good impression on Amelia," I said. "She came away from Marigold's tour feeling as if she'd met a delightful array of colorful, candid characters who took pride in their small community. Which is great, right?"

*I would think so.*

"Unfortunately," I said, "most people aren't as tolerant as Amelia. Most people wouldn't enjoy a run-in with Bossy Peggy and Gabby Sally. The tour would give most people the impression that the villagers are a bunch of opinionated blabbermouths who are too stiff-necked to get along with a neighboring village."

*A neighboring village . . . ? Did Marigold Edwards take it upon herself to tell Amelia about the Finch-Tillcote feud?*

"Marigold gave Amelia an explicit warning about the feud," I said. "Why would she even bring it up? If you were trying to sell a cottage in Finch, would you tell a prospective buyer that her future neighbors are actively pursuing a vendetta?"

*If I were an estate agent, would I disclose the existence of a local feud to a client? Probably not.*

"There you are," I said triumphantly. "Marigold is sabotaging her own sales and I think I know why." I made a wry face and continued reluctantly, "You may find it hard to believe, Dimity, but I got the idea from Bill's aunts."

*I find it almost impossible to believe that you would agree with them on any point whatsoever, but I'm listening.*

"Marigold is working for a developer." I shuddered as I recalled the chilling scenario Charlotte and Honoria had outlined in the drawing room at Fairworth House. "Marigold's job is to drive down property values in Finch so her big-shot developer client can buy up cottages cheaply. He'll annoy the villagers by making a ridiculous amount of noise and mess refurbishing the cottages, and when they complain—"

*Which they will.*

"—he'll plant the idea of living in a quieter place," I went on. "He'll wave a lot of money around and before you know it, the whole village will be in his hands, only it won't be a village anymore. He'll turn it into a . . . a *summer retreat*." I spat out Honoria's detestable phrase, but it still left a bad taste in my brain.

*A bit of noise and dust wouldn't drive the villagers out of Finch, Lori.*

"A huge amount of noise and dust combined with a tempting offer might do the trick. Most of the villagers are living on fixed incomes," I continued. Though it pained me to parrot Charlotte, I couldn't deny the truth in her taunt. "People living on a fixed income might find it difficult to turn down a developer's cold, hard cash."

*Mr. Barlow seemed to think that Peggy Taxman would purchase the empty cottages.*

"Peggy won't be able to compete with a professional developer," I said scathingly. "No, Marigold Edwards is laying the groundwork for someone a lot richer and more experienced than Peggy Taxman. I'm going to find out who it is and put a spoke in his wheel. Or her wheel. It could be a woman."

*What spoke do you propose to put in his or her wheel?*

"No idea," I said, "but I'll think of something."

*I'm sure you will. Your meeting with Marigold Edwards should prove to be quite instructive.*

"Don't worry, Dimity," I said. "I'll wangle the truth out of her."

*I have the greatest respect for your wangling skills, Lori, but before you employ them on Finch's behalf, may I make a suggestion?*

"Fire away," I said.

*You have thus far spoken with three people about Marigold Edwards.*

"Mr. Barlow, Lilian Bunting, and Amelia," I said, nodding.

*It's a rather small sample upon which to base such a momentous conclusion, don't you think? I suggest you spread your nets wider. Chat with Peggy and Sally and the rest of your neighbors. Ask them to describe their encounters with Marigold's clients.*

"Why bother?" I said. "I already know what they'll say. They'll claim they behaved with perfect propriety."

*Perhaps they did. The only way to know for sure is to ask them. If the encounters went well, you may have to rethink your suspicions. If they went badly, your suspicions will be vindicated. Either way, you'll be better prepared for Friday's meeting.*

"Okay," I said. "I'll take Bess for a stroll through the village tomorrow. I'll chat with whoever met Marigold's clients. And I'll try not to let my suspicions get in the way of the facts."

*Excellent. Now, about Charlotte and Honoria . . . What on earth inspired them to discuss Finch's fate with you?*

"They were discussing it with each other," I said. "And they weren't simply discussing Finch's fate—they were inventing it. They can't imagine why anyone would live in Finch year-round, so they came up with a story about a developer transforming it into a summer retreat. When they finished taking potshots at Finch, they took aim at Amelia."

*Was William present?*

"Most of the time," I said. "When he was in the room, the Harpies pretended to be concerned about Amelia because they have it on good authority that all artists are drunk, drug-addicted lunatics."

*What utter nonsense. I hope William leapt to Amelia's defense.*

"He calmly explained to them that Amelia isn't a drunk, drug-addicted lunatic," I said. "I would have gone after them with a hatchet, but I'm a little more excitable than William." I smiled mirthlessly. "I'm also on to their game, which he isn't."

*What did they say about you?*

"Let's see . . ." I counted on my fingers. "I'm old, I'm fat, I'm a lousy dresser, and I'm ruining Bill's career by forcing him to stay away from the office because I'm also a lousy wife and an incompetent mother. Oh, and Bess should be called Elizabeth because only ignorant peasants like me use nicknames."

*What kept you from going after them with a hatchet?*

"I didn't have a hatchet," I said. "I had Bess, though, and she was terrific. Once she started howling, the aunts couldn't get rid of us fast enough."

*Why was Bess howling?*

"I'm not sure," I said. "She had a full belly and dry diapers and she certainly wasn't lonely."

*Perhaps she objected to her great-aunts' unkind remarks.*

"Bess is barely fifteen weeks old, Dimity," I said, giggling. "If she understood a word they said, we may have a genius in the family after all." I stretched my legs out on the ottoman and got ready to astound Aunt Dimity. "Speaking of geniuses, you'll never guess where we went after we left Fairworth House."

*I presume you went to the Emporium to purchase a hatchet.*

"You're not even close," I said, laughing. "Bess and I went to Hillfont Abbey to visit the Summer King. The faux abbey matched your description. It's a whimsical country house loosely based on a historical model, but it's more than that, Dimity, much more. . . ."

I told Aunt Dimity everything I'd told Bill, but in far greater detail. My eyelids were drooping by the time I finished my epic tale, but it was such a pleasure to talk about Arthur Hargreaves instead of Bill's aunts that I couldn't bring myself to stop.

"I've never met anyone less uppity than Arthur," I concluded. "He's as unpretentious as his mix-and-match tea set and he's the exact opposite of mean-spirited. If Peggy Taxman could see him with Bess, she'd change her mind about him. And his allegedly mysterious corporate connections aren't mysterious at all. He traveled the world, giving lectures to students who later became CEOs. It's as simple as that."

*He has since turned into a recluse, however, so Charles and Grant weren't entirely wrong to refer to him as the Hermit of Hillfont Abbey.*

"If Crabtree Cottage were half as interesting as Hillfont Abbey," I said, "Charles and Grant would become the Hermits of Crabtree Cottage. I can understand why Arthur loves his home. Besides, someone has to look after the children."

*You've always had a hungry mind, Lori. It sounds as though Arthur fed it.*

"That's it," I said enthusiastically. "You've hit the nail on the head, Dimity. Arthur's like a walking, talking encyclopedia, but he wears his knowledge lightly. He dispenses it with a diffidence and a sense of humor that makes you forget how much you're learning. He must have been a fantastic lecturer. I could listen to him all day, only he wouldn't let me because he's as curious about people as I am." I sighed happily. "I don't think I could ever be bored at Hillfont Abbey. I don't think anyone could."

*I'm not sure your neighbors will agree with you. Will you tell them that you strode willingly into enemy territory?*

"Enemy territory," I scoffed. "Arthur Hargreaves isn't my enemy. If the villagers give me the stink-eye for saying so, so be it. Their disapproval won't keep me away from Hillfont."

*Their disapproval might, however, interfere with the friendly chats you intend to have with them tomorrow.*

"True," I acknowledged. "It's awkward to chat with people who've turned their backs on you. I'll save my scandalous news for another day."

*A wise decision. I'm somewhat surprised that Arthur made no mention of the feud.*

"I think he's as oblivious to it as his great-great-grandfather was," I said. "And I'm not going to be the one who brings it up with him. It makes the villagers look moronic."

*Blind prejudice is moronic. The only way to combat it is with education.*

"Everyone's a teacher," I said, smiling fondly as I repeated Arthur's words. "Maybe my job is to teach my neighbors to stop being such idiots."

I pressed the Test button on the baby monitor, to make sure that it was still working.

*Is something wrong, Lori?*

"I think it's called twitchy mommy syndrome," I replied. "I thought Bess would be fussy after her action-packed day, but I haven't heard a peep out of her."

*Perhaps she's conserving her lung power. She may need to rescue you from Bill's aunts again.*

"If Bess can plan that far ahead," I said, "we *definitely* have a genius in the family." I stifled a yawn, then glanced again at the monitor. "If you don't mind, Dimity, I think I'll look in on my little genius before I turn in."

*I don't mind in the least. You, too, have had an action-packed day. I look forward to hearing the conclusions you draw from tomorrow's tour of Finch.*

I didn't think my tour of Finch would alter my opinion of Marigold Edwards one iota, but I was too groggy to debate the point.

"I'll let you know what I find out," I said. "Good night, Dimity."

*Good night, Lori. Sleep well.*

The curving lines of royal blue ink faded slowly from the page. I returned the blue journal to its shelf, twiddled Reginald's ears, turned off the lights, and went upstairs to the nursery.

The baby monitor hadn't misled me. Bess was sleeping as peacefully as I would be as soon as my head hit my pillow. I glanced at Bianca, wondering if the white unicorn had the same calming effect on my daughter that my pink bunny had always had on me. Smiling, I gazed down at Bess.

"If you did rescue me from the aunts," I whispered to her, "keep up the good work. As long as we have your howl, we won't need my hatchet."

# Seventeen

**B**ill had opened up a can of worms when he'd suggested that Didier Pinot reexamine his will. The busywork he'd concocted for the sole purpose of avoiding his aunts had, much to his dismay, turned into real work. He couldn't stop at home after Tuesday's school run because he had to rush in to the office to discuss further changes Monsieur Pinot wished to make.

"Hoist by his own petard," I said to Bess. "Or, to put it another way, it serves Daddy right!"

It was nearly eleven o'clock. Bess and I were in the Range Rover and on our way to Finch. I'd hoped to leave for Finch earlier, but the clean-dirty diaper cycle and a series of volcanic eruptions from Bess had delayed our departure. I was in my third blouse of the day. Bess was in her fourth onesie.

The weather couldn't have been lovelier. A brief rain shower in the small hours had left the world gleaming. I made a mental note to thank the Summer King for his handiwork the next time we met.

Guilt assailed me as we passed Willis, Sr.'s gates. Had I been Amelia, I would have had three weeks' worth of debilitating headaches, but she was less devious than I was. The aunts were no doubt torturing her over brunch at Fairworth House.

Raindrops glistened on the bushy bay tree that concealed the entrance to the old farm track. I assumed the track had flooded overnight and felt a rush of gratitude to Willis, Sr., for suggesting a safer route to Hillfont Abbey.

I slowed to a crawl when we reached the humpbacked bridge, in part because the bridge was dauntingly steep and narrow, but mainly because the view from its tallest arch was so pretty. Finch lay before me, basking in the midday sun. Its honey-hued stone buildings, with their crooked chimneys and lichen-dappled roofs, faced one another across the cobbled lane encircling the village green, like a cluster of gossips leaning in for the latest news.

Peacock's pub, Taxman's Emporium, and the greengrocer's shop sat with their backs to a rising landscape of shadowy woods and sheep-dotted pastures, while Sally Cook's tearoom, the vicarage, and the old village school edged the water meadows that dropped down to the willow-draped banks of the Little Deeping. Homely cottages rubbed shoulders with the small business establishments. The geraniums, petunias, pansies, and impatiens in their carefully tended window boxes added splashes of vibrant color to the mellow scene.

Mr. Barlow lived at the foot of the bridge. He was in front of his house, working on the vicar's black sedan, when I entered the village. I waved to him and he raised an oily wrench in response, then motioned for me to pull over. I stopped the Rover beside the vicar's car, rolled down my window, and prepared myself for the first friendly chat of the day.

"Met William's sisters this morning," he informed me, resting his arms on the window's sill. "He brought 'em in after breakfast to show 'em the village. Snooty pair of cats, aren't they?"

Mr. Barlow was as bad as I was at mincing words.

"You don't know the half of it," I said.

"Don't think I want to," he declared.

"Was Amelia with them?" I asked.

"No," said Mr. Barlow. "She had to leave bright and early for Oxford. Something to do with setting up a new exhibit of her paintings."

Since Amelia had said nothing to me about a new exhibit, I suspected that it was a fabrication invented for the sake of self-preservation. She might lack my flair for duplicity, I told myself, but she wasn't a masochist.

"Been meaning to tell you," Mr. Barlow went on, "I was wrong about Peggy buying Rose Cottage and Ivy Cottage. She wanted to, right enough, but Jasper put his foot down."

"I'll bet he put it down softly," I said.

"His soft ways work with Peggy," Mr. Barlow reminded me. "They had enough on their plate, he told her, with the Emporium and the greengrocer's. No need to go looking for more."

"Thanks for letting me know about Peggy," I said. "Has anyone looked at the empty cottages today?"

"Not yet," he said. "Haven't seen hide nor hair of Marigold Edwards for a couple of weeks."

"She must be having a hard time lining up prospective buyers," I said. "Have you met any of her clients?"

"I've met all of 'em," he replied. "Marigold always tracks me down when she's showing a cottage. Stands to reason, doesn't it? Who else can tell her clients about the cottages' quirks?"

"Quirks?" I said alertly. "You told me that Rose Cottage and Ivy Cottage are as sound as a bell."

"They are, but every house has its quirks," Mr. Barlow said easily. "It's best to know about them beforehand. Take Rose Cottage, for example. The pipes knock when you run the hot water, the back door sticks in damp weather, and the chimney flue will need replacing in a year or two."

"And Ivy Cottage?" I asked.

"Whoever takes it on will have to take on the garden as well," Mr. Barlow replied. "If they don't, the whole village will have something to say about it. It'll be a lot of work, I tell 'em, but it's the kind of work that gives a real gardener pleasure." He straightened. "Better get back to my own work. Mrs. Bunting'll need the car this afternoon for meals-on-wheels. Nice talking with you, Lori."

"Nice talking with you, Mr. Barlow," I said and I meant it. It was clear to me that Marigold Edwards used Mr. Barlow's expert knowledge to underscore the empty cottages' shortcomings. As I restarted the engine, I murmured, "Strike one."

I parked the Rover in front of the Emporium, took Bess from her car seat, and carried her inside.

" 'Morning, Lori!" Peggy Taxman boomed from behind the shop's long wooden counter. " 'Morning, Bess!"

I always expected Bess to flinch at the sound of Peggy's voice, but she seemed to find it hilarious.

"Got a postcard for you from Jack and Bree," Peggy went on. She let herself into the post office cage at the counter's far end and handed the postcard to me through the cage's little window. "They're in Wellington—that's in New Zealand—and the weather's atrocious. Gale force winds, Bree says, blowing straight up from the Antarctic."

Postmistress Peggy considered it her sworn duty to read each and every postcard that passed through her hands.

"It's winter in New Zealand," I pointed out.

"They should have gone there in summer," she retorted.

I waited for Peggy to lecture me about the correct way to carry an infant, but she plunged into another topic altogether.

"William brought his sisters in here this morning," she thundered. "I'm not one to speak ill of a man's nearest and dearest, Lori, but those sisters of his should be shut up in a box and shipped straight back to America."

"If you figure out how to do it," I said, "I'll cover the postage."

"Like that, is it?" she roared, giving me an appraising look.

"It's exactly like that," I replied. "I hear you're not buying Rose Cottage or Ivy Cottage."

"Jasper was against it," she shouted. "It's a pity, because they'll never be cheaper, but he's right. We're busy enough as it is."

"How cheap are they?" I asked.

"Not cheap as chips," she hollered. "But reasonable."

"You'd think someone would have taken advantage of the reasonable prices by now, wouldn't you?" I said.

"I would," Peggy bellowed. "Don't know why someone hasn't."

"Maybe the buyers Marigold Edwards has lined up are persnickety," I said. "Have you met any of them?"

"Of course I have," Peggy roared. "Marigold always brings them in here for a bottle of water or a tube of sun cream or some such. That's when I give them my volunteer sign-up sheets." A manic gleam lit Peggy's eyes as she shook a meaty index finger at me. "I tell them not to bother moving here if they don't intend to pull their own weight. I tell them we need all hands on deck in Finch. Flower shows and church fêtes don't happen by accident, I tell them." She folded her beefy arms and squared her broad shoulders. "Then I give them my sign-up sheets and send them on their way."

I'd heard all I needed to hear. I thanked Peggy for the postcard and left the Emporium, ready to cast my nets wider.

I left Bess in her car seat while I removed the all-terrain pram from the Rover.

"Reasonable prices wouldn't scare off house hunters," I explained to her as I unfolded the pram and locked its safety latches, "but Marigold's machinations would. First she lets Mr. Barlow tell them what's wrong with the cottages, then she lets Mrs. Taxman bury them in a mountain of sign-up sheets. They'd have to be crazy to stick around after that." I put Bess and the diaper bag in the pram, then gazed across the green at the tearoom. "Let's find out what Mrs. Cook has to say about Marigold's clients."

Sally Cook had a lot to say.

"They come in here, asking for sugar-free, fat-free, cholesterol-free snacks," she said, sounding highly affronted. "No cream, no eggs, no sugar, and above all, no butter. How am I supposed to make pastries without butter? God knows I don't like to send folk away hungry, Lori, but they give me no choice. Pack of food-faddy fools, the lot of them." Her round face grew pink with exasperation. "The architect and his wife ordered *wine*, for heaven's sake. Does my tearoom look like a wine bar? I sent *them* to the pub."

I was ninety-nine percent certain of the torture the architect and his wife had endured at Peacock's pub, but I trundled Bess across the green again to hear a firsthand account of it from Christine Peacock.

"I remember those two," she said disdainfully as she served me a large glass of water. "They were no better than the rest of folk Marigold's brought in here lately. Wine snobs, every last one of them. If a bottle doesn't have a fancy label, it's not fit to drink. Dick tries to pry their closed minds open by giving them a taste of his homemade wine, but they never get past the first sip." She sniffed disparagingly. "There's no pleasing some people."

I drank my water and left the pub, feeling as though my suspicions were being amply vindicated.

"Mr. Peacock's wine upset Daddy's tummy once," I told Bess, recalling the revolting aftermath of Bill's stint as a judge in Dick's wine-tasting competition. "At least Marigold's clients had the good sense to stop at one sip."

"Lori!"

I turned to see the Handmaidens bearing down on me. Opal Taylor, Millicent Scroggins, Elspeth Binney, and Selena Buxton were eager to tell me that they, too, had had the dubious pleasure of meeting Charlotte and Honoria.

"William's sisters dress beautifully," Selena began.

Then the others jumped in.

Insulting comments whizzed through the air like thrown daggers, each of them prefaced with: "I don't wish to insult William's relatives, but . . ." By the time the collective diatribe was over, every possible criticism of Bill's aunts had been aired, re-aired, and aired again. I could have hugged the quartet individually and as a group.

"At least they're not moving into the empty cottages," I said. "I imagine Marigold Edwards's clients are more polite than William's sisters."

"Oh, they're splendid," Opal said effusively, her eyes glowing. "The young lawyers we met are from Tunbridge Wells originally, but they've been living in a London flat for the past year, poor things. They'll keep the flat, of course—so handy for their work—but they'd like a quiet place in the country for weekends."

"Marigold's Mr. Partridge is a martyr to hives," said Millicent. "He's on medication, but I told him an oatmeal bath is what he needs. His wife wants him to find a less stressful job, but I don't see it happening. He's spent the whole of his working life in advertising. At his age—he'll be fifty-five next April—he won't find it easy to start over."

"He's better off than the banker," said Elspeth. "He has a rash all over his . . . private area. I recommended lashings of calamine lotion."

"They're both better off than Mr. Fortnam," Opal declared,

adding for my benefit, "Mr. Fortnam is an Oxford don. His life has been in tatters ever since his wife left him for one of his students, but why it took him by surprise, I'll never know. The girl was half his age! A mature woman would make him a better wife, and so I told him."

"There was the surgeon as well," said Selena. "Hands like velvet and clothes to die for—all of them tailor-made, right down to his shoes. He's had trouble with his hair plugs—they keep getting infected—but I told him he doesn't need hair plugs. Bald men are very attractive, especially when they work out as often as he does." She tossed her head. "Not like that pudgy computer hardware engineer . . ."

"He can't help gaining weight," Millicent objected. "It runs in his family. His mother and father were simply enormous. . . ."

The Handmaidens went on and on, sharing a wealth of personal information they could have obtained only by subjecting Marigold's clients to the kind of interrogations usually reserved for hardcore criminals. I'd long since grown accustomed to their impertinence, but someone facing them for the first time would, I was certain, feel as if he'd been stripped naked by a flock of budgies.

Bess was eyeing my chest beadily by the time the Handmaidens trotted off to refresh themselves at the tearoom. I was about to wheel her back to the Rover when Grant Tavistock called to me from behind Crabtree Cottage's white picket gate.

"Charles is preparing lunch," he said when I was within chatting distance. "It was supposed to be brunch, but his culinary reach exceeded his grasp and he had to start over. Join us?" Grant opened the gate and crooned enticingly, "He's making his chocolate mousse."

I suspected that the proposed meal would include a heaping

helping of questions about Arthur Hargreaves, but I didn't mind. I
had a few questions of my own to ask Grant and Charles, so I accepted the invitation with one caveat.

"I'll have to feed Bess first," I said.

"We'll avert our eyes," Grant said, tutting impatiently. "Come in!"

# *Eighteen*

C harles, Grant, and I had lunch at the claw-footed oak table in their back garden, surrounded by old-fashioned flowers and fragrant clumps of thyme.

Well-fed, dry-diapered, and sheltered from the sun by the crab-apple tree that had given the cottage its name, Bess dozed in the pram's bassinet, waking occasionally to chew on her toes or to watch Goya, Charles's golden Pomeranian, and Matisse, Grant's lively Maltese, prowl around our ankles. The dogs paid absolutely no attention to her. Their eyes were fixed adoringly on Charles, who fed them under the table when Grant wasn't looking.

Charles's titanic efforts in the kitchen had paid off handsomely. The dishes he'd prepared—twice—were light, flavorful, and, by Finch's standards, epicurean. Sally Cook's tearoom menu didn't include chilled cucumber soup with crème fraîche and a watercress garnish, bruschetta with tomato tapenade and a pesto drizzle, or a spectacular, eight-layer vegetable terrine, but if it had, I would have eaten lunch there every day.

"Charles has been reading cookbooks again," Grant said, smiling wryly as we surveyed the feast Charles had placed before us.

"Lucky you," I said.

"Thank you, Lori." Charles gave Grant a frosty glance as he seated himself at the table. "It's nice to be appreciated."

Charles was a temperamental chef at the best of times. When he was "reading cookbooks," he could be as prickly as a porcupine.

"I wasn't criticizing you," Grant protested.

"Of course he wasn't," I said placatingly. "How could anyone criticize a man who produced such beautiful dishes?" I gazed at the food as adoringly as the dogs gazed at Charles. "You've outdone yourself, Charles. The great Escoffier himself would envy us."

"Now you're being silly," Charles said with a modest smile, but his mood improved perceptibly from then on.

The meal began, as did the inquisition I'd anticipated.

"Have you run into Arthur Hargreaves since we last saw you?" Grant asked with feigned nonchalance.

"As a matter of fact, I have," I replied. "Bess and I spent a few hours with him yesterday at Hillfont Abbey."

Charles gasped and Grant choked on his cucumber soup.

"You penetrated the *inner sanctum?*" Charles said incredulously.

"He showed me around his library," I said.

"Did you see the da Vinci sketch?" Grant asked wheezily, pressing a napkin to his lips.

"I may have," I said. "There were lots of technical drawings hanging on the walls. One of them may have been done by Leonardo."

"Why didn't you ask?" Grant demanded.

"We were talking about other things," I replied. "But I promise to ask Arthur to point out the Leonardo the next time I'm in his library."

" 'The next time I'm in his library,' " said Charles, mimicking my carefree tone. "Do you intend to make a habit of visiting Hillfont Abbey?"

"I don't know if I'll make a habit of it," I said, "but I do intend to go back. I like it there. I like Arthur, too." I looked from Charles to Grant and sighed deeply. "You've got him all wrong, you know."

"Not all wrong, surely," said Grant.

"You're right about him being rich and having exquisite taste," I acknowledged, "but he's not a crazy, cave-dwelling spider-guy. He's a homebody, not a hermit, and he doesn't control the corporate world by twanging a thread in his web. He offers friendly advice to a few bigwigs who used to be his students."

"Was he a teacher?" Charles asked interestedly.

"He gave scientific lectures all over the world," I told him. I remembered the tired expression that had crossed Arthur's face as he'd gazed at his framed maps. "I think he got sick of the lecture circuit, sick of the attention as well as the traveling. If you ask me, the attention embarrassed him. He's super-smart, but he's not a showoff. If he doesn't give interviews, it's because he's too humble to toot his own horn." I finished my soup and helped myself to a piece of bruschetta. "But don't take my word for it. Let me introduce you to Arthur. Honestly, guys, if you met him, you'd like him as much as I do."

"We'd also risk losing friends in the village," said Grant.

"If you lose them so easily," I said, "they weren't real friends to begin with."

"We still have to live with them," Grant pointed out.

"Maybe you should set an example for them," I said. "If I praise Arthur, I'm a lone voice in the wilderness. If the three of us praise him, we're a trio. A trio is louder than a lone voice. We might be able to persuade others to sing along with us."

Charles gazed reflectively at a cluster of blowsy peonies.

"Arthur Hargreaves is a humble homebody who gives friendly advice to former pupils," he mused aloud. "You've smashed our preconceptions to bits, Lori. I don't know whether to be glad or sad."

"You should be glad," I said sternly. "Blind prejudice doesn't suit you."

Charles accepted the scolding with good grace, but neither he nor Grant offered to join me the next time I visited Hillfont Abbey. Peer pressure, it seemed, was more powerful than curiosity.

"We met William's sisters this morning," Grant said. "I was dead-heading the roses in the front garden when they happened by."

"I was still in my dressing gown," said Charles, the late riser, "but I threw on some clothes and ran out to greet them."

"I hope it was worth the effort," I said.

"Oh, it was," Charles assured me. "They were tremendously entertaining."

"Entertaining?" I said doubtfully. "In what way were Charlotte and Honoria entertaining?"

"They're like a pair of wicked schoolgirls," Charles said happily. "All dolled up and simply *oozing* with nastiness."

"I wasn't entertained by them," said Grant. "I found them——" He broke off and regarded me apologetically. "Forgive me, Lori. I don't wish to criticize your relations, but——"

"They aren't my relations," I broke in emphatically. "They're Bill's aunts and he can't stand them."

"Amelia doesn't seem to be keen on them, either," Grant observed. "They were expecting her to join them for brunch, but she scurried off to Oxford instead."

"Coincidence?" said Charles, eyeing me waggishly. "I don't think so."

"It's going to be a long three weeks for Amelia," said Grant.

"It'll be a long three weeks for all of us," I said. "Except William. He *is* fond of them. Heaven alone knows why."

"They amuse him," said Charles. "I could see it in his eyes. They're the king's jesters. Jesters can get away with anything."

"Almost anything," I corrected him. "If they take things too far with Amelia, King William will have their heads."

"Let's hope they take things too far," said Grant, raising his glass.

"You're both taking them far too seriously," Charles said breezily. "I love a good pantomime villain. I hope William brings them to church on Sunday. I can't wait to hear what they have to say about the vicar's sermon."

"I can't wait to hear what they have to say about you," I said pointedly.

Charles opened his mouth to reply, closed it, and became absorbed in serving the terrine. Grant smothered a satisfied grin with his napkin and after chatting about Bree Pym's latest postcard, the vicar's car repairs, and the purple begonias in Opal Taylor's window box, I brought the conversation around to the subject that was uppermost in my mind.

Their faces lit up when I mentioned Marigold Edwards.

"If it hadn't been for Marigold, we would have bought a place in Upper Deeping," said Grant, as if he were describing a fate worse than death. "Finch wasn't even on our radar until Marigold put it there. She insisted that we see Crabtree Cottage."

"She wouldn't take no for an answer," said Charles, chuckling, "and how right she was. Crabtree Cottage was perfect. The minute we saw it, we felt as if we'd come home."

"No quirks?" I said swiftly.

"*Oodles* of quirks," Charles said delightedly. "The floors aren't level, the walls bulge, the timbers creak, the windows rattle——but those are the things that give a place character. We weren't looking for a flawless, soulless box. We wanted a house that lived and breathed."

"We had our doubts about Finch," Grant allowed. "We thought it would be too quiet for us."

"We thought we'd be bored to death," Charles interjected.

"Then Marigold showed us around the village," Grant went on, "and we fell in love with it."

"The villagers treated us like movie stars," Charles gushed. "They simply pelted us with questions. Better still, they were completely indiscreet about one other. Was Christine Peacock's new track suit really two sizes too small for her? Would Elspeth Binney's cat portrait win a ribbon at the art show? Would Opal Taylor ever manage to sell her hideous lamp?"

"We felt as if we'd stepped onstage in the middle of a play," said Grant. "We couldn't wait to find out what happened next."

"I sometimes think we moved to Finch for no other reason than to see Opal's lamp for ourselves," said Charles.

"Sally Cook's jam doughnuts were sublime," Grant said reminiscently, "and Dick Peacock's wines were so ridiculously dreadful that we couldn't resist tasting them all."

"And Peggy's sign-up sheets!" Charles exclaimed, clasping his hands together in pure ecstasy. "Do you remember her volunteer sign-up sheets, Grant? She wouldn't allow us to leave the Emporium without them."

"Peggy was a bit daunting," Grant admitted, "but we could tell that she was devoted to Finch. She made us feel as though we could each play a valuable role in village life." He looked at Charles. "We liked the notion of being needed."

Charles nodded, then turned to me.

"Once we'd settled into Crabtree Cottage," he said, "we went back to the Emporium with two of Peggy's sign-up sheets. I'd volunteered to run the cake stall at the church fête and Grant had volunteered to paint scenery for the Nativity play."

"We've been volunteering ever since," said Grant.

"And we owe it all to Marigold," said Charles. "I shudder to think of how dull our lives would have been if she hadn't brought us to Finch."

"Did Marigold warn you about the Finch-Tillcote feud?" I asked.

"She dropped a few hints about it," said Charles. "We were enchanted by the notion of an absurd, eons-old feud dividing the two villages. It added just the right touch of melodrama to Finch."

"We adore melodrama," said Grant.

"It sounds as though you adore Marigold," I said.

"We do," said Charles. "We keep our distance while she's working, of course, but we're always pleased to see her when she calls on us." He began to collect our empty plates. "Dessert, anyone?"

"Relax," Grant told him. "You prepared the meal. I'll clear the table *and* serve dessert."

After a short interlude, during which Grant took the dirty dishes into the kitchen, Charles took Bess for a stroll around the garden, and I took stock of the information I'd collected, we returned to the table to partake of Charles's masterful chocolate mousse.

I'd heard about my hosts' experiences with Marigold, but I still hadn't heard about their encounters with her clients. I allowed myself to savor one spoonful of mousse in blissful silence, then resumed my inquiry.

"It sounds as though Marigold has shown Rose Cottage and Ivy Cottage to quite a few people," I said. "Have you met any of them?"

"We missed the fat computer chap, the balding surgeon, and the London lawyers," said Grant, "but we met the itchy banker, the aging ad exec, and the cuckolded Oxford don."

"I thought you kept your distance from Marigold while she was working," I said.

"We do," said Grant, "but she always calls on us before she leaves. She can't ask her clients to wait in the car while she chats with us, can she?"

"Of course not," I said. "As relative newcomers to Finch, you must identify with her clients."

"We can almost read their thoughts," Grant confirmed. "They're as worried as we were about living in such a small, out-of-the-way place."

"They're afraid they'll be bored to death," said Charles. "We tell them not to judge a book by its cover."

"We assure them that, appearances notwithstanding," Grant said, "Finch is an exciting place to live."

"Because of the village-wide events?" I hazarded.

"We let Peggy Taxman fill them in on events," Charles said dismissively. "We fill them in on the highlights Peggy doesn't cover."

"What highlights?" I asked with a flutter of apprehension.

"Our burglary, of course," said Grant, "and the fire at the tearoom."

"We practically reenact the slanging match Peggy and Sally had last year on the village green," said Charles.

"We also think it's important to mention that people aren't left on their own when the river floods," said Grant. "We assure them that the entire village pitches in to clear away the mud whenever the Little Deeping spills over its banks."

"If there's time," said Charles, "we describe the day the village was trashed by the yahoos attending the Renaissance Festival."

"Whether there's time or not," said Grant, "we won't let them leave until they've heard our pièce de résistance."

"What would that be?" I asked uneasily.

"We tell them about Crabtree Cottage's previous owner," Grant replied.

"You don't tell them she *died* here, do you?" I said, appalled.

"Why shouldn't we?" Charles retorted. "It's the most thrilling thing that ever happened in Finch and it happened in *our* cottage."

"When they first come to Finch, they think it's a sleepy village," Grant said complacently. "Charles and I let them know that it's wide awake."

I smiled weakly and finished my chocolate mousse.

# Nineteen

I was not in a jolly mood when I drove home from Finch.

"Burglaries!" I sputtered furiously. "Fires! Floods! Feuds! Slanging matches! The green trashed by tourists! A corpse in Crabtree Cottage!" I thumped the steering wheel with my fist. "I'm not surprised that the empty cottages are still empty, Bess. The wonder is that *anyone* moves to Finch, *ever!*"

Bess was less disturbed than I was by the interviews I'd conducted in the village. She fell asleep before we reached the cottage and stayed asleep until I placed her on her padded mat in the study. While she tried and tried again to roll over—a maneuver she had yet to conquer—I addressed a few cogent remarks to Reginald.

"It's been a long time since I observed our neighbors with an outsider's eye," I told my pink bunny. "Remind me not to do it again. It's terrifying."

Reginald's black button eyes gleamed consolingly. I touched a finger to his snout, then took the blue journal from its shelf. Instead of flinging myself into one of the study's tall leather armchairs, however, I sat on the floor within arm's reach of Bess, so I could offer her toys, tickles, and encouraging pats on the back while I spoke with Aunt Dimity.

"Dimity," I announced as I opened the journal. "I've just returned from Finch, where I did as you suggested. I collected firsthand accounts of meetings between the villagers and Marigold Edwards's clients."

I pursed my lips grimly as Aunt Dimity's old-fashioned hand-writing curled and looped across the blank page.

*Good afternoon, Lori. Thank you for following my advice. Did your conversations with the villagers confirm or assuage your doubts about Marigold's motives?*

"I went into the exercise with an open mind," I said almost truthfully. "I came away from it believing that Marigold Edwards is a conniving, two-faced, underhanded, self-serving rat who's doing everything in her power to destroy the village."

*I see. Reading between the lines, I would guess that your doubts were confirmed.*

I laughed involuntarily.

"My doubts weren't merely confirmed," I told Aunt Dimity. "They are now carved in stone. Peggy Taxman told me that Rose Cottage and Ivy Cottage are listed at 'reasonable' prices, but after speaking with her and a few others, I'm convinced that Marigold's fear tactics will force the prices down even further."

*Are you certain you spoke with enough people, Lori? Did you spread your nets as widely as possible?*

"I chatted with Mr. Barlow, Peggy Taxman, Sally Cook, Christine Peacock, Charles Bellingham, Grant Tavistock, and the four Handmaidens," I replied. "I had to quit after that because I couldn't take any more."

*You couldn't take any more . . . what?*

"Craziness!" I expostulated. "Honestly, Dimity, I could have filled a trawler with the lunacy I dredged up in my nets today."

*Can you be more specific?*

"I certainly can," I said. I nudged a polka-dotted plush dinosaur closer to Bess, then leaned back against the ottoman and began to present my findings to Aunt Dimity. "Do you remember what Mr. Barlow told me when I asked him if Rose Cottage and Ivy Cottage were in good shape?"

*I believe he informed you that they were as sound as a bell.*

"Those were his exact words," I said, nodding, "but they're not the words he uses when he speaks with Marigold's clients. Instead of treading gently around the cottages' minor flaws, he reels off a detailed list of every loose floorboard, squeaky hinge, and wobbly door knob because, according to him, every cottage has its quirks and it's best to know about them beforehand."

*Mr. Barlow is an honest man.*

"Precisely," I said. "That's why Marigold turns him loose on her clients. She uses Mr. Barlow's honesty to make them think twice about buying a cottage with a back door that sticks or one with a garden that needs a lot of attention."

*Go on.*

"Marigold drags her clients into the Emporium to make small purchases," I continued. "Then she stands back and watches gleefully while Peggy Taxman scares the pants off of them."

*Peggy is rather overpowering. I've often wondered if she speaks loudly because she's hard of hearing.*

"It's not just Peggy's voice that scares them," I said. "It's her voice, her build, her demeanor, and her confounded sign-up sheets. Put them together and what have you got? You've got a tyrant who bullies newcomers into participating in village life whether they want to or not."

*Peggy's notion of mandatory community involvement is good for the village, but I can understand why it wouldn't appeal to everyone.*

"It doesn't appeal to *me*," I retorted, "but I go along with it because I've gotten used to it. I'm used to the Handmaidens, too, but if I were a house hunter weighing up the pros and cons of living in Finch, I'd put all four of them squarely in the cons column."

*Elspeth, Opal, Millicent, and Selena may be inquisitive, but they mean no harm by it.*

"The Handmaidens make Finch look like a refuge for the incurably nosy," I stated flatly. "And Marigold has inflicted them, en masse, on every single person she's brought to Finch."

*Oh, dear. Have they been intolerably intrusive?*

"They've grilled Marigold's clients mercilessly," I said.

*Mercilessly?*

"Mercilessly," I repeated firmly. "Let's review a few random snippets they collected from Marigold's clients, shall we?" I pulled my free hand away from Bess's back and raised a finger for each snippet I recited. "The advertising executive is a martyr to hives, the banker has a rash on his private parts, the surgeon has infected hair plugs, the computer engineer is struggling with his weight, the Oxford don's wife ran off with one of his students, and the young lawyers plan to keep their London flat while they spend weekends here." I snorted derisively as I ran out of fingers. "I'm sure they walk away from their encounter with the Handmaidens thinking that Finch is a great place to live—if they want to live under a microscope."

*But one does live under a microscope in Finch.*

"Of course one does," I said, exasperated, "but there's no need to advertise it. Marigold uses the Handmaidens like a big, flashing neon sign. She might as well climb to the top of the bell tower and holler: 'If you move here, your life will no longer be your own!'"

*Her clients can't possibly find fault with Sally Cook's tearoom.*

"They can if they want fat-free food," I countered. "Sally doesn't have much patience with food-faddy fools, as she calls them. Clients who wish to avoid cream, sugar, eggs, and butter are out of luck at the tearoom because Sally sends them packing."

*Anyone who goes to a tearoom in search of fat-free foods should be sent packing.*

"I agree, Dimity," I said, "but if they can't enjoy a bite to eat at the tearoom, where can they enjoy one?"

*The pub, of course.*

The naiveté of Aunt Dimity's response made me giggle semi-hysterically.

"People who refuse to eat eggs and butter aren't going to stuff their gullets with pickled eggs, pork scratchings, and sausage rolls," I told her. "But Marigold doesn't take her clients to the pub for the sheer pleasure of seeing them look down their noses at Christine Peacock's pub grub." I cocked my head to one side and asked archly, "Can you guess why she *does* take them there?"

*Good grief. Marigold doesn't recommend Dick Peacock's wine to them, does she?*

"I don't know if she recommends it," I said, "but she doesn't knock it out of their hands when Dick serves it to them. Banana chablis, Dimity! Christmas pudding pinot noir! What further proof do you need of Marigold's duplicity?"

I eased Bess onto her back, gobbled her wiggly toes, and handed her the shark-shaped rattle Will and Rob had brought home from a trip to the baby boutique in Upper Deeping, then turned my attention to the new lines of handwriting that had appeared in the journal.

*I refuse to believe that Grant Tavistock and Charles Bellingham would let Finch down. They're conversant in art, music, literature, fine wine, and gourmet dining. If Marigold wished to emphasize Finch's faults, she wouldn't introduce her clients to its most sophisticated residents.*

"Unfortunately," I said, heaving a sigh, "Grant and Charles don't discuss civilization's high points with Marigold's clients."

*What do they discuss?*

"Finch's low points," I replied. "Their chosen topics include, but are not limited to, their break-in, Sally's kitchen fire, and the Little Deeping's spring floods. The exact list of crimes, disruptions, and natural disasters seems to vary, but Grant and Charles always finish up with their pièce de résistance or, as I prefer to think of it, their coup de grâce: Pruneface Hooper's death in Crabtree Cottage."

*Have they taken leave of their senses?*

"I did tell you that I'd dredged up a net full of craziness," I pointed out.

*It's imbecilic to present rare and isolated incidents as typical. Grant and Charles aren't imbeciles. Were they, perhaps, attempting to engage their listeners in some form of dark humor?*

"Nope," I said. "They were trying to make Finch sound exciting."

*Roller coasters are exciting, but I wouldn't care to live in one.*

"After one of Marigold's tours, you wouldn't care to live in Finch, either," I said.

A glance at the mantel clock told me that Bill and the boys would be home in about an hour. Although I could have rehashed my neighbors' failings in even greater detail, I decided to wrap up my report.

"To summarize," I said. "Today's friendly chats proved to me that, unlike the Handmaidens, Marigold Edwards intends to harm Finch. She's choreographed a dance between the villagers and her clients that drives buyers away and property values down. It's only a matter of time before her secret developer boss swoops in to pick up the empty cottages for less than reasonable prices."

*It's evident that Marigold introduces her clients to far too many villagers, far too quickly. Contrast their experiences with your own, my dear. You've gotten to know your neighbors gradually, over the course of many years. You've had numerous opportunities to observe their good qualities as well as their foibles. You've seen for yourself that, while they may be abrasive at times, they're never cruel. More often than not, they're helpful, generous, and kind.*

"They're good folk," I agreed. "But if I were selling a house in Finch, I'd lock them in their cottages until the deal was done."

*There'd be no need to lock them in their cottages if you were selling a house because you, unlike Marigold, wouldn't stage-manage their encounters with your buyers. You wouldn't introduce your clients to everyone, all at once. You'd allow them to dip their toes into the village, so to speak. You'd warn them about Dick's wine and Peggy's manner and the Handmaidens' insatiable curiosity. You'd charm Sally into producing a fruit salad or a watermelon sorbet for them. You'd let Mr. Barlow explain to them that a wobbly doorknob is of far less importance than a sound foundation.*

"I'd also tell them that there's been exactly one break-in, one small fire, and one minor flood in Finch since I moved here," I said. "And I wouldn't overdramatize Pruneface Hooper's death, either."

*Of course you wouldn't, because your only goal would be to sell your house. Marigold appears to have a quite different goal, but I'm less certain than you are of its precise nature. She may be working for a developer, she may be working for herself, or she may have a private score to settle with the empty cottages' current owners.*

"Maybe she's from Tillcote," I said, grinning. "Maybe she plans to avenge her village's honor by ruining Finch."

*Stranger things have happened, Lori. Your next task will be to find out what Marigold's real goal is. Once you've uncovered her hidden agenda, you'll know what must be done to protect Finch.*

"The showdown will commence at ten o'clock on Friday morning." I looked from Bess to Reginald, then gazed slowly around the study. "I wish I could see her sooner. It'll be weird to spend two whole days at home after so much hustle and bustle."

*I'm sure you'll find something to do.*

I made a wry face.

"I can always find something to do at home," I said. "Laundry, cleaning, cooking, letting Stanley out, letting Stanley in, looking after Bess, Bill, and the boys . . ." I let Bess seize my index finger and pull it into her slobbery mouth for a good gumming. "Don't get me wrong, Dimity. I enjoy taking care of my family. But I've also enjoyed the past few days."

*You're allowed to enjoy both, you know. Too much routine is as wearing as too much hustle and bustle. True contentment lies at the midway point between the two.*

"It's all about balance, eh?" I said.

*I believe so. And while you're engaged in your household chores, you can devise a strategy for your meeting with Marigold.*

"Any suggestions?" I asked.

*You might begin by telling her that you're interested in Rose Cottage and Ivy Cottage.*

I threw my head back and laughed.

"I wouldn't even be lying," I said as Bess laughed with me. "I *am* interested—*very* interested—in the empty cottages." I gave another hoot of laughter. "She'll probably give me a sales pitch."

*I hope she does. Her sales pitch would be quite revealing.*

"I'll coax one out of her," I promised. "Marigold may be able to bamboozle her clients, but she won't bamboozle me."

*I should think not. You're a Finch-trained snoop!*

"I shall do my utmost to live up to my training," I said, inclining my head graciously toward the journal. "In the meantime, however, I have to get dinner ready and throw another load of diapers into the wash. I'll let you know what happens with Marigold."

*Thank you, my dear. Good luck!*

# Twenty

*A*s Aunt Dimity had predicted, I took a great deal of pleasure in resuming my disrupted routine. I wasn't an ob-
sessive homemaker, but I liked to bring a certain degree
of order to the chaos of living with two little boys and a baby. I
plunged into my chores with a gusto I hadn't felt in ages.

I took over the school run as well because Bill had been thrust
into his pre-Bess routine by Didier Pinot, who'd decided to tear up
his old will and create a new one from scratch. Oddly enough—or,
perhaps, not oddly at all—Bill didn't mind. His inadvertent return
to the office had allowed him to get back in touch with a profession
he loved. Though he intended to keep his vow to spend more time at
home with his family, he was not averse to becoming reacquainted
with his clients.

"It's all about balance," I reminded Bess wisely, as I carried a tee-
tering tower of sneakers up to the boys' room on Wednesday.

I telephoned Amelia after Thursday's school run for an update on
the situation at Fairworth House.

"I believe William is taking his sisters to Stratford today," she
informed me.

"You believe?" I said, puzzled. "Aren't you going with them?"

"Sadly, I can't," she replied. "I'm needed in Oxford."

"Ah, yes," I said as the penny dropped. "Your exhibition. I imagine you'll be extremely busy over the next couple of weeks."

"I will," she declared unequivocally. "I'm afraid I won't have much time to get to know William's sisters better during their visit."

"Oh, I think you know them well enough already," I said dryly.

"You and Bill are still coming to dinner on Saturday, aren't you?" she asked with a hint of anxiety in her voice.

"We'll be there," I assured her, "but I don't think we'll eat much. Have fun in Oxford."

"It's work, Lori," she said.

"Of course it is," I said. "I'll see you on Saturday."

I then telephoned Deirdre Donovan.

"William and the two tartars are on their way to Stratford," she confirmed. "Declan's driving them. I feel sorry for him, but I won't mind having Fairworth to myself for a while."

"How are you holding up?" I asked.

"My jaw's a bit sore from gnashing my teeth," she said, "but other than that, I'm fine. Will we see you and Bill on Saturday?"

"You will," I said. "You'll see Bess, too. We're leaving Rob and Will at Anscombe Manor with Emma Harris, but we're bringing Bess with us."

"Good," said Deirdre. "You and I can take turns hiding in the nursery."

"That's the plan," I said, grinning, and returned cheerfully to my housework. The thought of waiting hand and foot on Bill's aunts for three solid weeks made my own chores seem positively delightful.

By Friday, the cottage was looking much better than it had on Wednesday and I was feeling recharged and ready to do battle with Marigold Edwards. Instead of driving home after the school run, I brought Bess into the school to meet her big brothers' classmates and teachers. While the teachers took turns cuddling Bess, Will and Rob showed me their latest project. I kept one eye on the clock and the other on their fully operational papier-mâché volcano until it was time for Bess and me to go.

The Edwards Estate Agency was located on a quiet street near Upper Deeping's bustling main square. I parked the Rover directly in front of the building, put Bess in the pram, and paused on the sidewalk to scrutinize the small advertisements displayed in neat rows on the agency's plate glass windows. The ads featured photographs of properties for sale in a number of nearby towns and villages, but I failed to spot Rose Cottage and Ivy Cottage among them.

"Big surprise," I muttered sarcastically to Bess. "If your aim is to discourage buyers, it doesn't pay to advertise."

The agency's glass door opened suddenly and a slender woman with graying hair and a soft voice greeted me tentatively. When I acknowledged that I was, indeed, Lori Shepherd, the woman introduced herself as Mrs. Dinsdale and ushered us into the outer office. There was nothing luxurious about Mrs. Dinsdale's desk or the bank of metal filing cabinets behind it, but the chair she offered me was comfortable and her manner was professionally polite.

She pressed a button on her telephone and, at exactly ten o'clock, Marigold Edwards emerged from an inner office. I recognized her immediately as the petite blonde who'd shown Pussywillows to Amelia.

When I looked past my adversary's carefully applied makeup, I saw a bright-eyed, energetic woman in her early fifties. She was dressed in a pale pink fitted blazer, a matching pencil skirt, and black pumps, and her nails were as meticulously manicured as Charlotte's and Honoria's. I wanted to dislike her on sight, but I couldn't automatically dislike anyone who beamed so warmly at Bess.

"What an adorable little—" She broke off and looked at me questioningly.

"Girl," I filled in for her. "Her name is Bess."

Marigold put her pencil skirt to the test by squatting down to look Bess in the eye.

"How do you do, Bess?" she said. "My name is Marigold."

Bess giggled.

"It's a funny name, isn't it?" Marigold said, wrinkling her nose good-naturedly at Bess. "But I hope your mummy will use it instead of calling me Mrs. Edwards."

"I will, if you'll call me Lori," I said. "Do you have children?"

"A son and a daughter," Marigold replied, straightening. "They're grown and flown now, but my son, at least, will be back to work for us after he finishes his degree. How lucky you are to have a little one. I miss having a baby around the house." She tilted her head toward the door to the inner office. "Please, come through."

Marigold's office was nicely appointed, but it struck me as businesslike rather than posh. Her teak desk wasn't antiseptically tidy and a row of bulging three-ring binders sat atop her teak filing cabinets. If she was receiving kickback money from a developer, I thought, she wasn't spending it on fancy fittings for the agency.

I parked Bess next to the chair facing the desk, checked her diaper, wiped her dribbly chin, and handed her the shark rattle before seating myself. Marigold, who'd remained standing, asked if she could get anything for me.

"If it's not too much trouble, I'd like a glass of water," I said, adding ruefully, "Nursing makes me thirsty."

"Say no more," she said with an understanding smile. "I nursed both of mine."

She left the office and returned a moment later with a liter bottle of water and a tall glass. She insisted on filling the glass for me before she took her place behind her desk. Try as I might, I couldn't fault her attentiveness nor could I deny her charm. On the face of it, she seemed to be a thoroughly pleasant woman. I had no trouble understanding why my neighbors thought so highly of her.

"I can't tell you how pleased I am to meet you, Lori," she began. "I met your husband, of course, when he was looking for office space in Finch. I hope Wysteria Lodge is serving him well?"

I stared at her in stunned silence, feeling like the world's biggest dunce.

"Are you all right, Lori?" she asked, eyeing me with concern.

"Y-yes," I stammered, still shaken by my own stupidity. "You caught me off guard, is all. To tell you the truth, I'd forgotten that Bill worked with an estate agent when we first moved to Finch."

"Baby brain," Marigold said sympathetically. "It happens to us all. When my two were Bess's age, I could scarcely remember my own name, let alone something that happened over a decade ago." She leaned forward and folded her hands on her desk. "I believe you inherited your property."

"I did," I said.

"Are you thinking of selling it?" she inquired.

"No," I said, much too loudly. I took a long drink of water to steady myself, then said calmly, "I have no desire whatsoever to sell my home."

"I'm glad," she said. "It's such a pretty cottage. Are you, perhaps, interested in acquiring another property?"

"I'm interested in Rose Cottage," I said, relieved to find my place in the script.

"I see." Marigold's brow furrowed. She lowered her eyes briefly, then leaned farther forward, looking as solemnly compassionate as an undertaker. "Will your husband remain in your cottage?"

"What?" I said blankly.

"After the divorce," she clarified in the same gentle tones. "Will your husband remain in your cottage while you move into Rose Cottage? Or will it be the other way around?"

"What are you talking about?" I said. "Bill and I aren't getting a divorce."

"Wonderful," Marigold said, her face brightening. "I'm a little confused, though. Why would you wish to purchase Rose Cottage if neither you nor your husband intend to live there?"

"We're . . . we're planning to use it as a rental property," I improvised.

"What a pity," she said with a sigh. "I hate to disappoint you, Lori, but Rose Cottage isn't available as a rental property."

"Ivy Cottage, then," I said quickly.

"I'm afraid you wouldn't be able to rent Ivy Cottage to a third party, either," Marigold informed me regretfully. "As is the case with Rose Cottage, subletting would violate the terms of the lease."

"The terms of what lease?" I asked.

"Jack MacBride and the Blandings lease their respective properties from the freeholder," she replied.

"You'll have to be patient with me, Marigold," I said. "I'm afraid I don't know what a freeholder is."

"You're a freeholder," said Marigold, smiling. "In simple terms, a freeholder is a property owner. A freeholder may choose to live in his property or he may choose to lease it to a tenant."

I frowned at her, perplexed. "Are you telling me that Jack MacBride and the Blandings don't own their own cottages?"

"I am," she said "They're tenants. They lease their property from the freeholder."

"Who is the freeholder?" I asked.

"It's a what rather than a who," Marigold explained. "Ivy Cottage and Rose Cottage are owned by a private company."

"A company?" I said. "What company?"

"I'm surprised you have to ask," said Marigold. "The same company holds the lease on your husband's place of business, Wysteria Lodge."

I blinked as another wave of confusion swept over me.

"I thought my husband owned Wysteria Lodge," I said.

"I'm afraid not," said Marigold. "He leases it from the company that owns the freehold."

"How many properties in Finch does this company own?" I asked.

"All of them," Marigold replied, "apart from the church, the vicarage, and the schoolhouse, which are, obviously, owned by the Church of England."

"Obviously," I said faintly. I cleared my throat, took another drink of water, and resumed, "Just to be clear: You're saying that Peggy Taxman doesn't own the Emporium or the greengrocer's shop. She leases them from a private company."

"Correct," said Marigold.

"What about Mr. Barlow's house?"

"Leased."

"Sally's tearoom?"

"Leased."

"Dove Cottage? Wren Cottage? Plover Cottage? Larch Cottage?" I said, picturing the Handmaidens' modest abodes.

"Leased, leased, leased, and leased," Marigold replied. "As I said before, every building in Finch, apart from those owned by the church, is leased from the same company."

"How can one company own an entire village?" I asked, thunder-struck.

"It's not an unheard-of arrangement," Marigold said imperturb-ably. "I work as a managing agent for a number of entities that own large tracts of housing."

"Forgive me for saying so," I said, "but you don't seem to be man-aging Finch's housing very well. Ivy Cottage and Rose Cottage have been vacant for months, yet I don't see their photographs in your window."

"I'd like to put them there," Marigold said, "but I'm compelled to follow the company's instructions."

"I don't understand," I said. "Why would a company refuse to advertise its properties?"

"Every company has its own way of doing business," she said with a small shrug.

I paused to collect my thoughts, then said, "It seems as though your clients meet a lot of people when they come to Finch to see a house because you make a point of introducing them to just about everyone in the village. Do you follow the same procedure in every village or have you been instructed to treat Finch differently?"

"I've been instructed to immerse my clients in Finch," said Mari-gold. "I'd prefer to take things a little more gradually, but orders are orders."

I paused again. I was willing to believe that Marigold Edwards was an innocent dupe, but I was unwilling to exonerate the company that had given her such bizarre and unprofitable instructions. Noth-ing she'd said had dispelled my belief that a developer meant to have his way with Finch. His private company might find it difficult to dislodge sitting tenants, I reasoned, but it could make sure that no one replaced those who chose to leave. Eventually, there would be nothing but empty cottages in the village. Then the company could move ahead with its plan to convert them into high-priced holiday homes.

"Who gives you your instructions?" I asked. "May I have a name?"

"Again, I hate to disappoint you," said Marigold, "but I'm not at liberty to divulge that information. The company prefers to use me, the managing agent, as an intermediary. I can, of course, forward any questions or comments you might have to the appropriate department."

Here, at last, was the evasiveness I'd expected from Marigold Edwards. She was clearly determined to conceal the name of the company that had slyly and secretly taken control of Finch, but I was equally determined to pry the name out of her. I folded my arms and fixed her with a level gaze, but before I could demolish her defenses with my finely honed snooping skills, her telephone buzzed.

She picked up the receiver, listened intently, said, "Thank you, Mrs. Dinsdale," and returned the receiver to its cradle.

"I'm sorry, Lori," she said, "but you'll have to excuse me. I'm showing a house in Tillcote in"—she glanced at her watch—"thirty minutes. If I don't leave now, I'll be late and I don't like to keep my clients waiting."

Bess made a noise she'd never made before, a pathetic mewl I didn't associate with any of her usual needs. I bent over her, but I could discover nothing wrong. She wasn't clamoring for a feed or complaining about anything in particular. Her diaper was dry, her clothes weren't bunched up, the pram's safety harness was fastened correctly, and there were no red marks to indicate that she'd whacked herself in the head with the rattle.

I was about to pick her up for an all-purpose cuddle when Marigold spoke.

"Poor thing," Marigold cooed. "Is she hungry?"

I gazed into Bess's deep, dark eyes and thought fast.

"Yes," I lied. "She's used to having a meal about now." I sat up and grimaced apologetically at Marigold. "Would you mind if we . . ." I let my voice trail off in an unspoken appeal.

"Of course I wouldn't mind," she said. "We mums must stick together." She took a file from a desk drawer, placed it in a briefcase she'd retrieved from beneath the desk, and stood. "It was a pleasure to meet you and your daughter, Lori. If you ever decide to sell your home or to purchase another, I hope you'll think of me." She beamed at us and strode to the door, saying, "Take all the time you need. I'll make sure Mrs. Dinsdale doesn't disturb you."

"Thank you," I said, lifting Bess from the pram.

"Not at all," said Marigold.

She left the office, closing the door quietly behind her. I waited until the tap-tap-tap of her heels had faded into the distance, then kissed Bess all over her face, returned her to the pram, and darted behind the desk.

"Who's the clever baby?" I said while I scanned the file cabinets. "If I didn't know better, I'd say that your timing was perfect." I looked over my shoulder at Bess, who was once again chewing contentedly on her shark, and laughed at my own silliness. As a mother of three, I knew for a fact that infants had terrible timing.

Happily, the file cabinets were arranged in alphabetical order. I opened the drawer containing the F files and began to rifle through the folders.

"I *knew* something fishy was going on," I said to Bess. "What kind of company refuses to advertise? What kind of company throws its clients off the deep end in Finch? Aha!" I crowed as my fingers touched a folder labeled FINCH.

I yanked the folder from the drawer, opened it on Marigold's desk, and froze.

There, lying atop a thick sheaf of papers, was a dog-eared photocopy of a map I'd seen recently—a faded, yellowing, hand-drawn map of Finch.

I told myself it meant nothing. I told myself that the map could have been photocopied long before it had come into Arthur's possession. I told myself that there could be no possible connection between the beneficent Summer King and a vile developer. I pushed the dog-eared photocopy aside to examine the sheet of paper that lay beneath it.

My legs gave way and I sat heavily in Marigold's chair.

The letter sent by Monoceros Properties, Limited, to Marigold Edwards had been printed on stationery embossed with a simple line drawing of Hillfont Abbey. I traced the outline of the abbey's square tower with a trembling fingertip, then let my gaze drop slowly, almost fearfully, to the letter's closing.

" 'Sincerely yours,' " I whispered, " 'Arthur Hargreaves.' "

# Twenty-one

I fixed my gaze on Bess and waited for my heart to stop pounding. Then I took a deep breath and read Arthur's letter from start to finish. It was a brief, cordial acknowledgment of Marigold's "most recent report" and a directive enjoining her to "continue to act in accordance with our agreement."

"What report?" I muttered. "What agreement?"

I began to make my way through the file, scanning each piece of paper with a growing sense of perplexity.

Although there was no official title attached to Arthur's name, it rapidly became apparent that he was Marigold Edwards's principal contact at Monoceros Properties, Limited. Her job as the company's managing agent required her to compile reports for him concerning the house hunters she brought to Finch.

Her reports did not, however, contain standard real estate agent notes. They said nothing about a client's age, marital status, financial situation, employment record, or housing preferences.

Instead, Marigold had written detailed notes describing her clients' personality traits, such as the young lawyers' workaholism and the surgeon's narcissism, and their private tribulations. Her descriptions of the advertising executive's hives, the banker's rash, the surgeon's infected hair plugs, the computer engineer's weight issues, and the Oxford don's failed marriage were alarmingly familiar.

I skimmed her reports on other clients as well, clients the Handmaidens hadn't mentioned to me—a financial consultant, an obstetrician, a radiologist, and the economist Lilian Bunting had encountered at St. George's—and they all followed the same pattern: a personality assessment followed by a litany of ills.

Marigold concluded her reports with a description of each client's reaction to the total-immersion tour of Finch. Though her wording varied—some clients were "annoyed and offended," while others were merely "spooked"—the responses were uniformly negative.

The sound of approaching footsteps spooked me. I shoved the folder back in its drawer, threw myself into my chair, and had Bess in my arms within seconds, but by then the footsteps had retreated.

Bess, on the other hand, had advanced, making it abundantly clear that she wasn't going anywhere until I'd kept my part of the bargain. I adjusted my top accordingly and while she dined, I telephoned Bill.

"Hello, love," he said. "What's up?"

"Do you rent Wysteria Lodge?" I inquired.

"Yes," he replied.

"Who collects your rent?" I asked.

"No one," he answered. "I pay it online."

"The online account must have a name," I pointed out.

"I pay my rent to Monoceros Properties, Limited," Bill said with a soft chuckle.

"What's so funny?" I asked.

"Nothing, really," he admitted. "I'm sure Monoceros is a perfectly respectable family name, but it's also the name of a constellation. The constellation's name is derived from a Greek word."

"Greek may have been on your private-school syllabus," I said impatiently, "but it wasn't taught in my public school. Translation, please."

"Monoceros," said Bill, "is the Greek word for unicorn." He chuckled again. "I like the idea of paying rent to a mythical creature."

"Bianca," I breathed, envisioning the gift Harriet had bestowed upon Bess.

"Sorry?" said Bill. "Did you say something, Lori?"

"Not really," I said, feeling dazed. "Look, Bill, I have to go. I'll talk to you later."

"Are you all right?" he asked.

"I'm fine," I said. "I just need to think."

I dropped my cell phone into the diaper bag and gazed distractedly into thin air as I recalled the not-too-distant memory of standing beside Arthur in his splendid library while his dark-haired, impetuous granddaughter deciphered her family's coat of arms. The bulldog stood for tenacity, she'd explained, the honeybee stood for hard work, and the unicorn . . .

"The unicorn," I murmured, "represents the power of the imagination."

Had it amused Arthur to name his company after a potent family symbol? I asked myself.

"Why did he choose the unicorn?" I asked Bess. "Why not the bulldog or the honeybee? What does the power of the imagination have to do with Finch?"

I glanced suspiciously at the file cabinets, wondering how many more files on Finch I would find if I went through them thoroughly. I had a strange feeling that Marigold had sent Arthur reports, not only on the house hunters, but on everyone who lived in or near the village.

"Arthur knew things about me he shouldn't have known," I said to Bess. "The first time we met him, when he came to fix your pram's axle, he called me Lori because he knew that everyone calls me Lori. He knew that I was from Finch and he knew that I had two young sons."

Bess reached up to toy with my lips and I nibbled her fingers.

"Do you remember what Arthur said about your grandfather?" I asked her, somewhat indistinctly. "He knew that Grandpa was a retired attorney with a passion for orchids. He also knew about Grandpa's upcoming wedding. He knew things about Emma, too," I went on. "When we were in the library, he called her 'the other American' and talked about her riding school. He claimed that he 'heard' things about Finch in a general way, as one does in the country. But maybe he heard about me and Emma and Grandpa from Marigold."

I looked at the file cabinets again.

"What's his game?" I asked Bess. "Why is he so interested in Finch?"

I couldn't picture the Summer King as a developer.

He already owns the village, I argued internally. If he wanted to convert his properties to holiday homes, he wouldn't have allowed Amelia to lease Pussywillows. He wouldn't have allowed Elspeth, Opal, Millicent, and Selena to lease their cottages. He would have kept Mr. Barlow from leasing the house near the bridge and he would have had Marigold Edwards tell Bill to look somewhere else for office space.

I stroked Bess's pink cheek.

"Arthur Hargreaves isn't a greedy corporate creep," I told her. "He's a . . . he's a . . . a teacher."

My voice trailed away into horrified silence as I realized how Arthur might bring the power of the imagination to bear on Finch.

"They're scientists," I said in hushed tones. "They like to conduct experiments."

Arthur's grandson was an astrophysicist, his son was a rocket scientist, and his wife was a structural engineer. While they pursued advanced scientific careers, Arthur's younger grandchildren conducted experiments just for the fun of it.

There was Emily, who buried chicken bones for later excavation; Stephen, who used his Meccano set to construct complex machines; and Colin, the prankster, who thought it would be a good joke to make his grandmother's carriage clock run backwards. Even Harriet's pinwheel cookies were an experiment.

Then there were the kites, the marvelous kites that had been designed and built by a veritable horde of Hargreaveses.

It seemed as though the entire Hargreaves family was fond of experimentation, including Arthur's second nephew, the financier who was "creative, yes, but not in a good way."

"And let's not forget Great-Great-Grandpa Quentin," I said, "the inventor who built experimental models." I caught my breath as another piece of the puzzle fell into place. "No wonder Arthur bought a da Vinci sketch, Bess. Leonardo da Vinci was a scientific genius. He spent his whole life jumping from one experiment to the next."

My horror morphed into anger as my train of thought picked up speed.

Had Arthur decided to conduct an experiment in Finch? I asked myself. Were my neighbors and Marigold's clients unwitting participants in a social engineering project he'd designed? Did he pick and choose residents based on criteria he'd devised? Did he plot the results of the immersion tours on a graph? Did he illustrate them with details taken from Marigold's reports? Was he planning to *publish* his findings?

The answers seemed all too obvious.

"How *dare* he?" I growled. "How dare he sit on his hill and look down on the rest of us? How dare he tinker with people's lives?"

Bess didn't react to my growling because she was asleep. I laid her gently in the pram, shut down the snack bar, and got to my feet. My meeting with Marigold Edwards had proved to be more revealing than Aunt Dimity could have imagined, but I'd gleaned all the information I could glean from Marigold.

To obtain the truth, the whole truth, and nothing but the truth about Monoceros Properties, Limited, I would have to confront Arthur Hargreaves.

I drove directly to Fairworth House, transferred Bess from her car seat to the pram, and headed for the orchid wood. I entered the Hillfont estate through the wrought-iron gate in the boundary wall, crossed the broad meadow, and walked beneath the arched opening in the outermost inner wall.

I passed through the apple orchard, the berry garden, the herb garden, the burgeoning vegetable garden, and the minor courtyards, and I found my way to the fountain court, guided by the distinctive shapes of the half-ruined walls I'd passed when I'd followed Arthur.

The fountain court was abuzz with activity. Stephen, Colin, Emily, and Harriet were there along with five other children I didn't recognize. The nine children appeared to be attaching tails to nine simple but brightly colored kites.

Dressed in a faded Hawaiian shirt, worn blue jeans, and battered sneakers, and adorned with his grape-wreath crown, Arthur stood in their midst, answering questions, giving advice, and lending a helping hand where one was needed.

"Bess!" Harriet cried when she spotted us. "Look, Grandad! It's Bess and Lori!"

She and the rest of the children dropped their kites and clustered around the pram to admire my daughter. Arthur smiled warmly and trailed after them.

"Hello again, Lori," he said pleasantly. "You've arrived just in time to witness a mass launch."

I refused to blow my stack in front of the children, but I didn't return Arthur's smile with one of my own.

"I'm not here to witness a launch," I said coldly. "You and I need to talk."

Arthur studied my face for a moment, then said lightly, "Harriet? I'll allow you to be launch leader if you promise not to be too bossy. Children? Take your kites to the meadow and give them a proper flight test. Lori?" He inclined his head toward the French doors. "Shall we repair to the library?"

While the chattering children collected their kites and ran out of the fountain court, I parked the pram beside the French doors, slung the diaper bag over my shoulder, and detached the bassinet. Arthur stretched out his hand, as if he wished to help me, but I pulled the bassinet out of his reach and carried Bess and the diaper bag into the library.

I placed bag and bassinet on the rug in front of the sofa and stood over them until Arthur had closed the French doors behind him. I then marched across the room to point accusingly at the map of Finch while I glared at him.

"Arthur Hargreaves!" I roared. "We are not your lab rats!"

# Twenty-two

*I*f I'd written the ensuing scene, Arthur would have thrown his head back and rattled the rafters with a mad scientist's cackle of laughter. A bookcase would have swung outward to reveal the hidden entrance to his secret laboratory. There would have been thunder and lightning and, perhaps, the distant howl of a ravening wolf.

In real life, the scene was a bit less dramatic.

Arthur tilted his head to one side and inquired politely, "I beg your pardon?"

"Don't play dumb with me," I snapped, straightening. "I've spoken with Marigold Edwards. I know all about Monoceros Properties, Limited."

"I see," said Arthur. He rubbed his chin thoughtfully. "If it's not too much trouble, would you mind telling me what you've learned about Monoceros Properties, Limited?"

"It's a cover," I said furiously. "You're using it to control access to housing in Finch."

"Why would I wish to control access to housing in Finch?" he asked.

"Because you're an evil genius!" I expostulated. "You bought up the village on the sly so you could use it in some sort of crazy social experiment."

"Interesting," he said without the least hint of rancor. "I've been called a genius many times before, but you are, to my knowledge, the first person to describe me as evil."

"Evil may be too strong a word," I admitted, blushing, "but unethical genius doesn't pack the same punch."

"No, it doesn't," Arthur agreed. "How did you find out about Monoceros? Did you run my name through a computer search engine?"

"I don't use computers to spy on people," I said disdainfully. "I spoke face-to-face with my neighbors. Then I rifled through Marigold's files."

Arthur's mouth twitched. He made an odd, choking noise. Then he began to laugh. It wasn't the cackling laugh I'd half hoped to hear from him, but the hearty guffaw of a man who'd just heard a delicious joke. He staggered a few steps farther into the room and sank onto an armchair across from the sofa, where he continued to chortle helplessly while I stood my ground, glaring at him with a mixture of uncertainty and seething indignation.

"Forgive me, Lori," he said finally, wiping his eyes. "I don't mean to be disrespectful. We all have certain lines we refuse to cross. Yours apparently include computer searches, but exclude the rifling of files."

He allowed himself one last, hiccuping chuckle, then took a shaky breath and contained his mirth.

"I'm perfectly aware of how contradictory I sounded just then," I said haughtily. "I told you about the files because I didn't want you to think that Marigold had betrayed your confidence. She seems like a nice person and I wouldn't want her to get into trouble for something she didn't do. But the fact remains that I don't trust the Internet. I do trust the evidence of my own eyes and ears."

"I, too, prefer firsthand evidence," he said. "In this instance, however, I'm afraid your own eyes and ears have led you astray."

He raised a hand to silence my protest.

"You're on the right track, I'll grant you, but you've ended up at the wrong destination." He nodded at the sofa. "Have a seat and I'll tell you where you went wrong."

He seemed so relaxed and so sure of himself that I began to have serious doubts about my hasty accusations. I glanced at the yellowing map of Finch, then crossed to sit on the sofa, with the bassinet at my feet.

"I'm listening," I said. "So is Bess."

"I'll try not to disappoint either one of you." Arthur leaned back in his chair, crossed his legs, and began, "I didn't buy Finch, Lori. I inherited it and all the responsibilities that came along with it."

"Did your father buy the village?" I asked.

"My father, too, inherited the village, as did his father and his father's father," said Arthur. "The original purchase was made by my great-great-grandfather."

"Quentin Hargreaves," I said. "The man who built Hillfont Abbey."

Arthur nodded.

"To understand my family's relationship with Finch," he said, "you must first understand Quentin." He paused, then lifted his arm in a gesture that encompassed the entire library. "Look around you, Lori. Tell me what you see hanging on the walls."

I gave the walls a cursory glance and said, "I see what I saw before, Arthur—maps, technical drawings, the family coat of arms. Why? Is it important?"

"What's important is what's missing," he told me.

"You're talking in riddles," I said impatiently. "I'm not good at solving riddles."

"You'll solve this one," he assured me. "Try again. Ask yourself what you would expect to find hanging on the walls of a library as old as this one."

I sighed irritably, but when I turned my head to study the library's walls, the answer came to me in a flash.

"Portraits," I said, feeling absurdly pleased with myself. "I'd expect to find family portraits. Where are they? Did Quentin build a special gallery for them?"

"If you go through the whole of Hillfont Abbey, you won't find a single family portrait," said Arthur. "I'm not talking about family snaps. We have plenty of those. I'm talking about the grandiose portraits of powerful ancestors painted as props to support a family's sense of self-importance. You won't find any of those in the abbey."

"Why not?" I asked.

"They foster laziness," Arthur replied. "They allow one to rest on someone else's laurels. Quentin was proud of his ancestors, most of whom were blacksmiths and armorers, but he refused to take credit for their accomplishments. He believed that each generation should set its own goals and achieve them through"——he pointed toward the coat of arms—"imagination, hard work, and persistence. Quentin inculcated his children with the belief that the only aristocracy worth preserving is the aristocracy of the mind."

"Arthur," I said, "you don't have to convince me that you come from a long line of high-achieving smarty-pants. I already know that cleverness runs in your family. I kind of got that message when I met your astrophysicist grandson. Maybe my tiny brain is missing the point, but I don't see what any of this has to do with Finch."

"You will," Arthur said. "As I told you the other day, Quentin was a manufacturer. He built factories, streamlined methods of mass production, employed hundreds of workers, and made millions of pounds. He believed in progress, in the future, but he also kept one foot planted firmly in the past."

"He preserved the Roman fountain," I said, nodding, "and he

filled his home with handcrafted furnishings. Also," I went on, like a student eager to show off, "he built a whimsical country house loosely based on a historical model."

"Well done," said Arthur. "Full marks."

"Once a teacher, always a teacher," I said with a reluctant smile. "You told me Quentin bought a large estate so he could pursue his dreams in peace. Was Finch part of the estate?"

"It was not," said Arthur. "He bought Finch one cottage at a time. Within ten years he owned the entire village, with the obvious exceptions of the church, the vicarage, and the schoolhouse."

"Which were owned by the diocese," I put in.

"Correct," said Arthur. "Quentin also purchased every parcel of land within a ten-mile radius of Finch."

"A ten-mile radius?" I echoed. "That means he bought Anscombe Manor and the Pym sisters' house and . . . and *Fairworth House*?"

"He did," said Arthur. "We still own each of those properties."

I gaped at him. "You're William's *landlord*?"

"I'm afraid so," Arthur said apologetically. "But I can assure you that the terms of his lease are not onerous. We gave him our permission to renovate the house and we contributed to the cost of the renovation."

"And he never knew it was you?" I said, astonished.

"I don't believe so." Arthur smiled mischievously. "I never received a thank-you note."

"But my cottage is mine, isn't it?" I asked, too preoccupied to react to Arthur's mild attempt at humor. "Marigold called me a freeholder."

"There's nothing preventing my family from selling all the properties Quentin acquired," said Arthur, "but it has, in fact, happened only once, when Dimity Westwood purchased her property. A great deal of money was involved in the transaction——land prices had risen sharply since Quentin's time——but Miss Westwood wished to leave the cottage to you without encumbrances."

"Wow," I said, stunned.

A squawk from Bess gave my reeling mind time to focus again. Once I'd freed her to practice push-ups on a blanket I'd spread across the rug in front of the sofa, I sat beside her and peered curiously at Arthur.

"I don't get it," I said. "Quentin was proud of being a self-made man. He didn't want to be a lazy aristocrat, living off the achievements of his forefathers. Why would he suddenly decide to become the lord of the manor?"

"That's exactly what he *didn't* do," said Arthur. "He bought Finch and its environs on the sly, to use your colorful phrase, by utilizing various intermediaries. He created a company——Monoceros Properties, Limited——to shield his identity. He made it virtually impossible to trace the transactions directly back to him."

"He bought Finch anonymously," I said, feeling utterly at sea. "Why would he buy a village if he didn't want to lord it over the villagers?"

"Quentin had no wish to lord it over anyone," said Arthur. "He bought Finch because the villagers despised him. They thought he was an upstart, a parvenu, a grubby tradesman who didn't deserve their respect. They called his house Quentin's Folly and made rude remarks about him whenever he ventured into the village."

I eyed Arthur doubtfully.

"I don't mean to pry," I said, "but did Quentin have a taste for . . . abuse?"

"Not at all," said Arthur, laughing, "but he did have a great liking for honesty. He found their attitude refreshing and wholly admirable. The people in Tillcote treated him with undue deference. They tugged their forelocks when he passed by and came crawling to him, cap in hand, asking for jobs and favors."

"They treated him as if he were an aristocrat," I said, with a glimmer of comprehension, "which is the one thing he didn't wish to be."

"Precisely," said Arthur. "He was accustomed to the rough-and-tumble world of industry. He preferred Finch's bluntness to Tillcote's toadying. He mistrusted kid gloves."

"He liked boxing gloves better?" I said.

"They're more direct," said Arthur. "Quentin wished to do something for Finch, but he didn't want the villagers to feel indebted to him."

"Why not?" I asked.

"To make them grateful would be to encourage subservience," Arthur explained. "He also agreed with the Greek philosopher Seneca, who wrote: Let him who has done a good deed be silent."

"Quentin wanted to do a good deed for Finch," I said, "but he wanted to do it anonymously."

"Yes," said Arthur. "When a dispute over stolen pigs arose between Finch and Tillcote, therefore, he sided with Tillcote."

"He offended Finch on purpose," I marveled, "so he could help the villagers without hurting their pride."

"It seems back to front," Arthur acknowledged, "but Quentin had to distance himself from the village in order to protect it."

"Protect it?" I said. "Protect it from what?"

"From housing estates, industrial parks, motorways, and suburban sprawl," said Arthur. "The countryside was already under threat in Quentin's time. He realized that the only way to protect Finch was to create a buffer zone around it."

I turned Bess over and let her play grab-and-chew with my fingers.

"A buffer zone would explain why Quentin bought the surrounding land," I said to Arthur, "but it doesn't explain why he bought the village."

"Quentin foresaw the day when country cottages would become a rare and valuable commodity," Arthur informed me. "He was bitterly opposed to the gentrification of small villages. He loathed the idea of the wealthy driving out those of lesser means."

"So he bought the cottages in order to control housing costs," I said, as understanding finally dawned. "He transformed Finch into a . . . a rent-controlled village where ordinary, everyday people could afford to live."

"It's been that way ever since," said Arthur. "We see to it."

"How do you keep Finch from being overrun by bargain-hunters?" I asked.

"The buffer zone helps," said Arthur. "No one can build a leisure center or a cinema or a minimall within ten miles of Finch. Their absence gives the village a highly desirable air of dullness."

"Finch has its limitations," I said wryly.

"We also rely on word of mouth rather than advertising to attract new residents," said Arthur. "When a property becomes available, we list it with one small estate agency in Upper Deeping and we give them strict instructions to wait for interested parties to come to them."

"The Edwards Estate Agency," I said. "Your family's current intermediary."

"They've served us well for nearly a hundred years," said Arthur.

"I suppose the total-immersion tour is another way of reducing demand," I said.

"So you found out about the tour as well," Arthur said admiringly.

"You have done your homework. I must admit that your name for it is catchier than ours."

"What do you call it?" I asked.

"An introduction to Finch," Arthur replied. "One moves into a community as well as a cottage."

"So I've been told," I said, hearing the echo of Aunt Dimity's words in Arthur's.

"The introduction," Arthur continued, "allows people to test the waters before they make a commitment. It's not an infallible system. People sometimes overestimate their tolerance for Finch's uniquely potent form of neighborliness."

"Not everyone enjoys living under a microscope," I said.

"No, indeed," said Arthur. "For example, the woman who leased Pussywillows before Amelia Thistle—"

"Dervla Ponsonby," I inserted.

"Miss Ponsonby," Arthur went on, "believed she could shut her door on the village. She failed to realize that the villagers would never stop knocking on it. The constant attention drove her mad. Eventually, it drove her out of the village. Mrs. Thistle, by contrast, welcomed the knocks."

"So did Charles Bellingham and Grant Tavistock," I said. "They loved the tour. When they moved to Finch, they were eager to get in on the gossip. They wanted to know as much about the villagers as the villagers wanted to know about them."

"If one is to live happily in Finch," said Arthur, "it helps to take an interest in one's neighbors."

"And yet," I said, "you're not allowed to take an interest in yours."

"Oh, I do take an interest," said Arthur, "from a distance."

"Still doing good deeds in silence, eh?" I said.

"Obviously not," said Arthur. "I believe you and Bess have heard every word I've said."

"Why is that?" I asked. "Why have you broken the code of secrecy? Why are you spilling the beans to me?"

Arthur stood and crossed to gaze through the French doors at the fountain court.

"We knew you'd come along one day," he said. "Not you in particular, but someone like you."

"Someone who noticed odd things going on in the village and dug around until she found an explanation?" I said with a touch of pride.

"No," he said. "Someone who tripped the wire."

"The . . . what?" I said, thrown off base.

"The wire," Arthur repeated, turning to face me. "Of course, it's not a wire anymore. It's an infrared sensor, but it serves the same function." He pointed at the ceiling. "It makes the flag on the tower fall to half mast."

"Are we back to riddles?" I asked, mystified.

"Forgive me," said Arthur. "I'm getting ahead of myself. Let me start again." He returned to his seat and leaned forward with his hands loosely clasped between his knees. "We placed an infrared device in the corner of our boundary wall. It shines a beam across the old cart track. When the beam is broken, an alarm sounds in the abbey and our flag falls to half mast. I saw the flag drop and knew that someone had come up the path."

"I thought you heard Bess crying," I said reproachfully.

"I couldn't have heard her through the racket the children were making," said Arthur. "Though, of course, I did hear her when I approached the wall. She has a fine pair of lungs."

"Never mind about her lungs," I said indignantly. "Do you climb over the wall for every rambler who breaks the beam? Your alarms must be going off all the time."

"Ramblers rarely use the track," said Arthur. "They're worried about flash floods. They've triggered the alarm only three times in the past seven years. They weren't the reason it was installed." He nodded at me. "You were."

"You're creeping me out, Arthur," I said. "You may be a visionary, but you couldn't have foreseen me."

"Sorry," he said, raising his hands in a pacifying gesture. "I misspoke. I wasn't referring to you specifically, but to you as an adult resident of Finch. You, Lori, were the first adult resident of Finch to use the track since the villagers abandoned it nearly a hundred years ago."

"You're kidding," I said.

"The breech between Finch and Hillfont Abbey was absolute," he said. "It traveled down through the generations. In the meantime, the track deteriorated and became flood prone. Even if a villager had been willing to ignore the taboo, he would have thought twice about using such a dangerous route to approach the abbey."

"Okay," I said, "but why is using the track so important?"

"Quentin felt that when an adult villager ventured up the track and spoke civilly to a member of his family, it would be time to repair the old cart path and to reestablish the connection between Hillfont and Finch." Arthur cocked his head to one side and smiled. "You ventured up the track. You spoke civilly to me. You, Lori, are Hillfont's emissary."

"I don't recall volunteering for the position," I said.

"It's yours, whether you volunteer for it or not," said Arthur, chuckling. "You've already told someone about meeting me, haven't you?"

"Only my husband," I protested. "And Grant Tavistock and Charles

Bellingham. And Lilian Bunting. And . . ." I suddenly recalled mentioning my first meeting with Arthur to the group of women gathered around Bess in the churchyard after the Sunday service. I cleared my throat. "And I take your point, Arthur. I'm not very good at keeping my mouth shut."

"Which is why you'll be a wonderful emissary," he said.

"Can I tell them everything?" I asked.

"It's entirely up to you," he said. "If you want your neighbors to know that the only thing keeping them in their homes is a form of charity, then by all means, tell them everything. There's a remote possibility that the media might pick up the story, but your neighbors are strong enough to handle it. It wouldn't dent their pride to be known in Tillcote, for example, as charity cases."

I smiled wryly.

"Another point taken," I said. "Your secret is safe with me." I turned my head to gaze at the yellowing map of Finch, then looked up into the Summer King's blue eyes. "If it weren't for your family, Arthur, Finch wouldn't be Finch. I'll never let the villagers know how much they owe you, so you'll have to let me thank you on their behalf." I rolled onto my knees and leaned forward to kiss his weathered cheek. "Thank you, Arthur. Thank you for protecting my village."

"Shall we join the children?" he proposed, his eyes dancing. "Shall we watch the kites?"

"We shall," I said. "After I change Bess's diaper."

Arthur's laughter filled the room and this time I joined in. There would always be kindly laughter, I thought, in the realm of the Summer King.

# Twenty-three

I had every intention of sharing Arthur's remarkable story with Bill and with Aunt Dimity on Friday evening, but life got in the way. A flat tire during the school run, a cricket ball through the kitchen window, and an exploding diaper that would have taxed the cleanup skills of a fully trained hazmat team made me glad simply to crawl into bed at an early hour.

I spent Saturday morning persuading Will and Rob not to pack every toy, book, and piece of clothing they possessed for their overnight at Anscombe Manor. I spent Saturday afternoon brushing lint from Bill's tux, searching my closet for an evening gown I could squeeze into, and listening to Bill grumble about his aunts. By the time we finished dressing for dinner, I was ready to stuff a sock in his mouth, but I thought I looked pretty good.

I'd chosen a strapless gown in midnight-blue silk satin primarily because it would allow easy access to the snack bar, but also because its mermaid shape flattered my motherly figure. Bill was too busy girding himself for battle to notice.

I'd dressed Bess in a pretty pale-blue cotton frock Sally Cook had made for her, then added a few backup onesies to the diaper bag in case she needed a quick change en route. The diaper incident was still fresh in my mind.

At half past seven, we climbed into the Rover and drove to Fairworth House. Deirdre Donovan greeted us at the front door, looking as lovely and as unflappable as ever.

"William and Amelia are in the drawing room with the tartars," she murmured as she relieved us of our coats and the diaper bag.

"How do you do it?" I said quietly. "You've had to kowtow to them for nearly a week. Why haven't you ripped your hair out by the roots?"

"It's simple," she said. "I've discovered what they like to eat."

"Diet pills?" I hazarded.

"Vodka martinis," said Deirdre. "Stirred, extra dry, no olives. They lap them up like a pair of thirsty puppies, then doze off. They're not bad company when they're asleep."

"Ingenious," I said.

"Let's get this over with," Bill growled, squaring his shoulders.

I gave Deirdre a speaking look.

"Stay cool, Bill," she said. "I'll have you out of here by ten."

"Nine would be better," Bill muttered.

"Eat fast," she advised.

Deirdre opened the drawing room door and announced us, then stood aside to allow us to enter the room ahead of her. Honoria and Charlotte rose from their chairs to welcome their nephew effusively while favoring Bess and me with perfunctory smiles. William and Amelia kissed me on both cheeks and told me how lovely I looked before taking Bess with them to show her the Staffordshire spaniels on the mantel shelf. I sat on the Regency settee and waited for World War III to begin.

"Bill needs a drink, Donovan," Charlotte said gaily as Bill escorted her and Honoria back to their seats and their martini glasses.

"A drink for Bill," said Honoria, snapping her fingers at Deirdre.

"Nothing for me, thank you, Deirdre," Bill said, joining me on the settee.

"Not even a small one?" Charlotte coaxed. "To celebrate your release from home detention?"

The muscles in Bill's jaw began to work, but he kept his cool.

"I'm driving," he explained.

"We're not!" Honoria crowed.

She and Charlotte raised their glasses to Bill, drained them, and motioned imperiously for Deirdre to refill them. Though Deirdre filled the glasses to the brim, the sisters didn't spill a drop as they went on speaking. I was impressed.

"You'll never guess who we ran into at L'Espalier last month," Charlotte said, naming one of Boston's most exclusive restaurants. "Pamela Grove! Dear, sweet Pamela. You remember Pamela, don't you, Bill?"

"She was Pamela Highsmith when you dated her," said Honoria.

"I remember Pam," Bill said woodenly, putting his arm around me.

"Her son is the same age as Will and Rob," said Charlotte. "He's already finished his first year at Beresford."

"I'm sure you remember your old prep school," Honoria said playfully.

"I remember my prep school," said Bill.

"Imagine our surprise," Charlotte continued, "when dear Pamela informed us that you hadn't put your sons' names down for Beresford."

"*Our* sons," Bill said, tightening his hold on me, "won't be attending Beresford."

"If you don't send them to Beresford," said Honoria, "where will you send them?"

"Lori and I aren't sending them anywhere," said Bill. "Will and Rob are happy where they are."

"My dear boy," said Charlotte, "prep school isn't about happiness. It's about making the right friends."

"Friends who share the same background," Honoria elucidated. "Friends who will stand them in good stead for the rest of their lives."

"Will and Rob aren't likely to meet their own sort in this godforsaken corner of the world, are they, Bill?" Charlotte asked silkily.

"Will and Rob have many friends," Bill said through gritted teeth.

"But what kind of friends?" Charlotte asked with a dissatisfied moue. "Farmers' sons? Shopkeepers' sons? Public schools are good enough for ordinary people"—her eyes darted to me—"but are they good enough for *your* children?"

I could almost see the faint wisps of steam coming out of Bill's ears. I willed Bess to break the rising tension with a well-timed wail, but she insisted on cooing contentedly in her grandfather's arms.

"We realize that you were pressured into moving here, Bill," Honoria said, sending another malevolent glance my way, "but you mustn't allow the same kind of pressure to jeopardize the twins' futures."

"They're your sons and heirs, Bill," Charlotte said gravely. "Don't you think they deserve to have the same advantages your father gave you?"

The vein in Bill's right temple was throbbing. His face was flushed and his jaw muscle looked as if it might snap. I felt the hand clasping my waist curl into a fist, and braced myself. The outbreak of war seemed imminent.

Then the doorbell rang.

"See who it is and send them away," Honoria said peremptorily to Deirdre.

"This is a family occasion," said Charlotte. "Interlopers are not welcome."

She directed her last comment at Amelia, but Amelia deflected it with a gracious smile. The week in Oxford had evidently rendered William's fiancée immune to his sisters' jibes.

"You haven't invited one of the villagers to dine with us, have you, William?" Honoria drawled. "The ramblings of a country bumpkin will do nothing to elevate the tone of the——"

She broke off as Deirdre returned to the drawing room, looking faintly disconcerted.

"A gentleman to see you, sir," she said to Willis, Sr.

"Gentleman might be overstating the case," said a familiar voice from the entrance hall. "I prefer to think of myself as a humble scholar."

Arthur Hargreaves strode into the room, dressed in a spotless tuxedo, an immaculate shirt, a flawless bow tie, and gleaming black leather shoes, with his grapevine wreath tilted at a rakish angle over one eye. He struck a wide-legged pose before Charlotte and Honoria, thrust his hands into his trouser pockets, and grinned roguishly at them.

"*You,*" Charlotte gasped as the color drained from her face.

"*Arthur?*" Honoria breathed, looking horror-struck.

"Hello, girls," he said cheerfully. "I hear you've become proper ladies."

The color rushed back into Charlotte's face in a crimson flood. Honoria's mouth moved, but no sound emerged.

"Deirdre," said Willis, Sr. "Would you please take my granddaughter to the nursery? I believe her diaper requires attention."

Deirdre, who'd been staring delightedly at Arthur, came out of her happy trance and, with many a backward glance, took Bess from the room.

"I do apologize for bursting in on you," Arthur said, extending his hand to shake Willis, Sr.'s and Bill's. He raised Amelia's to his lips before releasing it. "I'm Arthur Hargreaves and I live next door. Lori thought we should get to know one another." He cocked his head toward Honoria and Charlotte. "No need to introduce myself to those two. Honey and the Shark are old pals."

"Honey and the Shark?" I said, feeling as though Christmas had come early.

"That's what they called themselves back in the day," Arthur said brightly, beaming at Bill's aunts. "We met in Boston when I was lecturing at MIT. They were party animals back then. Haven't changed a bit, have you, girls? Still downing your drinky poos?" He began to stride jauntily back and forth in front of the sisters. "I was a callow fifteen-year-old, but Honey and the Shark liked the look of me. Fixed me up with a fake ID, took me barhopping." He came to a halt and gazed wistfully into the middle distance. "I'll never forget the sight of them, dancing on a pool table with their dresses hiked up around their . . ." He sighed reminiscently. "It was quite an education."

The martini glasses fell to the floor. The sisters stood.

"Excuse me, William," Charlotte said, her eyes downcast. "I am unwell."

"As am I," Honoria mumbled.

They sped from the room. The sound of their footsteps on the marble staircase suggested that they were unwilling to wait for the elevator.

"Is it true?" I asked Arthur, clasping my hands to my chest as I rose from the settee. "Oh, please, let it be true."

The answer came from an unexpected quarter.

"It is true," said Willis, Sr. "My sisters were legendarily wayward young women. My father had to bail them out of jail on five separate occasions. My recollections of their youthful indiscretions have always made it difficult for me to take their conversion to respectability seriously."

"Thank you, Arthur," I cried, throwing my arms around him.

"I had to protect our emissary," he said, his eyes twinkling, when we broke apart. "And some good deeds can't be done in silence."

"Mr. Hargreaves?" said Amelia. "Would you care to join us for dinner?"

"I would be honored," said Arthur.

"The honor," said Bill, grinning from ear to ear, "is entirely ours."

And though darkness had fallen on the slumbering world, the sun shone that night in Fairworth.

# Epilogue

*T*he wedding was a joyous occasion. Willis, Sr., and Amelia were equally radiant and the love they felt for each other seemed to fill every heart in St. George's. Peggy Taxman, Sally Cook, and Christine Peacock held their husbands' hands, Grant Tavistock rested his head against Charles Bellingham's shoulder, and the Handmaidens couldn't help smiling through their copious tears.

My matron of honor dress fit me like a dream and though I wasn't as slender as the young bridesmaids, my curves won their fair share of admirers. Bill looked debonair in his morning suit and Will and Rob performed their roles as ring bearers flawlessly—after Amelia showed them the cookies she'd hidden in her bouquet.

The sunlit reception at Fairworth House was more fun for some than for others. Charlotte and Honoria led the rest of Bill's relatives in welcoming Amelia to the family, then took the first flight back to Boston. Bree Pym and Jack MacBride presented the newlyweds with a matching pair of didgeridoos they'd picked up in Australia, then regaled us with tales of their journey, finishing each other's sentences with an ease that left little doubt in anyone's mind that the vicar would soon be performing another wedding.

Arthur Hargreaves, his wife, and as many of their children and grandchildren as they could gather together at one time trooped through the wrought-iron gate to attend the reception. They came bedecked in flowers and bearing kites that quickly filled the clear blue sky. The villagers I'd failed to reach in my role as emissary were too entranced by the sight of a dragon chasing a biplane to remain standoffish. Harriet won over the last holdout by informing Jasper Taxman quite seriously that his wife had the most magnificent speaking voice she'd ever heard. After that, Peggy boomed to anyone who would listen that the Hargreaveses weren't so bad after all.

The old cart track was paved, the drainage system was repaired, the encroaching shrubs were trimmed, and the low-hanging tree branches were removed. Charles and Grant were the first to ride their bicycles on it, but Emma Harris was the first to use it as a bridle path. More often it's used as a walking path by ramblers and villagers alike. No one in Finch wants to miss a launch day.

Arthur was happy to show Grant and Charles his da Vinci and to employ them to frame the botanical painting he'd commissioned from Amelia as a birthday gift for Harriet, who, as it turned out, was a budding botanist, which explained her experiments with cacao beans.

The wrought-iron gate is seldom still. Will and Rob visit Hillfont Abbey to play in the faux ruins, Amelia goes there to paint the flowers in the broad meadow, and Willis, Sr., spends long hours chatting with Arthur in the library. Bess and I return there often and when we do, we're treated like members of the veritable horde.

"Harriet was right," I said, looking down at the blue journal. "Everything—*everything*—begins with the imagination."

It was August. The hedgerows bordering my little lane were beginning to look dusty and the pastures beyond the hedgerows were becoming parched, but the study was cool and pleasantly shadowy, sheltered from the harsh sunlight by the strands of ivy that crisscrossed the diamond-paned windows above the old oak desk.

I glanced at Bess, who was kicking up her heels in her bouncy chair, then at Bianca the unicorn, who, I'd decided, would share Reginald's niche until Bess was old enough to refrain from eating her, before returning my gaze to the journal to watch Aunt Dimity's elegant copperplate curl and loop across the page.

*Quentin Hargreaves had a far-reaching imagination. Not many men could have foreseen the fates that would befall so many small villages in England. Even fewer could have conceived of a scheme that would keep one of the smallest from suffering a similar fate.*

"Bill and I drove to Tillcote this morning, after we dropped the boys off at the stables," I said. "Rich people live in the old houses, the old guard lives in council housing, and the highway's hum followed us wherever we went. The rector at All Saints wanted to charge us ten pounds—apiece—for a churchyard tour."

*Tillcote went the way of the modern world. Thanks to Quentin and his descendants, Finch didn't.*

"Thanks to you, I own our cottage," I said. "I still don't understand why Monoceros Properties, Limited, agreed to sell it to you. You didn't live here as a full-time resident after you moved to London. I'm surprised the Edwards Estate Agency didn't write you off as an absentee tenant."

*Old Mr. Edwards did write me off as an absentee tenant, but I convinced him that my heir wouldn't be an absentee. I told him that she would build a life here for herself and her family. I promised him that she would do her bit for Finch, that she would give back more than she took, that she would be willing to do the real work of the village.*

"Your imagination was as far-reaching as Quentin's," I said, smiling.

*Fortunately, my pockets were as deep as his, too. I clinched the deal by paying the company three times the cottage's fair market value.*

"Good grief," I said weakly.

*It was purely a matter of self-interest, I assure you. I'd detected a pattern in the agency's choice of tenants. I suspected that a wealthy American heiress wouldn't be allowed to lease my cottage. By purchasing it and bequeathing it to you, I made my own dreams come true. My cottage has become your home. My village has become your village. And I've had the great good fortune to be by your side—in a manner of speaking—every step of the way. I can hardly wait for you to embark on your next adventure.*

"I'm pretty sure my next adventure will involve teething," I said. "It may be a little less pleasant than solving the mystery of the empty cottages."

*Less pleasant for you and for Bess. Are the cottages still empty?*

"Yep," I said, "but Marigold brought a potter to see Rose Cottage yesterday. He liked Peggy's sign-up sheets and he ate two of Sally's jam doughnuts. He didn't drink a full glass of Dick's wine, but he didn't spit out his first mouthful. He gave as good as he got with the Handmaidens, he found the wall paintings in St. George's fascinating, and he lapped up Grant's and Charles's tales of woe. So the signs are good, Dimity. The potter may be a contender."

*Fingers crossed, as the saying goes.*

"Well," I said, making a face at Bess, "I'd better get moving. I promised Harriet I'd bring Bess to Hillfont today."

*Enjoy the warm weather while it lasts. The Summer King's reign will come to an end next month.*

"The Summer King's reign will never end," I said. "Even in the depths of winter, Arthur will find a way to make the sun shine—within a ten-mile radius of Finch." I thought of the man in the grapevine wreath crown and felt my heart swell with gratitude as I cried, "Long may the Summer King reign!"

# Harriet's Pinwheel Cookies

Makes about 5 dozen cookies.

## Ingredients

3 cups all-purpose flour
½ teaspoon baking powder
½ teaspoon salt
1 cup unsalted butter, softened
1 ⅓ cups granulated sugar
2 eggs
2 teaspoons vanilla extract
2 ounces unsweetened chocolate, melted and cooled

## Directions

1. In a large mixing bowl, stir together flour, baking powder, and salt.

2. In another large mixing bowl, beat the butter and sugar with an electric mixer for about 2 minutes, until light and fluffy. Add the eggs, one at a time, beating after each addition. Add vanilla.

3. Add the dry ingredients to the wet ingredients and beat on low until just combined.

4. Divide the dough in half. Form one half into a 4-inch by 4-inch square. Wrap in plastic wrap and set aside.

5. Return the other half of the dough to the mixer. Add the melted chocolate to the dough in the mixer and beat until just combined. Form the chocolate dough into a 4-inch by 4-inch square. Wrap in plastic wrap.

6. Refrigerate both doughs for at least 30 minutes.

7. On parchment paper, roll the vanilla dough into a 16-inch by 13-inch rectangle, about ⅛ inch thick.

8. On another sheet of parchment paper, roll the chocolate dough into a 16-inch by 13-inch rectangle, about ⅛ inch thick.

9. Place the chocolate dough rectangle on top of the vanilla dough rectangle, to make two layers. Peel away both sheets of parchment paper.

10. Cut the layered dough in half. Roll each half into a tight log. Wrap each log in plastic wrap. Refrigerate for at least 3 hours or overnight.

11. Preheat oven to 350 degrees F.

12. Line medium cookie sheets with parchment paper.

13. Cut the logs into ¼-inch-thick slices. Space 1 inch apart on cookie sheets.

14. Bake for 8–10 minutes, or until vanilla swirls are lightly golden.

15. Cool on cooling racks or eat them while they're still warm from the oven. Your choice!

If you love Nancy Atherton's
novels featuring

# Aunt
# Dimity

go to
**www.headline.co.uk**
to discover more in the series

# THRILLINGLY GOOD BOOKS
# FROM CRIMINALLY
# GOOD WRITERS

CRIME FILES BRINGS YOU THE LATEST RELEASES FROM
TOP CRIME AND THRILLER AUTHORS.

SIGN UP ONLINE FOR OUR MONTHLY NEWSLETTER AND BE THE FIRST
TO KNOW ABOUT OUR COMPETITIONS, NEW BOOKS AND MORE.